**The look she gave** ~~him~~ **was pure misery.**

"Oh, hell, Lina," he said and rose, pulling her to her feet and into his arms. For a moment she stood stiff. He was about to release her when she made a muffled sound, leaned on him and seemed to go boneless. They stood like that for a long time. Inhaling her scent, he cradled the back of her head with one hand while he held her up with his other arm.

The hard mound of her belly felt odd wedged between them. It was like a purse or a—no, not a basketball—a soccer ball. Maybe one of those kid-sized ones. Then he had the dazed thought that what he felt between them wasn't kid-sized—it *was* a kid. A whole, complete person in the making.

The fact that this particular baby might be his was something he couldn't let himself think about, not yet.

Dear Reader,

As you may have noticed by now, I have a thing about men who have trouble admitting to the softer emotions. Of course, many of my heroes are cops, who have to be tough guys. How else can they protect themselves from the awful things they see every day? But honestly, as with so many of the themes I come back to over and over, I suspect this one has to do with my own family and childhood.

I remember meeting my paternal grandfather, who was probably a good man but was cold enough to make you shiver. I'm willing to bet that man never in his life told a woman he loved her, never mind his two sons. Dad grew up in the Depression in the worst of poverty, his mother an invalid, his father trying to keep them together. Result: a man who cared deeply, but had a really hard time issuing compliments or saying such simple words as *I love you.* Dad has been gone for fifteen years now, but I still sometimes think I hear his truck coming down the hill to my house. He'd show up, mow my lawn or clean my gutters, and leave, sometimes even without stopping in the house to say hi. But I always knew that was love in action.

My heroine in this book, Lina Jurick, was betrayed by a man once and doesn't know how to trust Bran Murphy, emotionally remote. I hope you enjoy their struggle—his to accept what he feels and articulate it, hers to understand that love can be expressed in many ways.

*Janice Kay Johnson*

# JANICE KAY JOHNSON

---

## The Baby He Wanted

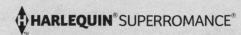

**HARLEQUIN**®SUPERROMANCE®

Recycling programs
for this product may
not exist in your area.

ISBN-13: 978-0-373-60956-7

The Baby He Wanted

Copyright © 2016 by Janice Kay Johnson

Printed in U.S.A.

An author of more than ninety books for children and adults, **Janice Kay Johnson** writes about love and family—about the way generations connect and the power our earliest experiences have on us throughout life. An eight-time finalist for a Romance Writers of America RITA® Award, she won a RITA® Award in 2008 for her Harlequin Superromance novel *Snowbound*. A former librarian, Janice raised two daughters in a small town north of Seattle, Washington.

### Books by Janice Kay Johnson

**HARLEQUIN SUPERROMANCE**

*Brothers, Strangers*

*The Closer He Gets*

*The Baby Agenda*
*Bone Deep*
*Finding Her Dad*
*All That Remains*
*Making Her Way Home*
*No Matter What*
*A Hometown Boy*
*Anything for Her*
*Where It May Lead*
*From This Day On*
*One Frosty Night*
*More Than Neighbors*
*To Love a Cop*

*Two Daughters*

*Yesterday's Gone*
*In Hope's Shadow*

*The Mysteries of Angel Butte*

*Bringing Maddie Home*
*Everywhere She Goes*
*All a Man Is*
*Cop by Her Side*
*This Good Man*

*A Brother's Word*

*Between Love and Duty*
*From Father to Son*
*The Call of Bravery*

**SIGNATURE SELECT SAGA**

*Dead Wrong*

Visit the Author Profile page at Harlequin.com.

# CHAPTER ONE

COMPANY OF ANY kind wasn't on Bran Murphy's mind when he walked into the tavern. His plan was to find a stool at the bar well away from anyone else.

But there she was, sitting alone, with hair the color of dark honey laced with sunbeams flowing in waves down her back.

He let his gaze pause on her only briefly before he scanned the entire room. As with most cops, looking for trouble had become automatic. He didn't spot any tonight. A local country band played a ballad and three couples shuffled on the small dance floor. A crowd hooted and called good-natured insults around the pool tables. People seemed to be having a good time.

He locked onto her.

She'd chosen to sit at one end of the bar, six stools separating her from the closest patron, a man hunched morosely over his drink. Completely still, she looked even more alone than the physical distance suggested. Her head was bent and she seemed to be gazing into her drink as if the glass held tea leaves that would reveal arcane secrets.

Nothing about her suggested that she sought companionship. Giving in to impulse for the second time tonight, Bran took the stool only one away from hers anyway.

She glanced his way, giving him a glimpse of a perfect oval face and gray-green eyes filled with grief or anger, he couldn't be sure. Then she went back to pondering the mixed drink she hadn't touched.

"Are you all right?" he asked, even though he hadn't walked in here with any intention of being sociable, either. In fact, he didn't know why he *was* here. He should have stopped at the store for a bottle of whiskey or a couple of six-packs of dark beer and gotten stinking drunk in the privacy of his apartment. But the first impulse of the evening, a sudden one, had made him turn into the tavern parking lot instead.

Hell, maybe this was smarter. He wouldn't let himself get so drunk he couldn't drive home, which meant he wouldn't feel quite so shitty come morning.

On his wedding day.

"I'm not sick, if that's what you mean," the blonde said, softly enough he had to lean toward her to hear.

Bran signaled the bartender, ordering a pitcher instead of the whiskey he'd intended.

Looked like he had something in common with the blonde. Sure as hell, neither of them was here to celebrate.

He nodded his thanks for the pitcher and poured himself a glass, then took a swallow.

"You want to talk about it?"

She gave that some thought before answering. "No." This time she studied him. "If you're planning to hit on me, you're wasting your time."

"Hadn't crossed my mind," he told her, although that wasn't entirely true. No, it hadn't, but it would have eventually, and now that the subject had been introduced, his mind stuck on it.

"Oh. Okay," she said.

Damn, she was beautiful. Her tan was more pale gold than brown, her nose small, her mouth pretty... Skinny jeans molded to slim legs that he thought might prove to be reasonably long. Well-rounded hips and generous breasts suggested she had a genuine hourglass figure. Bran liked curves.

Paige hadn't had many of those.

She went to the gym almost daily, determined to pare every hint of extra flesh from her body. As the wedding approached, she'd become fanatical about her diet and exercise, striving for some notion of perfection that wasn't his. He'd given up reasoning with her. In fact, he hadn't had much chance, since wedding preparations made her even more unavailable than she'd already been.

Paige wasn't here. A beautiful blonde was.

As he watched, she finally picked up her glass and guzzled what looked like a mixed drink as if it was water and she was parched. A shudder went through her before she plunked the glass down on the polished bar.

The bartender, a balding guy in his forties, appeared. "You want another one? Whiskey sour, right?"

"Yes, please."

Her choice suggested she wasn't much of a drinker.

Bran was on his second glass when the band began another ballad. Out of the corner of his eye, he saw the dance floor empty.

"Would you like to dance?" he asked.

The blonde blinked as if she was having trouble bringing him into focus, but her voice sounded clear. "Okay."

She slid off the bar stool and into his arms as if she belonged there. She might be five foot six, he guessed, which made his shoulder a perfect resting place for her head.

He barely moved his feet. Mostly, they swayed. He didn't press her as close as he would have liked, figuring it wouldn't be gentlemanly, given that he had a serious hard-on. Bran closed his eyes and rested his cheek against her head, inhaling a familiar scent that threw him back a lot of years. Mint.

A patch of the plant had grown beside the back steps of his childhood home. Even brushing the leaves was enough to awaken the fragrance. His mom used to make a sweetened drink with orange and lemon juice, orange peels and mint leaves pulled from that plant.

Until this moment, he'd forgotten all about that drink and how much he loved it. Twenty-five years was a long time.

He nuzzled the honey-colored hair, as smooth and luxuriously textured as heavy satin. The woman in his arms moved her head a little, as if she was rubbing her cheek against him. She gave a small sigh that shot straight to his groin.

The last notes of the song died, but neither of them moved for a minute. Finally, reluctantly, he released her. Her hands slid down his chest and she stepped back, shy.

Back on their bar stools, he said, "I'm Bran. Short for Brandon." He held out a hand.

She slowly extended her much smaller, fine-boned hand. "Lina. Short for Alina."

"Lina." He liked that. "Well, Lina, what do you usually do for fun?"

She crinkled her nose. "Not this. Um… I'm a huge reader. Movies are fine, but usually I'd rather read."

He smiled. "Me, too."

"Really?" She brightened, her expression almost…hopeful.

He felt strange for a minute, as if his heart had contracted, briefly depriving him of oxygen. His voice came out husky when he said, "Really. A lot of nonfiction. Mysteries and thrillers, anything random that grabs me."

She liked mysteries, too. They compared authors, then argued about a few books one of them had loved and the other hated. She suggested an author he hadn't tried, and he did the same. Eventually, they segued to movies, then music. She swam laps three or four times a week at the high school pool, she told him, and admitted to having been on a youth team and her high school team.

She made a face. "I'm not built to be fast, though."

His gaze dropped to her breasts, and his blood headed south again. As far as he could see, she was built just right.

They slow danced a couple more times. Lina didn't seem any more interested in line dancing than he did.

She had a couple more drinks. He finished his

pitcher but figured he was still—barely—safe to drive, given how long he'd been working on it.

When the bartender came to offer her another refill, Bran shook his head. Lina scowled at him. "Why'd you do that?"

"Honey, you're sloshed."

"I'm not your honey." She slipped off the stool and wobbled, grabbing it to restore her balance. "Not anyone's honey."

He was glad to hear that. "You planning to drive home?"

"Don't know."

"You're not." He took out his wallet and tossed down enough bills to cover both their drinks. "I can call you a taxi, or drive you home."

Her eyes narrowed. "How come you're not shlosh...*sloshed*, too?"

"I'm bigger than you. I can drink more without getting hit as hard." When he stood, his head swam, but his balance was okay. He wrapped an arm around her, gratified when hers slipped around his waist and she leaned into him.

"'Kay," she murmured.

They stepped outside into a too-warm June night. A slap of cold air would have felt good. Bran looked around the now-crowded parking lot in perplexity, unable to remember where he had left his Camaro.

He had keys, he knew he did. He patted his pocket. There they were. Just no car.

The neon sign right across the road from the tavern drew his eye. Motel. Vacancy. The "No" part was turned off. As lodging went, it was pretty basic, but decent as far as he knew. It wasn't on the sheriff's department radar for drug dealing or prostitution, at least.

"We should get a room," he decided.

"No hitting on me. You said."

"I changed my mind," he admitted. "But if you just want to sleep, that's what we'll do."

"I changed my mind, too," she confided in a small, husky voice.

Rocketed to full arousal that easily, he steered her across the road into the motel office, where a bored kid who looked to be barely of legal age swiped Bran's credit card and asked for a signature.

Bran took the key—yes, a real key—as well as the card with their room number on it and collected Lina from the chair where he'd parked her.

The flight of outside stairs was a challenge, but they made it, Lina giggling as he tried to jam the key in the lock. Hell, he *was* drunk. Sloshed. Plowed. It worried him that she was, too. Did this qualify as taking advantage of her?

The key finally turned and he pushed the door open. He all but fell in. Lina giggled again.

Oh, yeah, she was drunk.

She closed the door behind them and flipped a switch that turned on lamps on each side of the queen-size bed. Bran stood, doing battle with his conscience.

"Will you kiss me?" Lina asked timidly.

He cleared his throat. "I'd like to kiss you. But Lina... Are you going to be sorry in the morning?"

He waited, suspended in fear that she'd come to her senses now. Of course she would. She wasn't a one-night-stand kind of woman. But, *God*, he hoped she wouldn't change her mind.

Little worried lines formed on her forehead as she scrutinized his face. "You won't hurt me, will you?"

"No!" He framed her face in hands that shook with an unfamiliar tremor. "Never." He hesitated. "I'm a cop, Lina."

"Oh." She nibbled uncertainly on her lower lip as her eyes continued to search his. "Do you have, um, you know? A condom? Because I don't. And I'm not on anything."

"I do. I have a couple in my wallet."

Paige had refused to go on the pill or a birth control patch until after the wedding. *Didn't he know how all those hormones made women gain weight? No way was she messing with her body right now!* Bran had really hated the necessity of wearing a condom, but right this minute, he didn't want to think about how he'd have felt if he hadn't had one.

Lina laid a hand on his shoulder and rose onto tiptoe. "Then I won't be sorry," she murmured, and brushed her mouth over his.

The kiss exploded. He drove his fingers into that mass of silky hair, tilting her head until he found the perfect angle. Her arms came around his neck and he closed one hand over her bottom, lifting and pressing her against him. That fast, his hips rocked. He had to have her *now*.

Their clothes flew. T-shirts first, which caused her to start kissing and stroking his chest. Desperate, he found the catch on her bra and released the most beautiful breasts he'd ever seen. He propelled her backward until she came up against the bed, then lifted her and laid her down, his mouth capturing a nipple before her back hit the mattress. He licked and teased until she gripped his head and repeated, "Please, please, please." And then he suckled. The little noises she made had him groaning and pulling back.

He told her how beautiful she was while he yanked off her boots and peeled tiny panties and stretchy jeans off her curvaceous hips and down those long legs.

For a second, one knee planted on the bed between her thighs, Bran stopped just to look. He had never even imagined a woman as sexy as this one. Her body was both delicate and voluptuous, her lips puffy from his kisses, her eyes heavy-lidded. And then there was that richly colored hair, masses of it spread across the bedspread. The disconcerting idea struck him that she also looked vulnerable. If she hadn't been drunk, she'd be grabbing for something to cover herself.

He reared back to kick off his shoes and un-button his jeans. Lucky he'd gone into the tavern unarmed, rare for him. His gun was locked in a safe beneath the driver's seat of his Camaro. A tavern parking lot wasn't the best place to leave an expensively restored vintage sports car...but damn...he'd never wanted anything in his life the way he did this woman.

His jeans fit so tightly at the moment, he emp-tied his pockets onto the dresser top before he cautiously unzipped. Jeans and boxers gone, he pulled out the couple condoms from the wallet, tossing one packet onto the bedside table and rip-ping open the second one. His hands were still shaking. He lifted his gaze to see that she had risen up onto her elbows and was staring with an expression that did amazing things to his ego. A blush rose on her cheeks even as her tongue came out to touch her lips.

He got the condom on and crawled forward until he could kiss her again, voraciously this time.

He bypassed her glorious breasts and splayed a hand on her belly, circling until his fingers encountered the nest of curls the same honey shade as her hair and just as silky.

She was already so wet, his finger slid between her folds and right into her. She cried out and grabbed his arms.

"Now. Please, now."

He stroked her for another few seconds, the limit of his self-control, before he spread her thighs and thrust deep.

She looked at him in astonishment and whispered, "Oh," after which her eyes closed and she tipped her head back.

Considerate was beyond him. Bran couldn't have gone slow if he'd had a gun to his head. He set a hard, fast rhythm that she matched, clutching at him as her hips rose and fell. He couldn't have stopped the orgasm that lifted him like a monster wave and swept him forward, either. But she cried out at the same time, her tiny convulsions part of the staggering pleasure.

THEY MADE LOVE twice more. In the middle of the night, Lina had come back from the bathroom to find him awake, waiting for her.

This morning, she'd slid out of an amazing dream to find it had been real. A man's hard body spooned her. His erection pressed against her butt and his fingers played between her legs.

She groaned and arched convulsively. He gave a low, husky laugh and closed his teeth on the bundle of muscle and nerves that ran between her neck and shoulder. Then he lifted her leg and slid into her. It felt…amazing. Unlike the night's tumultuous lovemaking, this time he moved lazily, teasing her by not going as deep as she craved. His fingers circled and pressed until she heard her own small, broken cries.

Suddenly, he groaned, half lifted her to her knees, and drove hard and fast. She came by the third stroke, taking him with her.

They both collapsed. After a moment, he groaned.

"Now, *that's* how I like to wake up."

Lina hadn't known it was possible to wake up to anything like that. "It was…really good." She wasn't even sure she was 100 percent awake. An awareness that she felt queasy suggested she was. Nothing like a hangover to ground her.

"I need a shower," he said, kissed her nape and pushed himself out of bed.

She heard him gathering his clothes from the floor, but didn't roll over. She hadn't even seen his face yet this morning. Lina closed her eyes, glad at least that she could picture him. Big, solid, broad-shouldered. His dark auburn hair had been disheveled. Her fingers remembered how silky that hair was. His face was all male, but too rough-hewn to be handsome. It was his bright blue eyes, sharp, that had captivated her. Now she wondered what he'd seen when he looked at her. Had he known from the beginning that she could be coaxed into bed?

She moaned. God, what had she done? How stupid was this, getting drunk and checking into a cheap motel for a one-night stand with a guy she'd met at a tavern? A guy whose last name she didn't even know?

Really, really stupid, that's what.

Worse yet, she couldn't help wondering if she had half intended to do just this. Why else had she gone to the tavern? She could have gotten drunk at home.

The shower came on. Lina rolled to her back and covered her eyes with her hands. She had to have been desperate for confirmation that she was an attractive woman. There was no other explanation for her idiocy. Finding out that David had cheated on her had damaged her self-esteem as much as her heart.

The divorce had been finalized in December. *Merry Christmas to me.*

She would have said she was over him until she was hit by yesterday's nugget of news about

David and his new wife. Now she couldn't even kid herself that he'd ever loved her.

Still…sex with a stranger in a seedy motel room?

He hadn't felt like a stranger by the time he kissed her. He'd felt like a guy she had really liked. They had things in common. He seemed… decent. Not to mention sexy. He'd given her an out, and she believed he'd have accepted a *no* if she'd said it.

A funny sensation blossomed in her chest, pushing out the shame. Hope? Yes, hope. Maybe he'd really liked her, too. Maybe this wasn't as sleazy as it seemed.

*Please, God*, she thought.

Deciding she needed to be dressed when he reappeared, Lina slipped out of bed and saw that he'd laid her clothes neatly on the dresser as he picked up his own. Which meant he was considerate, too.

Her first clue that she'd screwed up majorly was the icky feeling that she was leaking between her legs. Something was running down the inside of her thighs.

Panic squeezed her. Oh, God. He'd used a condom the first two times they'd…not made love… had sex. But not this morning. She had the awful memory of him tossing a single packet on the bedside stand while tearing open the other one.

He hadn't had three.

"That *bastard*."

Lina calculated quickly. It was late enough in the month, she should be safe—unless he took strange women he picked up in bars to motels on a regular basis and didn't use condoms.

Her chest felt horribly tight and she was all but panting for breath. Get dressed. That was what she had to do next.

In the act of reaching for her clothes, she saw everything he'd left on the dresser top. A wallet, a set of car keys, a Harris County Sheriff's Department badge and a square piece of heavy vellum paper with a crease suggesting he'd folded it to jam it in a pocket. An invitation. Her heart hammered sickeningly as she looked down at it.

*Mr. and Mrs. Joseph Collins*
*Request the honor of your presence*
*At the marriage of their daughter*
*Paige Marie*
*To*
*Brandon Murphy*
*Saturday, June 23, at 3:00 p.m.*

Lina got stuck on the date. She read it over and over.

Today. He was getting married *today*.

Forget the bachelor party. He'd decided to have a last fling, and *she* had obliged him.

The shower turned off.

Shaking, panicked, desperate, she yanked on her clothes, not bothering to take the time to put on her bra. She had to be gone before he came out of the bathroom. Her car key was still with the money she'd brought in the pocket of her jeans. The realization that he must have paid for her drinks flitted into her head. And why wouldn't he have? It was still cheap sex.

She opened and closed the door as quietly as she could, trying to step lightly on the stairs. At the bottom, she took off at a run, barely pausing to check for traffic before tearing across the road. There were only three cars left in the gravel parking lot: hers, a beaten-up pickup truck and a glossy black Camaro. His, of course, she thought bitterly.

Gasping for breath, Lina unlocked the driver's door of her car and jumped in. She could see the motel in her rearview mirror. The door to their room remained closed. Either he was still in the bathroom, or he was relieved she was gone.

He was likely relieved.

When she pulled onto the road, gravel spit out from beneath her tires.

BRAN SAW THAT the room was empty the instant he opened the bathroom door. His first reaction was shock. Then he swore viciously. How could he be so freaking stupid as to leave his wallet and car keys out here?

Both were still there, at least, his badge beside them. Man, that would have been embarrassing if she'd taken it. Losing his driver's license would be a royal pain, too. He flipped open the wallet, relieved at the sight of not only the driver's license, but also his debit and two credit cards. A little cash was a small price to pay…

But it was there, too. He flipped through the bills, counted. Seemed about right. Had she not even picked up his wallet?

No, of course she hadn't. She wasn't that kind of woman. Of course she wasn't.

*Shit*, he thought, she did regret the night. The best sex of his life, and she'd run from him, ashamed. And it was his own damn fault. He'd *known* she didn't do things like this, that she was drunk and not thinking straight. What had he expected? That she'd be hanging around, wanting to flirt and talk about when they'd see each other again?

He'd find her…

Yeah, and how was he going to do that? Blonde woman, twenty-five to thirty-five years old, approximately five foot six. The tiny mole he'd seen on her shoulder? Only helpful for identification if she was found dead. For all he knew, she wasn't even from around here. If she was? Alina wasn't a common name…but he had no idea what her last name was, or what she drove. Where she worked, or what she did for a living.

He swore and leaped for the door, but wasn't surprised to discover he was too late. His Camaro sat out in front of the tavern, alone except for a rusting pickup he couldn't in a million years imagine her driving.

While he'd stood here counting bills, she'd made her getaway. Bran groaned and rubbed a hand over his face.

Maybe…she'd find him. If she'd even looked at his badge or opened his wallet, she had one up on him. *She* knew his last name and where he worked.

That was followed by the cold realization that if she didn't come looking, it meant she didn't want to be found, either.

And he had to honor that.

Pocketing the badge and wallet, he glanced down and saw the corner of a piece of paper sticking out from beneath the dresser. The maid could pick it up. Bran dropped a ten-dollar bill on the dresser, then walked out, feeling a couple decades older than he had a few days ago.

## CHAPTER TWO

WITH ONLY A week to go until Christmas, Lina Jurick felt exceptionally unfestive. Her parents weren't very happy that she wasn't flying home for the holidays, but pretending to be joyous was beyond her.

It wasn't like she was hiding anything from them. Well, not hiding very much anyway. Once she'd made the decision to carry the baby to term, she'd told them she was pregnant. The only part she'd refused to talk about was the identity of the father. *She* didn't want to think about Bran "short for Brandon" Murphy, who might or might not be married.

After she'd fled, it had occurred to her that he could have gone to the tavern for the same reason she had: he was bummed. Say, because his wedding had been canceled.

That idea was slightly more palatable than the alternative, that she was a last hurrah. But not a whole lot. If his bride-to-be had stood him up right before the wedding, what did that make her, Lina? Some kind of hey-she's-available fill-in?

All cats were gray in the dark, right? And in the morning, when it wasn't dark anymore, he'd had her from behind and never had to look at her face. If he hadn't gotten any sex on what should have been his wedding night, he'd certainly had plenty the night before.

Occasionally she let herself wonder if it had occurred to him he hadn't used a condom that last time. But, really, what difference did it make whether he'd just forgotten or made the decision to wake up the way he liked even though he couldn't protect her? The result was the same.

At least the morning sickness phase was long past. These days, all she had to combat was exhaustion. She needed to go to bed way earlier than normal if she was going to feel anything close to human when her alarm clock went off in the mornings. And, just her luck, middle school kids rode the same buses as high school kids, tying them to a similar schedule. No, worse: her first class was at the obscene hour of seven thirty. High school teachers were able to sleep in ten minutes later.

Today, she should count her blessings. With two weeks off for the holidays, she could sleep as much as she wanted. Catch up on sleep. Store it. If she could think of anything fun to do, she was free for that, too. Wild and crazy? Not a chance. She'd used up her quota the night she got pregnant.

She could take a nap after lunch, then go for a swim later.

A nap and exercise. As a way to spend her first day of vacation, it was such a thriller, even she was depressed. Maybe Maya could get away to have lunch with her.

Maya answered her call, muted the phone for a minute and came back to say, "Yes, please." She lowered her voice. "Mr. Floyd is driving me *nuts*. Must get out of here."

Lina changed from her sweats into maternity jeans and a warm sweater with enough stretch to cover her burgeoning belly and put on boots because they zipped and were less work than bending over to tie laces.

Her mood lifted during the short drive to the bank branch where Maya worked as a loan officer. Once she reached it, she idled briefly out front. Mr. Floyd, the branch manager, discouraged the use of the parking lot for friends and family. If she'd been absolutely determined, she could have squeezed her Kia into a minuscule spot behind a van, but she made a face and decided to skip it. Parking on the cross street made sense anyway; she could pick up a couple of things at the Walgreens on the other corner once she and Maya were back from lunch.

She locked up and walked past the drive-through and the ATM to the front doors, but when she tried to open one, she couldn't. They were locked. What on earth—

Belatedly, she focused on the printed sign plastered to the glass: "Temporarily Closed—Computer Network Issues. We Regret the Inconvenience."

How strange. Maya hadn't said anything, so whatever it was must have just happened. Lina peered in and couldn't see a soul, teller or customer, which wasn't a big shock since this bank had a conference room to the right just inside and restrooms to the left. The only other windows looked in at the currently empty conference room. Past the short hallway, a second set of doors led into the bank proper, and what view she would otherwise have had was partially blocked by one of those standing height desks where you could write a check or fill out a deposit slip before getting in line. From this angle, she could only see one teller window, with no one behind it.

Presumably, IT people were working frantically. Maybe everyone else was gratefully having a cup of coffee, or Mr. Floyd had decided to hold an impromptu staff meeting to be sure nobody was allowed to waste time. Sounded like him.

Still, Maya was entitled to her lunch break. She would surely have called or at least texted to say she was delayed. And, would they really lock the doors instead of letting customers come in for an explanation of the problem?

As Lina backed away from the doors, pondering, she took out her phone. No messages, no texts.

Darn it, people *had* to be inside. Driving past the parking lot, she'd noticed Mr. Floyd's dark gray BMW in its place of honor as well as a couple of other cars. Although those might belong to the IT people rather than customers.

Call Maya, she decided.

But her friend didn't answer her cell phone. Lina didn't leave a message.

Increasingly uneasy, she tried to decide what to do. She could wait in her car for a few minutes and then try again. Go to Walgreens and assume Maya would call when she was ready to leave. But the weirdness of this had her alarmed.

The back door was not only always kept locked, it was also steel and windowless. The only other place she could really see into the bank was the drive-through window, assuming they hadn't pulled down the shade. No cars had gone in or come out since she'd arrived. Why couldn't she use it as a walk-through to bring somebody to talk to her even if only to say, "Yes, we really are closed."

She went back the way she'd come and circled the corner of the building. Feeling almost as though she ought to be tiptoeing, she approached the double drive-through with the center island. Then she saw the explanation for the lack of traffic: a sandwich board blocked the entrance to the drive-through. She presumed the same sign was tacked to the other side.

Not understanding her trepidation, Lina inched up to the window.

The shades hadn't been pulled, but she still couldn't see anyone. Aliens had beamed everyone in the bank up to their spaceship. IT guys had taken employees hostage until they fully understood the hideous mistake someone had made that had frozen up the bank's computers.

Only…shouldn't someone be laboring on one of the computers? Unless the problem was offsite, but if that was so, why wasn't Maya answering her phone and *where was everybody?*

Lina's skin prickled. She shifted a few feet to the left and with a rush of relief saw four people standing in a cluster. Mr. Floyd and Maya and two men. Okay, she'd been silly—except…one of the men held a gun to Maya's temple.

*Oh, God, oh, God.* This was a bank robbery, happening right in front of her. Without taking her eyes off the scene inside, Lina fumbled for her phone at the bottom of her purse.

The bank manager shook his head. He looked

scared but mulish. At the same time, Maya saw Lina with her face pressed to the glass. Her eyes widened, the terror on her face changing to something else.

The next second, her head blew up.

And then the man who'd shot Lina's best friend turned and saw her.

LEANING BACK IN his desk chair, Bran unwrapped the sandwich he'd just picked up from the deli. He didn't love eating at his desk, but he was trying to cram some work in so he could leave early. He had an appointment to talk to a woman who had been a neighbor of his family when he was a kid. She and her husband had lived right across the street when Bran's little sister, Sheila, was murdered. Apparently Mr. Greaver had died a few years back, but his widow had stayed put. Bran and his brother, Zach, both cops, were trying to get in touch with everyone who'd lived nearby then. Sheila's killer had never been arrested. Despite having no jurisdiction, they intended to accomplish what the investigators at the time had failed to do.

So far, they'd only hit dead ends, but there'd been something in Mrs. Greaver's voice when Bran had talked to her yesterday—

The door behind him burst open.

"Murphy," his lieutenant snapped. "Warring. Where the hell is Warring?"

Bran spun in his desk chair, surprised by the edge in his boss's usually rock-steady voice. "Break room, to get a drink from the machine. What's wrong?"

"Armed robbery at Snoqualmie Community Bank. First responders are on the way. I want you and Warring on it. The caller says she saw a loan officer shot in the head. If they're still in there…"

Bran tossed the sandwich on the desk and jumped to his feet. "How did somebody manage to call out?"

"She didn't. She couldn't understand why the doors were locked midday, so she looked in the drive-through window."

"Where is she now?"

"The Walgreens across the street."

"We're on our way."

He caught Charlie Warring just as he emerged from the break room carrying a can of Pepsi. Seconds later, they jumped into an unmarked sheriff's car and rocketed out of the parking lot, Charlie still groping for the seat belt as he tried to keep from spilling his drink.

"What the hell?"

Bran told him what he knew. During the drive, they both listened to the chatter on the radio. By the time they screeched to a halt outside the bank, they knew that the robbers had been gone when the first deputies arrived. An ambulance rolled up behind them. Two patrol cars with flashing lights were outside.

Charlie and Bran walked in to find the expected chaos. The uniforms had corralled customers and employees in one area, where two women sobbed and everyone else appeared distraught. One of the deputies saw Bran and jerked his head toward the counter that normally separated tellers from customers.

He stopped at a swinging half door. On the other side, two bodies sprawled on the carpeted floor. It wasn't instantly obvious how the man in the suit had been killed, although blood soaked the carpet to one side of him. The woman's body was another story. Blood, brains and bits of bone spattered the wall beyond her. The information had been accurate; no question, somebody had shot her in the head, and from close range.

"Jesus," Charlie murmured. "I bank here. I think she's the loan officer. Pretty."

She wasn't pretty anymore.

Bran pointed to the pile of cell phones, which suggested the robbers had had some foresight. They'd made sure no one texted out or snapped a photo of them.

Another uniform approached. Despite his attempt at stoicism, he appeared shaken. "My partner and I were the first responders. I hope the lady who called this in saw something, because nobody else did. They all agree that two masked men shoved through the doors yelling and waving guns. Customers and tellers were herded behind the counter and made to sit on the floor, facing the far wall—" he nodded in that direction "—and told to clasp their hands on their heads. They could hear what went on, but didn't see anything. I didn't even ask questions, and they started to babble. They tried to be helpful, but they all had different estimates of height, weight, race…" He shook his head. "Don't think you'll get a lot of help there."

"Thanks," Bran said.

Charlie offered to get things started there while Bran went looking for the witness who'd called 911. Charlie Warring was about Bran's age. With any other detective in the department, Bran would have refused, but he and Charlie had developed a trust.

"You suppose the lieutenant has already notified the FBI?" Charlie asked.

"Undoubtedly," Bran said with resignation. He'd never worked with the feds before, but he'd have his chance now. They were all over any bank robbery.

He found the pharmacy doors locked. A man peered at him from a distance away. When Bran held his badge up to the glass, relief appeared on the man's face and he hurried to let him in. With a nod toward the back, he said, "The lady who saw what happened is with the manager. Should I keep the door locked?"

"No need now. The robbers are long gone. But locking up was smart."

Bran took a moment to determine that no customers had been present when the witness came tearing in. Then he strode down an aisle and, at the back of the store, found an unlocked door marked "Employees Only." Past a restroom and what appeared to be a break room was an office. He knocked and identified himself as police.

A woman called, "Come in."

There were two women inside, one with her back to him, the other behind the desk. She rose to her feet at the sight of him. From the nice suit, he guessed she was the store manager. "I'm Laverne Dailey," she said.

"Detective Bran Murphy."

"Are the robbers still in the bank?" she asked.

"No, they were gone by the time the first unit arrived. I can assure you we'll do everything in our power to identify and arrest them." He heard the coldness in his voice.

The sight of those bodies had hit him harder than usual, maybe because of the location and the identity of the victims. This wasn't a domestic, or the fallout from a bar brawl. The dead weren't drug dealers or gang members. The bank was the kind of business where people expected to be safe. To the best of his knowledge, there'd never been a bank robbery in this county. And bank robbers didn't usually kill.

"A uniformed officer will be stopping by to ask some questions, just in case an employee noticed activity by the bank."

During his speech, the woman sitting with her back to him hadn't turned around. In fact, she hadn't given any sign she'd even noticed his arrival. She hunched over, her arms crossed as if she was hugging herself. Traumatized, and why wouldn't she be?

Honey-colored hair was bundled on the back of her head. His gaze fastened on it. Some people's hair was all one color. Hers had threads of pale gold, brown and red amongst the predominant dark blonde. He bet if he studied it long enough, he'd identify a dozen or more colors that together added up to a gorgeous, heavy mass of hair that… he knew.

No. It couldn't be.

He grabbed the second chair in front of the desk, pulled it to face hers and sat down. "Miss—"

She looked up and his mouth went dry. The woman who had haunted his dreams for months looked at him with red-rimmed, puffy eyes.

"You," she said flatly.

So she had recognized his voice. Bran let his gaze move over her, and what he saw made his heart stop beating.

She was pregnant. The curve of her belly was unmistakable. Bran wasn't an expert on pregnancy, but she had to be past the first three months or so, when women didn't much show. She wasn't swollen so big he'd worry about her going into labor right now, either. If he had to guess—

Jesus. If he had to guess, he'd put her at five or six months.

Six months ago, almost to the day, he'd made love to her without using a condom. He'd worried about that for a long time, even as remembering what it felt like to have her without the irritating barrier of latex heated his blood.

When he lifted his stunned gaze to her face, he found wariness had joined the grief and myriad of other emotions already there. Bran opened his mouth but had just enough self-control to close it before he said the obvious. *Did you plan to tell me?* Later, when they were alone, he'd be asking that question. Right now, he had a job to do. And she'd seen something horrific enough, he wasn't about to kick her when she was down.

"Ms. Dailey, may we borrow your office or the break room?"

The manager understood what he was asking. "Please, stay here," she said, coming around the desk. "Lina, are you sure I can't get you a drink?"

"That's a good idea," Bran said. "Something with sugar. She's in shock."

"I don't need—" Lina's brief defiance collapsed. "Thank you. But no caffeine, please."

Laverne Dailey squeezed her shoulder. "Of course not."

Lina and Bran sat in silence until the manager returned with a 7Up. Bran cracked it open and handed it to Lina. "Drink. The sugar will steady you."

After a moment, she nodded. The door closed quietly behind Ms. Dailey.

Lina took a swallow, but her hand was shaking, so he took the can from her and set it on the desk. "I need your full name," he said, wincing at how stiffly that came out.

He read the desperation in her eyes. "I wasn't imagining things, was I? Maya is dead."

"I'm afraid so. Maya…?"

"Lee. She is…she was a loan officer. And my best friend," she whispered, desolate.

Battling the need to draw her into his arms, he said, "I'm sorry for your loss, and that you had to see something so terrible."

She sucked in a breath. "Jurick." She spelled it. "That's my last name. I'm Alina Jurick."

"You live locally, I take it." He couldn't help the wryness in his tone.

Her eyes slid away before meeting his again. "Yes. I live in Clear Creek and teach at the middle school."

"What do you teach, Lina?"

"Social studies."

Bran only vaguely recalled his long-ago middle school classes. Social studies had been a mishmash of history and government, maybe a little anthropology and archaeology thrown in. He'd have liked to ask more, like why she had chosen to work with kids that age, but made himself stay on topic.

"Okay. You came to do some banking."

She shook her head. "No, Maya and I were going to have lunch. I talked to her about fifteen minutes before I arrived. I parked on the street instead of in the lot, because her boss doesn't even let employees park there, never mind friends."

He heard about her perplexity when she found the doors locked in the middle of the day, and resisted asking why the hell she hadn't called the cops right then.

"It was the sign," she said.

"Sign?"

"It was taped to one of the doors." She told him what it said.

"It's not there anymore. Which means they grabbed it on the way out."

"I think there was another one at the head of the drive-through. If they were in a hurry, they might have left that one."

"Good," he said. "Give me a second."

Charlie answered immediately and promised to send someone out to check.

Bran returned his phone to his belt.

"It did seem strange," Lina said. "But…normal strange. You know what I mean? I sort of knew something was wrong. But, um, there's this feeling of unreality. Who expects something like…" She wobbled to a stop, then clapped her hand over her mouth.

Bran lunged out of his chair and grabbed the wastebasket, putting it in front of her. She bent over and retched. When she seemed done, he found tissues on a credenza and gave her a handful, then urged her to sip more of the soda. At some point in there, he'd come to be crouched beside her, rubbing her back.

The look she gave him held such misery, he said, "Oh, hell, Lina," and rose, pulling her to her feet and into his arms. For a moment she stood stiff. He was about to release her when she made a muffled sound, leaned on him and seemed to go boneless. They stood like that for a long time. Inhaling her scent, he cradled the back of her head with one hand while he held her up with his other arm.

The hard mound of her belly felt odd wedged between them. It was like a purse or a—no, not a basketball—a soccer ball. Maybe one of those kid-size ones. Then he had the dazed thought that what he felt between them wasn't kid-size— it *was* a kid. A whole, complete person in the making.

That this particular baby might be his was something he couldn't let himself think about, not yet.

Once he would have sworn her belly quivered, but probably all of her had.

Finally, she sighed and didn't so much ease back as collapse onto the chair. "I'm sorry. You must have more important things to do than wait while I freak out. I guess you need to hear what I saw, don't you?"

"I do, but you don't have anything to be sorry for. Anybody would have been shaken up."

He didn't recall ever being reluctant to push a witness to tell her story like this before. Bran hoped he was a compassionate man, but softer emotions weren't in his repertoire.

"I couldn't see anyone else. There had to be tellers in there."

She didn't want to ask whether they were dead, too, he guessed.

Bran resumed his seat. "Two tellers, two customers. The robbers made them sit on the floor
behind the counter, hands on their heads, facing
away from the confrontation you saw. They're
shaken up, but not hurt."

She gave a jerky nod, then continued, telling
him she hadn't really looked at one of the two
men, but she knew he'd worn a ski mask. "So I
couldn't have seen his face anyway. I think he
was shorter than the other robber. Mr. Floyd—
that's the bank manager—isn't tall. Like five foot
eight? They were about the same height. He was
thin. He had a gun, too."

This *he*, Bran supposed, was bank robber number two, not Mr. Floyd. "Was he facing you?"

"No, he was mostly turned away. I think he
was threatening Mr. Floyd, who was refusing to
do something." Her beautiful eyes widened. "Mr.
Floyd…was he hurt?"

"I don't have identities yet, but a man was
killed as well as your friend."

"Oh, no," she whispered. Her knuckles showed
white as she wrung her hands.

"I'm sorry," he said again, feeling helpless.
"Saying no to armed men threatening him wasn't
very smart."

"No." Lina was quiet for a minute. "Maya
didn't like him. I don't think any of the employees did. He was really full of himself, and sanc-

timonious. You know? It would be just like him to think he could stand up to those men because he was important and principled and of course they'd back down."

In other words, the guy was both a prick and an idiot.

He watched Lina collect herself. "The other one, he had the barrel of his gun pressed to Maya's temple. She looked so scared." She swallowed. "Maya saw me."

"What?"

"I think she kind of jerked and—" Lina did some deep breathing "—he shot her. Her head just…"

Bran covered her writhing hands with one of his. "Try to step back, as if it was a movie and not real. Did the guy pull the trigger because he was startled? Or do you think he'd been ordered to kill her?"

She stared at him, but he could tell she was replaying what she'd seen. "I think Mr. Floyd had been told that if he didn't cooperate, they'd kill Maya. And he wouldn't, so they did."

"That's what I think, too," Bran said gently. "Her seeing you had nothing to do with her death."

"Yes, but—" She gulped. "He shot her and then he turned. He saw *me*."

Bran's blood ran cold.

She shuddered. "And…and I saw *him*."

"He wasn't wearing a mask?"

She shook her head. "Why would he let anyone see his face?" she begged.

He didn't know. They must have known law enforcement would be watching the robbery within half an hour. Banks all had cameras.

"He couldn't shoot you through the teller's window," Bran said slowly. "They're bullet-proof."

"I don't know if he even came to the window. I ducked, really fast. And then I ran straight across the drive-through lanes and the side street instead of going to my car or…or to the alley to try to hide. In case he burst out the front or back door."

"That was smart." He fought to hide the rage and fear that made it hard to breathe. "Lina, did you recognize him?"

She shook her head, but some crinkles formed on her forehead. "Not really, although…he looked sort of familiar. Do you know what I mean?" she appealed to him. "He might just have had an ordinary face, but it's like, oh, if you see someone out of context and can't place them. They're a stranger, but not."

"Like a grocery checker you notice at the next table when you're eating out."

"Exactly like that," she said gratefully. "But it was such a quick glimpse…"

"If his face doesn't show up clearly on video,

we'll have you sit down with a police artist. However briefly you saw the man, I'm betting the artist and you can come up with a portrait."

She looked doubtful, but said, "I'll try."

"What worries me is that he saw *you*, Lina. You're memorable, not ordinary."

"I'm not."

"Yeah, you are. I had no trouble recognizing you." If he sounded a little dry, who could blame him?

"Yes, but you and I—" Color rose in her cheeks. "We…"

He knew what they'd done.

"I mean, we spent quite a while together. Talking and…"

Yep. *And.* They'd done a lot of that, too.

Blushing furiously, she said, "The other people in there must have seen *something*. And…and they'd have heard what was said."

"If we get anything useful from those who were in the bank, I'll worry less about you. From what I heard before I came over here, I'm not optimistic. It's also possible he'd just pulled the mask off when you saw him."

She stared at him, stricken. "If he did…that means he was going to kill Maya either way, doesn't it?"

"I'm afraid so" was the best he could do. The video could be grainy; the guy's face might be caught at an angle so that distinguishing features weren't clear. Or no camera had pointed the right way to capture his image at the moment he'd been unmasked. But her friend had had a close look at him.

"Oh, God." She hugged herself again.

Very aware of the passing minutes, Bran said, "Lina, I have to get back to the bank. You and I need to talk, but we'll save that for later. I'm only going to ask one thing right now. Is that baby you're carrying mine?"

She seemed to shrink into herself, making him feel like a bastard, but he had to know. After a minute, her head bobbed. "Yes."

Damn. It was like seeing someone running out in front of his car, knowing he would never be able to brake in time. His vision had sharpened and time slowed, but his reactions had slowed, too.

He could only nod. "All right." Really? It was all hunky-dory? *No problemo?*

*Do your job.* "Lina, I won't be able to get away for hours. I don't want you to go home until we know more, in case the guy did recognize you. Do you have family close by? Or a friend who will let you spend the night if necessary?"

She stared at him. "But… I don't have anything with me. Except my purse." Looking more like a satchel, it sat by her feet.

"As soon as I break free, I'll come get you. Then we'll figure out what to do. But if you're the only one who saw his face and this guy by any chance did know you, he can't afford to let you identify him. Do you understand?"

She nodded, her face so white he was afraid she might keel over. But her back stayed rigid. "Yes. I saw what he's willing to do."

Damn. She had.

"Tell me where you'll be."

"Let me make a call." She dug in the bag for her phone, and a moment later was talking to someone. She finished by saying, "I'll tell you all about it when I get there. Thank you, Isabel." The call ended. She told him the friend's name and address.

He took her phone from her and added his number to her contacts, then put hers in his phone. "I'll walk you to your car."

They both thanked the manager on the way out. As they crossed the street, Bran said, "I'm going to have you take a look at the parking lot. Do you remember what vehicles were here when you arrived?"

"Yes." They walked past the bank so she could see the lot. "Those are the same cars that were here then."

"Okay. Where did your friend park?"

"I noticed it on Maple." That was the street

they'd just crossed. My car is only half a block from hers."

"Is that why you parked where you did?"

"No, there wasn't any room in front of the bank." She saw something on his face. "They didn't park in the lot, did they?"

"No, they'd have gotten as close to the front door as they could. Preferably blocking any view of the bank from passing traffic."

"Close to the front...there was a gold Camry. I noticed it because my parents have one like it. And a cargo van. My car is really small, so I could have squeezed in between the van and the Camry, but I'm not very good at parallel parking and it would have been tight."

"Okay," he said, keeping his tone relaxed. He didn't want her to freeze up. "Describe the van to me."

"It was white, with panels instead of windows along the side. On the back, too, I'm pretty sure. I remember thinking I wouldn't like having to rely totally on mirrors."

"Was there a company name on the side or the door? A decal of any kind? A bumper sticker?"

But she was shaking her head. "Nothing. I doubt I'd have noticed a bumper sticker. I mean, I barely glanced at the back of the van when I was thinking of trying to squeeze in behind it."

"I don't suppose you noticed the license plate."

"Not a chance." She hesitated. "I guess it might have caught my eye if it had been an out-of-state license or a custom one."

That was his guess, too, given how extraordinarily observant she had proved herself to be.

With a hand on her arm, he nudged her into movement again. "Getting away was the smart thing for you to do. You had no reason to focus on the van."

Cops clustered outside the bank's front door. The medical examiner was just going in. Bran nodded at him.

"Which car is yours?" he asked Lina, looking to the cross street.

"The Kia."

He had her point out her friend's, too, before asking, "You feel steady enough to drive?"

She took a deep breath. "Yes. Anyway, it's not that far to Isabel's."

He insisted on walking her to her peanut of a car and watched as she wedged herself behind the wheel and adjusted and fastened the seat belt. How in hell did women who were eight months pregnant still reach the pedals?

Shaking the thought off, he waited until she had closed the door and then rolled down the window to look up at him.

"Okay," he said. "Keep an eye out behind you on the way. If any other vehicle seems to be sticking with you, I want you to come right back here. Call me, too. Don't wait until you get here. Do you understand?"

Lina bit her lip but nodded.

"And call if you remember anything else you think I should know."

"I will."

"If it looks like I won't make it before bedtime, I'll let you know. This Isabel understands you might have to stay, right?"

"Yes. She teaches at the middle school, too. We've gotten to be good friends."

One hand flat on the roof of her car, Bran looked down at her. "I'd suggest you have a glass of wine, but I guess you can't do that."

She actually tried to smile. "Probably one glass wouldn't hurt anything, but I made a no-alcohol, no-caffeine vow once I realized I was pregnant."

"You don't smoke, do you?"

"No. I never have. And I wouldn't."

Feeling foolish, he nodded. "I'll call, Lina."

Without another word, she pushed a button so her window glided up and put on her turn signal before pulling out onto the street. Afraid she'd get a ticket if she didn't? No, he thought; Lina Jurick was a law-abiding citizen. A good girl, who had done something very uncharacteristic the night she'd gone to a cheap motel with him.

Standing where he was for longer than he

should have, watching until the little Kia turned out of sight three blocks away, he wondered if his promise to call had sounded reassuring to her, or whether she'd taken it as a threat.

He swore under his breath. Would she ever have told him about the baby if they hadn't come face-to-face? Part of him was scared shitless. And part of him...he didn't know...and couldn't take the time to untangle it all.

Bran turned and walked into the bank.

# CHAPTER THREE

WAITING WAS REALLY HARD.

After one look at Lina when she first arrived at the Moreno's house, Isabel sent her two kids to their bedrooms. Then she sat Lina down in the kitchen and insisted she nibble on soda crackers and drink ginger ale while she told the whole, awful story.

Well, she didn't mention that, to complete the trauma, she had just come face-to-face with the father of her baby. Who happened to be the investigator.

Not even Maya had known who the father was. All Lina would ever say was that it had been a mistake. Admitting that she'd gotten drunk and willingly had repeated sex with a complete stranger in a cheap motel room? No.

Steadier, Lina was able to have a bowl of soup and half a sandwich with Isabel and both kids, who were told only that Lina was waiting for a friend to call. At three and five, they nodded incuriously and chattered away. Predictably, they were excited about Christmas. Their tree was up in the living room, but without gifts under it.

"Carmen might be able to keep her hands off them," Isabel said, once the children had trotted off to the living room to watch a Disney movie on DVD, "but Ricky never could. They've both been hyper from the minute I left work Tuesday."

Of course, the women's conversation reverted quickly to the horrific scene at the bank. Isabel had met Maya through Lina and had to deal with her own shock.

"In Clear Creek!" she kept exclaiming.

Lina felt the same. She read in the newspaper about things like this happening, but it never did in this small, rural county. Except now she wondered if she hadn't been naive. Crimes of some kind must occupy Bran and all those other cops she'd seen swarming the bank.

Eventually she wound down as if her battery was failing. She had to ask if there was someplace she could nap. She was afraid she'd have had to lay her cheek on the table and sleep right there otherwise.

Once alone, exhaustion claimed her before she could shatter. It was as if her body had to shut down.

Hours later, she woke up disoriented. Night had somehow fallen. She'd have been completely in the dark if not for a night-light glowing softly on the dresser.

She was in Carmen's room, Lina remembered. Posters, wallpaper border and curtains all featured horses. Five-year-old Carmen had told her earnestly that she wanted to grow up to be a horsie rancher and a ballerina. She was dainty enough to be a ballerina, but admitted to having been on a pony only twice. Mama and Papa— she had looked daggers at her mother—wouldn't buy her a horse.

Lina stumbled to the bathroom across the hall where she washed her face and brushed and braided her hair. For a minute, she stared unseeingly into the mirror.

*Oh, dear God. Maya.* She wanted it to have been a nightmare, but knew better.

From the smells, Isabel must be cooking. Lina felt queasy, as if the morning sickness had reappeared.

Isabel looked her over anxiously when she appeared in the kitchen. "You look better. Would you like a pop? Or juice?"

That might help. Lina poured herself a glass of cranberry juice and sat down. "I'm being useless. I'm sorry."

"No, no. I wouldn't have let you help," her friend said. She nodded toward the bag Lina had plopped at her feet. "You should call the detective. He called *me* because you weren't answering. I think you scared him."

"I didn't hear it ring." Lina checked her phone. He'd tried her four times and left two messages. Listening to them, she realized Isabel was right; he did sound worried.

He answered on the first ring.

"I'm sorry," she said before he could say anything but her name. "I took a nap. I must have really conked out."

"So Isabel said. She checked on you for me."

"She did?"

"I'm winding things up here. Why don't I come over? I can update you on what we've learned, and then I think you can safely go home."

"Oh, thank goodness! Does that mean the camera was pointing at him?"

"Not exactly. I'll explain when I get there."

Either somebody was within earshot or he was determined to sit down face-to-face with her.

Or it wasn't really the bank robbery and Maya he wanted to talk about. He wouldn't confront her about the pregnancy here, with Isabel and maybe Eduardo or the kids within earshot, would he?

If not, he'd want to follow her home. There'd be no escaping the conversation she dreaded.

*The one we have to have*, she reminded herself. She'd always known she would have to tell him about the baby and give him the chance to be involved in her life. She just…kept putting it off.

"Okay," she said. "I'll wait until you get here."

"Ten minutes," he promised, and was gone.

He hadn't asked for directions, but she supposed he could find any place, even if it was within the city limits and therefore not in his jurisdiction, which was unincorporated county.

Predictably, Isabel insisted they should at least stay for dinner. She'd made plenty. Lina thanked her, but said, "Detective Murphy is a police officer. He feels obligated to tell me some of what they've learned, but after that he'd probably like to just get home."

"But it will be ready—" Isabel laughed and shook her head. "I have this ridiculous need to feed people. I'm turning into my mother. Ignore me."

Laughing for the first time in many hours, Lina hugged her petite, dark-haired friend. "If you're turning into your mother, it can't be such a bad thing. And if you mean it about dinner, I'll ask Bran—I mean, Detective Murphy—when he gets here."

Isabel's eyes sharpened at Lina's slip, but she didn't comment on it. "Either way is fine."

Bran had been more than kind today, but the closest thing to real emotion she'd seen on his face was the shock when he recognized her…

and saw that she was pregnant. Otherwise, he'd been guarded, even remote. She couldn't imagine him wanting to sit down with a cheerful family to share their dinner.

When the doorbell rang, she let him in, feeling an immediate punch of awareness. He wouldn't have to say a word or do anything to dominate any gathering. He did that with just his physical presence and those piercing blue eyes that took in everything.

"Why don't you come in and meet my friend?" Lina suggested.

"Sure." He took one step in and inhaled. "God, that smells good. I'm starved. No lunch."

"We're invited to stay for dinner. Eduardo should be home any minute. They have two kids, though…"

His stomach chose that moment to rumble, and one side of his mouth tipped up. "Do you think there's really enough to go around?"

"I'm sure."

She'd barely introduced him to Isabel when they heard the garage door rising. Lina didn't know Isabel's husband well, but had liked what she'd seen of him. He was a strong, stocky man not that much taller than her, his skin much darker than his wife's. His kids raced to greet him, and he had a huge smile as he tossed each one into the air in turn before gently setting them down.

Then he looked at Lina. "Isabel called to tell me. What a terrible thing to happen, and for you to see it…"

"I appreciate Isabel taking me in. And—" she smiled at the little girl "—Carmen letting me borrow her bed for a nap."

She had started to introduce the two men when it became apparent they already knew each other.

The next thing she knew they were all seated around the dining room table eating chile verde con puerco with refried beans and warm corn tortillas. Lina guessed Isabel had been cooking all afternoon, but maybe it was one way she enjoyed using her days off. Lina barely nibbled at her dinner, hoping no one noticed, but Bran ate enough for both of them.

He answered a few questions from the adults about the robbery, careful not to say anything the kids shouldn't hear, then began talking to Eduardo about his business, Clear Creek Power Equipment. It sounded as if he had rented equipment from him a few times. He had also investigated a burglary from the business.

Isabel taught biology and coached the girls' soccer team. "They asked me to take over the basketball team, too," she joked, "but I had to admit it isn't my sport." They all laughed at that. Isabel might have been five foot one. Her husband teased her, saying she could make a basket if she were standing on his shoulders.

After accepting hugs and promising to call, Lina and Bran left.

"I'll follow you home," he said, his tone completely inflexible.

Shivering, Lina didn't argue. Snow had been forecast for the next day or two, and she wondered if it might start falling tonight. They could hardly stand out here on the sidewalk and talk.

Bran's black Camaro hugged her bumper all the way home. At her complex, he parked illegally but stuck something on his dashboard that she assumed said Police or the like, and followed her into the lobby where she collected her mail before leading him to the elevator.

As it rose, he said, "Your friends are nice people."

"They are. You already knew Eduardo."

"Because of the investigation."

The elevator doors opened and they went down the hall to her apartment. "And you rented equipment to work on your house," she said, curious about him.

"I live in an apartment, too. I've been helping my brother work on an old place he's restoring. I'd have said it was a dump, but it's starting to look good."

She unlocked the door. "You're lucky to have family nearby."

"He only moved here this spring. We'd…lost touch."

Lina wondered about the hesitation, but only nodded. Once inside her apartment, she watched as he assessed it, starting with the small, decorated tree that sat on a tabletop, then taking in her bookcases, furniture, the opening into the kitchen.

"Can I get you a cup of coffee?" she asked, as much to fill the silence as anything.

He shook his head. "Not when you won't be having any."

"It's no trouble…"

"Thank you, Lina, but no." He nodded toward her sofa. "Why don't you sit down?"

She did, her apprehension making her feel like a child who knew she was in trouble. So much for having the upper hand because this was *her* territory.

"What did you mean by *not exactly*? Did you or didn't you see his face?"

Bran sat in a maple rocking chair facing her across the coffee table. "There's not a good view."

"How can that be?"

He sighed. "Cameras are aimed in front of the tellers, not behind them. One placed to the side let us see your friend and the manager with the two men, but it wasn't a good angle. Both men wore knit ski masks. They stormed in, brandished weapons and yelled to intimidate the employees and the two customers who were in the bank at that point. Only one teller was at work, and she froze and didn't push the alarm. They took away everyone's cell phones. As I said, they were made to sit on the floor with their backs turned. According to one of the women, they were told that the first person trying to sneak a look would be shot."

"So none of them did."

"No. They were scared out of their skulls. None of them could even describe body types. They all agreed both men were big, which is typical when witnesses are scared. They did confirm that you were right about what was going on. The manager was refusing to open the vault. The robber who did the talking said they'd kill the woman if he didn't do what they wanted. He said no again."

A whimper escaped her.

He half stood, then sat again, his hands gripping the arms of the chair. "I'm sorry, Lina."

She took some deep breaths and was finally able to nod.

"When the guy grabbed your friend, she fought. From what we can see on the video, it looks like she hooked her fingernails in the knit mask and pulled it sideways. He wouldn't have been able to see at all. Subduing her, he couldn't fiddle with it to align the eyeholes, so he wrenched it off. After he shot her, he grabbed it and put it back on. He wasn't without it for more than a minute, if that."

"But Mr. Floyd would have seen him, too."

"Yeah. That was a death sentence for him, I'm afraid. That and— "

She could tell he didn't want to finish the thought. So she did. "And trying to stand up to them?"

"I'd have put it a little differently," Bran said. "If he'd cooperated from the beginning…"

Maya and he would both be alive. Lina swallowed and nodded.

"We'll definitely want you to sit down with the artist," he continued. "A couple of FBI agents arrived, and they're pretty excited that you saw him. It turns out they've been after these two for a while."

"What do you mean? Have they robbed other banks?"

"This is at least the third, and there's a possibility of others. These guys have used the signs before. They took them away when they left after the two previous robberies, but witnesses had noticed them and remembered the wording, which was identical to what you saw and to the one taped to that sandwich board. You were right— they did take down the one on the door as they fled, but left the one at the drive-through. Unfortunately, neither have any fingerprints. These guys are careful."

Hung up on what he'd said at the beginning of that last speech, she asked, "What do you mean, a possibility of others?"

"There've been a couple others in the past eighteen months that were so similar, it's likely the same two guys. Ski masks, yelling, making everyone sit behind the counter with their backs turned. No one saw signs."

"If no one happened to come to the door or try to go through the drive-through…"

"Exactly," he said.

"I remember the news mentioning several bank robberies not that long ago," she said, trying to recall details. "But weren't they down south?"

"The two where we know they used the signs were both in Pierce County. One in Tacoma, one in Lakewood." Two hours away, then. "The others that may be linked happened in Issaquah and Monroe."

So, midway. Both were at least an hour drive from Clear Creek.

"Because of the string of robberies, we're assuming the two men are not locals," Bran said. "The agent in charge of the investigation suspects that they live in Pierce County, but decided it was getting too hot down there for them to risk hitting another bank in the area. Some had taken additional precautions, including armed guards, and these two were smart to be nervous."

"That's why you think I don't have to worry." She felt lighter, suddenly.

"It's likely that the guy just had one of those faces that isn't especially distinctive."

"Have they killed anyone before?"

He shook his head.

Lina absorbed the information. So much anger rose in her, for that instant she was almost glad Mr. Floyd was dead, too. If not for him, Maya wouldn't have died. He'd put the bank's money ahead of her life.

They sat in silence for long enough, she had trouble making herself look at Bran. Could he tell what she was thinking? If she didn't say anything else, would he go away?

If he did, that would only give her longer to tie herself up in knots. *Ask. You have to ask.*

She took a deep breath. "Are you married?"

He jerked, rocking the chair. "What? Why would you think—" Then he fell silent.

"I saw the invitation. You left it on the dresser. It was…it was your wedding day."

"Oh, hell." He sounded weary. "That's why you took off, isn't it?"

"Yes."

"I'm not married, Lina. I wouldn't have slept

with you the night before my wedding, for Christ's sake. How could you think—"

"I didn't know you. I still don't know you." With an effort, she calmed herself. "But you were planning to get married."

"We'd called it off a couple days before I met you." He made an odd sound. "She called it off."

"It's not very flattering to me, either way," Lina said. "All I knew was that I'd been stupid." So much for calm. Every tumultuous emotion she'd felt today coalesced into a burst of rage. "You didn't use a condom!"

"No." Honesty and regret showed stark on his hard face. "I didn't even think about it until later. I'm sorrier than I can say. I…worried." He paused. "I tried to find you."

Because he was afraid he'd gotten her pregnant, not because he wanted to see her again. Good to know.

"If you saw the invitation, you knew my name."

She bent her head and focused on her hands, clenched into fists on her thighs. "Yes."

"Were you ever going to tell me?" For the first time, anger crackled in his voice, too.

"Yes." She made herself lift her head and meet those blue eyes. "I swear I was."

"When?"

"Soon." She'd been telling herself the same

thing for months. *Soon*. More honestly, Lina said, "Before she's born."

He looked stunned. "She?"

"Yes. I had an ultrasound. I'm having a girl."

"You mean, *we're* having a girl."

She didn't blame him for the renewed anger, even though she had good reason to be mad, too. "It's *we* if, well, you believe this is your baby. And you plan to take responsibility."

"Yeah," he said hoarsely. "I believe you. And of course I do. This is my fault."

"This?" She shot to her feet. "If you see this baby as some horrible mistake you feel duty-bound to take responsibility for, forget it!"

Instead of fighting back, he let out a pained sound and rubbed both hands over his face. "Lina, will you sit down?"

She wanted to tell him this was *her* baby and he could take a hike. But she suspected her volatile emotions had more to do with hormones and the horror of the day than with anything he'd said. Slowly, she lowered herself again to the sofa.

He sounded inexpressibly weary when he said, "You've had time to come to terms with it. I haven't."

"You're right," she said stiffly. "I'm sorry."

"Did you consider an abortion?"

She closed her eyes and made herself be honest. "Briefly. I was…pretty freaked out. But, you know, I'm thirty-two. I want to have children. I can be a good mother on my own."

"You won't be on your own."

She couldn't deny that financial support would be welcome. A teacher's salary wasn't fabulous. Even if she could work up until the birth, she would miss the last three months of the school year, which would eat up a fair amount of her savings.

"Do you have other children?" she blurted. Why hadn't she wondered before?

"No. God, no. I've never been married." A muscle twitched in his jaw. "You?"

"I'm divorced."

At her answer, emotion crossed his face. She couldn't quite decipher it.

At last he nodded. "There's more we'll have to talk about, but right now I just want to say one thing. From here on out, this baby ties us together. It would help if you could trust me."

He hadn't gotten mad. He almost sounded… gentle. Lina took some deep breaths and remembered the hope she'd felt that morning six months ago, before she saw the wedding invitation. What had he done that was really so awful? Face it, she'd readily agreed to spend the night with him. He had gone so far as to give her an out when he asked if she'd be sorry in the morning, and she knew in her heart he wouldn't have taken her to bed if she'd said yes, or even maybe.

Not using a condom had been unbelievably stupid, of course, but he'd probably been hungover.

She was making excuses for him.

Well, who was she to talk? The responsibility had been shared. Drowsy or not, *she* should have thought about a condom, too.

And…he was right. He would forever be her child's father.

"I…I think I can," she said shakily. "Trust you, I mean."

"Thank you." Instead of leaving, he asked, "Do you feel all right? You're not having any problems?"

"So far, no big problems. I was sick to my stomach for a couple months, but mostly right now I just need more sleep than usual."

He gazed at her, unblinking. "What do you mean, *so far*? And do you have problems that aren't *big*?"

"Nothing ominous." Although she worried constantly. "My blood pressure is a little higher than the doctor would like. She's leaning on me to get plenty of exercise, which I'm doing. Otherwise… things can go wrong later in the pregnancy, but that's rare. I've always been healthy. My mother had no difficulties in childbirth." When he failed to look convinced, she added, "It is all natural, you know."

"Do you feel the baby moving?"

She smiled and looked down to see that she had laid an open hand on her swollen belly. "Yes. It's amazing. The first time—" she lifted her head "—it was a flutter, like a butterfly inside me. But she's already getting stronger. She'll be kicking me before I know it."

He appeared unwillingly fascinated. "I've never really been around many pregnant women. Today I wondered how you'll manage to drive when you get further along."

She made a face. "I don't know. I want to work as long as I can, though, which means driving."

"At least you'll have the summer."

"Combined with maternity leave, it'll give me nearly six months off, thank God. I have a bad feeling that leaving her in day care will be hard."

Lina would swear he was making calculations, but he didn't share them with her. Instead he shook his head after a minute. "Man."

"I'll bet you wish you hadn't gotten out of bed this morning."

"But you were going to surprise me with the news one of these days anyway, weren't you?"

Lina didn't like the sardonic note in his voice. He didn't believe she would have told him. She'd have liked to be offended, but couldn't really blame him. After all, she'd procrastinated for months.

"I would have."

He rose abruptly and said, "I'll let you know when we get the sketch artist scheduled. The holiday may complicate that. I assume you're off work."

"We go back the fourth."

"Can you make yourself available tomorrow for the FBI agents to interview you?"

"Yes."

His gaze settled on her Christmas tree before returning to her. "Are you expecting family?"

She wasn't expecting anyone. Did she have to tell him the truth? He'd think she was pathetic.

"My family lives near Minneapolis. Flying didn't sound like fun right now—" she touched her stomach "—so I decided not to join them."

He frowned a little. "Won't you be celebrating with friends?"

"Maya—" Her voice hitched. "Maya was my best friend."

"I'm sorry I reminded you."

"Did you think I'd forget?" she asked incredulously.

"No." A man she suspected was rarely hesitant, Bran lingered, looking down at her. "You're likely to have nightmares, Lina."

"I didn't this afternoon when I napped."

"It'll all catch up with you." On that cheerful note, he nodded. "I'll call in the morning. Lock up after me."

She followed him to the door. He hovered momentarily just outside as if he wanted to say something else, but finally dipped his head again and walked away without looking back.

Lina closed the door and locked it, then sagged against it, the painted steel cool beneath her forehead. Thoughts and images tumbled in her head like clothes in the dryer.

*Maya staring at her. Her head... The monster seeing her. Tearing across the street, expecting a bullet to strike her any moment.*

And then the shock of having Bran walk in.

At least she'd gotten the dreaded meeting over with, but...

*From here on out, we're tied together.*

Lina moaned and bumped her head repeatedly against the door.

# CHAPTER FOUR

BRAN SHOULD HAVE gone straight home, but his car seemed to steer itself across town to his brother's house. Christmas lights glittered like icicles around the eaves, and a warm glow from the windows told him Zach and Tess were still up. He glanced at his watch: 7:34. Of course they hadn't gone to bed. Bran realized how unbalanced he felt. With a snort, he thought, *Unbalanced? How about stupefied?* His damn head was spinning. The day felt as if it had already lasted twenty-four hours at least.

He turned off the engine but hesitated. He should have called first. And…was he really ready to tell anyone else?

Bran guessed he must be, or he wouldn't be here.

With a sigh, he got out and crossed the lawn, bounding up the steps to the porch. He rang the bell and waited. No surprise, Zach had put in a new front door with a peephole. He worried about Tess, and for good reason. After the two of them witnessed an ugly crime committed by another sheriff's deputy, she had been terrorized. Even though Andrew Hayes, the deputy, had been convicted of attempted first degree murder for trying to kill Tess, Zach hadn't let down his guard. Bran didn't blame him.

Zach opened the door. If he was surprised, it didn't show. There was still tension between the two of them—reconnecting after twenty-five years wasn't easy—but tonight Bran saw only welcome.

"Hey, come in. I hear you had an exciting day."

He didn't know the half of it.

"It was a little out of the ordinary," Bran agreed. "I was heading home, but somehow I ended up here."

"Have you eaten? We have leftovers."

"Thanks, but I had a good dinner. I'd sent Lina—uh, our principal witness—to a friend's house, and when I went to get her, they fed us. Best Mexican food I've eaten in years, if ever."

A slightly raised eyebrow told him he hadn't distracted Zach from his slip. But it didn't matter—wasn't he here to spill his guts?

"Bran!" Tess had popped out of the kitchen and, smiling, came toward the two men. She rose on tiptoe and kissed him on the cheek, something she'd taken to doing lately. No, not lately—since her wedding day. She'd apparently decided Bran was her brother-in-law, so by God she'd treat him like family whether he liked it or not.

The odd thing was, he did like it, even if he hadn't said so. He liked Tess. She was a gutsy woman. He liked that she was making his brother happy. Their screwed up childhoods had left Zach determined never to marry or have a family, a resolve that crashed and burned when he couldn't run from Tess. Keeping her safe had meant keeping her close.

"If this is a bad time…"

She frowned. "Don't be silly. Do you want a beer?"

"Uh…thanks. Sure."

"Zach?"

"Yeah, I'll take one, too."

They got comfortable in the living room, which was one of the first rooms they had finished remodeling. The day Bran came to help replace the roof, the wood floors in the whole house were worn, and there had been holes in the walls in here. Zach had applied a thin coat of plaster over the new wallboard, and now they were a creamy white while the hardwood floor gleamed. The star on the Christmas tree in front of the window almost touched the ceiling.

This house looked like a home now. Disquieted, Bran realized it had come to feel more like home to him than his own apartment did. He had dinner here at least a couple times a week, and often spent one of his days off helping Zach work on the place.

Tess reappeared with two bottles of a dark German beer, smiled and said, "I'll leave you two to talk."

"No, you can hear this unless there's something you want to get back to," he heard himself say.

"Of course I want to hear." She plopped down on the sofa next to Zach, who wrapped an arm around her.

At first sight, anyone would have been able to tell the two men were brothers. Both were an inch or two above six feet, athletic. Zach's features were cleaner cut, making him handsome and Bran...not. At least in his opinion. Zach had dark hair, Bran a deep auburn darkened from the carrot-red he'd been born with. Both had blue eyes the same color as their mother's, a fact that disconcerted Bran when he thought about it. He'd turned his back on her a lot of years ago and still wasn't happy to have been forced to accept her in his life. Again, because of Zach.

Tess was a cross between sex goddess and girl-next-door with her scattering of freckles. She was tall enough to have modeled, had thick, glossy, maple-brown hair and green-gold eyes. Bran wasn't oblivious to her sexual appeal, but hadn't been slammed with it at first sight the way his brother was. Good thing, as it turned out.

Now Lina, she'd hit him hard. If he'd had her number, he'd have called her within twenty-four hours. Truth was, he hadn't so much as touched another woman since the night with Lina. He had convinced himself it was because of Paige and the last-minute cancellation of their wedding, but he knew better now. He hadn't been able to get Lina out of his head.

Nobody said a word. Their expectant expressions spoke for them.

He groaned and tugged at his hair, which was more characteristic of Zach than him. Getting started wasn't easy. "The night before my wedding—what should have been my wedding—I got drunk."

Zach nodded, even though he, like Bran, wasn't much of a drinker.

"I should have gone home, but I didn't. I went to a tavern, and I met a woman. We spent the night together, but I didn't know anything but her first name. When I got out of the shower in the morning, she had taken off."

"With your wallet?" his brother, the cop, asked.

"No. She hadn't touched anything. I made some attempt to find her, but with only a first name, I struck out." He hesitated, suddenly wishing he hadn't invited Tess to sit in on this confession. "I didn't use a condom."

"Oh, dear," she said.

He grimaced. "The one solid witness to today's bank robbery? It's her. Lina. Lina Jurick. And she's six months pregnant."

Zach swore.

"She didn't know how to find you, either?"

That was Tess, optimistic about human nature.

"She knew," he said grimly. "Turns out, I'd had the damn wedding invitation with me. While I was in the shower, she saw it. That's why she took off."

"O-oh," Tess breathed.

"She swears she was going to tell me before the baby was born. It's a girl," he added. "What it comes down to is, I'm going to be a father."

"Shouldn't you insist on some testing?" his brother asked. "To be sure you *are* the father?"

Bran shook his head, sure at least about this much. "Lina isn't like that. She teaches at the middle school. She's a thoroughly nice woman."

"Pretty?"

"Beautiful." He rubbed a hand over his jaw. "My head is spinning."

"How much did she see today?" Zach asked.

Bran told them about the robbery and about his own initial fear that the killer might know Lina. "Doesn't sound likely, though," he concluded. "She says he has one of those faces. Not ugly, not handsome. Not memorable. His head was shaved, and she isn't sure if he was partially bald or what. She thinks he might have had an earring but didn't see any tattoos. The feds will be sitting down with her in the morning, and the sketch artist as soon as we can line it up."

"But tomorrow is Christmas Eve."

"Yeah, that complicates things."

"So, back to Lina," his brother said. "What's your plan?"

Wheels had been grinding in his head since he'd set eyes on her at the pharmacy. "Spend time with her," he heard himself say. "Unless I don't like her, I'll marry her." He shrugged. "Why not? I intended to marry. I want a family. With her, I already have one."

Amusement glinted in Zach's eyes, but Tess gaped at him.

"Just like that?" She sounded outraged. "No special fondness required? If that's not a recipe for disaster!"

"Why would it be?" he countered. "I liked her when we talked. And we did talk quite a bit that night. We're attracted. We're having a baby together. Not so many years ago, that alone would have guaranteed a wedding."

"But it doesn't anymore. Bran, what if you fall in love with someone else? What if she does?"

He'd kill the son of a bitch, that was what. Bran blinked at the violence of his reaction to the idea. No, he decided, there was nothing surprising about it. She was carrying his baby. She was his, even if she didn't know it yet. He didn't share, and when he made a commitment, by God he kept it, and he expected the same of her.

"I'm closing in on forty," he said. "It's not happening."

"So you were drunk that night," Zach said thoughtfully, rather than asking how old Lina was. "What about her?"

Suddenly wary, Bran asked, "And that matters how?"

"She was at a tavern on her own, maybe getting plastered. Either that wasn't so unusual for her, which makes me think you should ask some more questions before she puts your name on that birth certificate, or it *was* unusual for her, in which case you have to ask yourself what was going on that had her there."

He stared at his brother, who was right. He should have asked himself exactly that. Why hadn't he? Because she seemed so nice? What kind of idiot was he?

After a minute, he nodded. "Okay."

"Does she have family in town?" Tess asked.

"No. Doesn't sound like she's going anywhere, either."

Her forehead crinkled. "She won't be by herself for Christmas, will she?"

"I don't know," he admitted. "I didn't get a straight answer." He hesitated. "The loan officer Lina saw killed? Maya Lee was her best friend."

A gasp escaped Tess, who pressed a hand to her mouth. Even Zach looked disturbed.

"She was there because they were supposed to have lunch together. In no time, it's going to occur to her that, if she'd suggested an earlier time, her friend would be alive. Or she'll come up with some other reason to start blaming herself. I told her she's going to have nightmares," Bran said. "I didn't like leaving her, but I didn't have a lot of choices."

"Do you think she'd join us tomorrow night?" Tess asked immediately, with the generosity he'd come to expect of her.

"Your dad will be here." Not, thank God, his mother, who had plans with her current husband—number five—and stepkids. Bran would have preferred never to see her again, but he had been polite at Zach's wedding. He wasn't looking forward to the next time he had to be polite to her.

"So?"

"I don't know, Tess. I'll…think about it. She may not want to."

"She's going to be the mother of your daughter, no matter what. That makes her family, in a way."

"I told her that, but I don't think she's quite over finding out why I was there getting plastered that night. She was offended to think I was supposed to get married the next morning. I think she figures she was some sort of stand-in."

His brother's eyebrows rose. "Wasn't she?"

Bran scowled. "No."

His brother smiled. "You being mad and depressed didn't have anything to do with you taking a woman you didn't know to bed."

"I wasn't depressed." He didn't deny the mad part. "I had no intention of picking up a woman. All I wanted was a few drinks. She and I hit it off. That didn't have anything to do with the damn wedding."

Zach's smile widened. "Then bring her tomorrow. Let us meet her."

He sighed and took the first swallow of his beer. "I'll try."

Zach asked about Mrs. Greaver and Bran's appointment to see her this afternoon. He had, at least, thought to call her instead of being a no-show. She'd sounded the tiniest bit relieved.

"If you're tied up with this bank robbery, I can get in touch with her," Zach offered. "Or has the FBI taken over the whole show?"

"Actually, these two haven't been bad to work with. They seem to want to collaborate."

His brother grinned. "You mean, they need minions to do their bidding, don't they?"

Despite his mood, Bran grunted a laugh. "Probably."

Not until he left half an hour later did he wonder if he hadn't stopped by to see Zach and Tess because he was hoping they'd suggest he bring Lina. Something about that small tree with only a few presents under it in Lina's apartment had saddened Bran, damn it, even though he wasn't big on holidays himself. This year, he hadn't bothered to decorate because he wouldn't be spending Christmas Eve or Day at his own place. Last year, he'd been stuck joining Paige's family. The year before, he ignored the holiday. This year was different. He had family again.

Discovering he was being driven by impulses lurking in his subconscious didn't make him happy. He used his head; he didn't make decisions because of emotions.

And, sure, he'd surprised himself with the announcement that he was going to marry Lina, but the decision itself was entirely rational. It disturbed him a little that his equally rational decision to marry Paige had blown up in his face the way it did, but he was grateful now it had. Lina was a better choice. He'd have stuck to the commitment he made to Paige, but the truth was, he'd been finding he didn't much like her as the wedding neared.

When she called it off, he'd been mad as hell. He'd never imagined himself in love with her, so it had been his pride that took the hit. Driving through the dark streets on the way back to his lonely apartment tonight, he admitted to himself for the first time that she had made the right choice for both of them. She wanted more than he could give. What he'd never seen before was that he had wanted more than she had to give, too.

Something was happening inside him, and it didn't feel good. His chest felt compressed as he tried to figure out what it was he did want, beyond wife and kids. Home.

He didn't have an answer.


THE PAIR OF FBI agents came to Lina's apartment. Never having met a real, live FBI agent, she felt intimidated as she let them in. One was a woman, which helped her relax. Probably in her forties, the first thing she asked was when Lina was due. The man, way younger, appeared increasingly uncomfortable as the two women discussed pregnancy and childbirth.

He finally growled, "Can we get on with it?"

His partner grinned. "Scared you, did we?"

They did get down to business, making Lina repeat everything she'd already told Bran and then some. They asked some good questions. She was able to make what she thought was a pretty accurate estimate of height for the robber who had shot Maya. She remembered that mud had splattered the tires and bottom of the doors and sides of the cargo van, something she didn't think she'd told Bran.

"It looked recent," she said, thinking it out. "I mean, it was dry, or mostly dry anyway, but if they'd driven for hours I'd have thought more of it would have fallen off. You know? It had to have been from the day before, when it rained."

"It might have rained here, but it didn't in Seattle," Agent Novinski, the woman, said flatly. She took out her phone and did a search. "Or in Tacoma."

"Ruts and holes on a dirt road can stay muddy for quite a while, though," Lina pointed out.

"That's true," Novinski agreed, but Lina could tell she wasn't satisfied.

They wanted a better description of both the men than she could give them. No, she had no idea what color the second man's eyes were. He had been looking at Mr. Floyd, not toward her. Wiry, short for a man. She was sure the hand that held the gun was encased in the kind of thin glove doctors and nurses wore.

They were even more dissatisfied when she

couldn't be sure what color eyes the guy who'd shot Maya had.

"But you say he stared right at you," the male agent said.

"Yes, but you know how thick the glass is, and I was looking through it at an angle. Plus, I'd just seen my best friend get shot." She glared at both of them. "It was horrible. Do you know what happens when somebody gets shot in the head?"

Clearly they did. Special Agent Novinski, the woman, had the grace to appear regretful.

"I was beyond shocked, and terrified, too. I can still see his face and the way he looked at me, but I didn't think, oh, he has blue eyes."

Naturally, at that moment she pictured Bran Murphy's eyes, a vivid blue. She wished, quite passionately, that he was here. He wouldn't let these two badger her.

"My best guess is hazel or light brown. You know, kind of in between." She frowned. "I don't think he had really dark hair, either. Even shaved, his head would have looked different if he did. His jaw would have been darker, too. He was definitely Caucasian." She spread her hands in a helpless gesture. "I looked at him for a total of maybe ten seconds. This is the best I can do."

Eventually they gave up and departed, leaving her feeling drained. Lunch might help, she thought, but didn't move. Even making a sandwich seemed like a herculean effort. She wished suddenly, selfishly, that she had gone home for Christmas. Maya would still be dead, but her death wouldn't be so brutally real. Lina wouldn't be the only person who could potentially identify one of the men who'd robbed at least three banks.

And, oh, yeah, she'd still be in deep avoidance about telling Bran he was going to be a father.

Her phone rang. His name came up. For some reason, she didn't hesitate to answer the call.

"Are they done with you?" he asked.

Stung, she said, "Hi. Yes, I'm fine this morning. Thank you for asking."

There was a short silence. "Are you really fine?" he asked, in a different voice.

"No." She closed her eyes. "I mean, yes, I'm okay."

"Have they come and gone?"

"Yes. I don't think I satisfied them, but I can't see through walls and ski masks, so they were bound to be disappointed."

"They were hopeful." Was that a smile in his voice? "Can I bring you lunch?"

Her stomach came to attention. "What kind of lunch?"

"I was thinking pizza, but if you'd rather I could stop for deli sandwiches."

In the interests of not gaining too much weight, Lina tried not to indulge often, but pizza sounded like exactly what she needed right now. "I would love pizza," she admitted. "Can you make mine half veggie?"

"You don't eat meat?"

"I just want to know I'm eating something healthy along with all the fat, okay?"

She heard a rusty sound that might be a chuckle. "Good thinking. Give me half an hour."

And he was gone.

"I DON'T LIKE the sound of that," he said flatly.

"Of mud?" Lina seemed bemused. "Why?"

He had set down his slice of pizza, wiped off his fingers and quickly checked his phone, to find that the last rain in south King County or Pierce County had been eight days earlier.

"Because it suggests they were staying up here for at least the previous day. They wouldn't have picked up mud on the highway or in town." The bank was actually outside the city limits because of recent growth the Clear Creek council members hadn't been farsighted enough to anticipate, to their current frustration over lost tax dollars. A good percent of homes in the rural county were on dirt or gravel roads that developed potholes and ruts. Very few homes on acreage had paved driveways, either.

"Well, doesn't that make sense anyway?"

Lina asked. "I mean, Tacoma to here is kind of a long commute."

He gave her a look she ignored. After two slices of pizza, she was full, which left her free to speculate.

"Plus," she continued, "surely they'd have wanted to, I don't know, scope out the bank in advance. Why did they pick that bank and not Chase or Opus or Whidbey Island Bank?"

He sighed. Starting at the crack of dawn, he'd watched videos from another local bank until his eyes were crossing. Charlie was doing the same, as were several borrowed deputies. The FBI had generously taken the footage from the bank that had been robbed. They'd let the locals waste time on banks the pair hadn't targeted.

"You're right. We're going back a couple of days, thinking we'll see the same face appearing at a couple of other banks. They are unlikely to have gone in together, because two men would draw more attention than one alone."

"What if one of them was in Snoqualmie Community," she suggested, "oh, ages ago and knew the layout was perfect and the only window on the street looks in at a conference room instead of the bank proper?"

"But why would he have been if he's not a local?"

"He has a girlfriend or just a friend up here

who needed to stop at the bank one day when they were together? He'd go in out of professional curiosity, wouldn't he?"

Bran did not want to believe either of those slugs had any reason to feel at home in Harris County, because if that was the case, the likelihood became greater that he had somehow encountered Lina and that the spark of familiarity she felt was because she had actually encountered the creep.

"We have to look," he said.

"I know." Sitting cross-legged on the sofa, she made a face. "I'm sorry. You know what you're doing. I won't think of anything you haven't already considered."

He braced himself. "I don't mind hearing ideas, but that's not what I'm here to talk to you about."

Her wariness showed. So did her belly. He was still shocked at the way arousal had slammed him when she opened the door. Not once had he ever noticed a pregnant woman at the grocery store and thought, *Wow, she's sexy.* Apparently Lina was different.

Part of it, he guessed, was the fact that she was carrying *his* baby. And then there were all the memories of that night, and especially of the morning when he'd made her pregnant. God, it had been amazing. He'd never felt anything like that before.

Also, unlike the day before, she wasn't making any effort to disguise her pregnancy. No coat or thigh-length sweater. Nope, over black leggings she wore a stretchy black top that clung like a second skin to the generous curves of her body. Maybe she'd planned to do yoga or something. Her feet were bare, too. He kept finding himself fascinated by her long toes and high arches. With the nails unpainted, her feet looked innocent. Maybe she couldn't reach them anymore, it occurred to him.

Her cheeks were turning pink, which meant he was staring.

He felt some heat in his own face. "Do you have plans tonight?"

"Why?"

"Because my brother and sister-in-law suggested you join us for dinner."

Her mouth fell open. "You told them about me?"

"Shouldn't I have?"

"I don't know! We haven't decided anything!"

"You decided to admit that you're pregnant with my child."

"*Yours?* Like you *own* her?"

"You know that's not what I mean," he said, exasperated. Why would she flip out because he'd told his brother she was pregnant?

Her eyes narrowed. "Did you tell them how it happened?"

Until this minute, it hadn't occurred to him that she might mind, and why. Oh, crap. Should he lie? Be honest?

No lies, he decided, not ever. "I did," he admitted.

Lina's glare felt like the midday, equatorial sun. He'd wake up in pain tomorrow. Her voice, in contrast, was exquisitely polite if also steely. "Then you may tell them thank you, that I appreciate their kindness, but no, I can't join them tonight."

He had to fix this. "They're not judgmental people, Lina. Once they knew your due date, they'd have figured out when you got pregnant. That alone would tell them I'd done something stupid."

"Which stupid thing are you talking about? Not wearing a condom? Or did you mean, being careless enough to leave the wedding invitation lying in plain sight? But wait. Maybe you did that on purpose to make sure I didn't hang around with any illusions, like hoping that we'd just had a beautiful beginning."

"We did have a beautiful beginning," he snapped, then was shocked when he realized what he'd said. But he tried to be honest with himself, and he'd felt something unfamiliar that morning.

The timing might have sucked, but the woman and he had meshed in a whole lot of ways.

She blinked a couple times, obviously taken aback. "Why would you say that?"

Bran rolled his shoulders. "Because it's true. I don't make a habit of picking up women in bars. Yeah, I had too much to drink, and yeah, having Paige dump me at the last minute like that stung, but that's not why I wanted you. You're beautiful, and you seemed sad, and I liked you." He felt awkward. "I would have asked you out if you'd still been there when I came out of the bathroom."

"Oh." Lina nibbled on her lower lip for a moment. Her gaze shied away from his momentarily before connecting again. "I would have said yes."

"Good." It was too soon to suggest marriage, even if he'd like to have it settled. His plan to create a family had stumbled over an obstacle, but now he had another chance. One he liked even better.

*One step at a time*, he told himself. Zach was right, he'd need to find out why *she'd* gotten drunk and had sex with a stranger. This wasn't the moment, though, especially not if he wanted to spend Christmas Eve with her.

So, keeping his voice gentle, he said, "You didn't answer my question about tonight. Do you have plans?"

After a moment, she shook her head.

"Then won't you come with me to Zach's? I'd really like you to get to know my brother and sister-in-law."

She searched his eyes, her own betraying more vulnerability than she'd probably like. "Are you sure I'm welcome?"

"I'm sure."

Her knotted hands clenched and tightened a couple times. "Okay. I admit, I wasn't looking forward to tonight, especially not after...you know."

He nodded. "I do know. Uh... I'd better get back to work. I'll pick you up at five thirty, if that works."

"Thank you," she said with dignity. "Can I bring anything? I mean, food?"

He guessed there'd be plenty, but he said, "Don't rush out to the grocery store, but if there's a dish you can make easily, Tess would probably appreciate it. I know she's baking a ham."

She told him she'd think of something, and escorted him to the door. Bran wanted to touch her, but the way she held herself aloof told him that wouldn't be smart. *Soon*, he told himself. He'd just achieved a significant win. He shouldn't get greedy.

# CHAPTER FIVE

"I'LL HELP YOU clear the table." Lina pushed back her chair and began gathering dirty dishes before anyone could argue.

But as it happened, none of the men, which included Tess's father, leaped up and insisted that in fairness they should handle the cleanup.

Already holding two empty serving dishes, Tess smiled. "Thank you."

In the kitchen, Lina said, "I suppose you cooked the entire meal."

Tess laughed. "I did. To be fair, though, Zach worked a shift today, while I stayed home. My partner and I decided not to open the store. Who was going to shop for carpet on Christmas Eve?"

Lina had learned that Tess was half owner of Fabulous Interiors, which offered flooring, window coverings, tile and more. The house Tess and Zach were still restoring had benefited from her ability to buy materials at cost. The gorgeous tile in the bathroom was a good example. Lina had had several opportunities to admire it and the claw-footed tub. As frequently as she needed a bathroom now, she was afraid she might as well move into one the last month.

Bran had told her that Zach was also a sheriff's deputy. He was probably lucky not to be out patrolling this evening. Law-enforcement agencies couldn't shut down for holidays.

"I like your dad," she said tentatively. He'd been positively courtly to her.

"I'm glad. I feel lucky to have him." Tess glanced over her shoulder and then lowered her voice. "He had a massive stroke almost three years ago. Rehab was slow, and I keep waiting for him to have another one. I feel blessed every day he's still here."

"That must keep you on edge. He looks good, though."

"He does," Tess agreed. "Better all the time."

"It seems like he and Zach are good friends."

"They are." She laughed. "Now."

Lina returned to get another load of dirty dishes while Tess started rinsing off plates and loading the dishwasher. Lina was feeling increasingly comfortable with the woman who, it had occurred to her during the evening, would be her baby's aunt.

"I'm glad you're here," Tess said unexpectedly, after she'd started to slice two of the pies. "Bran is so alone."

"Do you think so?" Lina asked, startled. "I

would have said he's guarded, but he's been..."
How to put it? "More generous and open than I expected, I guess. I thought he'd be mad at me for not telling him right away about the baby."

"I'll bet you could hardly wait to have *that* conversation."

"It was like staring up at Mount Everest, and I was supposed to climb it without oxygen."

They were both giggling when Bran appeared in the kitchen. He eyed them cautiously. "Tell me you weren't talking about me."

They laughed again.

With a glint in his eyes that might have been humor, he asked if the coffee was ready.

"It is," his sister-in-law said. "I'll pour if you'll go take orders for pie."

"Do you have ice cream?" he asked hopefully.

Tess patted his cheek. "Of course I do." She paused for a moment, watching him go. "He's loosening up."

"What do you mean?"

"I don't think he liked me at first. Or he didn't *want* to like me. Or he liked me, but didn't know how to show he did. Or—" She made a face. "I feel as if I still don't really know him. He and Zach have reasons for not being very trusting—" At the sound of footfalls, she broke off.

"Two blueberry, one apple," Bran reported. "Ice cream all around."

The women decided to each try the other's pie.

The men had been talking about college football and the upcoming bowl games when the women served them, but lost interest the minute they had forks in their hands.

"I like football," Lina said into the silence as they dug into the pie. "Mostly pro. Since I grew up in Minnesota..."

The men all groaned.

Eventually, they got around to talking about the next day. Zach was working the day shift again. With not much seniority, he hadn't been given a choice. He shrugged. "I'd have volunteered anyway. The guys with kids should have the holiday off. We can celebrate anytime."

"We're planning to gorge again tomorrow night," Tess said cheerfully. "I have a humongous turkey and we'll open our presents after dinner. Please join us, Lina."

She groped for a polite out. Her daughter might be family, but she wasn't. "That's kind of you, but I can't."

Bran's hand found hers under the table. "Please," he said softly.

Face burning, Lina looked around to see only friendly, encouraging expressions. Why were they being so nice to a woman Bran had picked up in a bar, for heaven's sake? But she knew.

However they felt about her, she was carrying Bran's baby.

"I can't," she repeated. "I haven't had a chance to buy gifts for any of you, and—"

"And we haven't for you, either," Tess said briskly. "But I can't stand to think of you alone tomorrow night."

Isabel had invited her to join her family, too, but Lina had already declined. It was better to be alone than feel like an outsider.

Although, somehow she hadn't felt like an outsider tonight. She thought it was possible she and Tess might become friends. And Bran was either an amazing actor, or he really wanted her to say yes.

After a moment, she smiled shakily. "Then thank you. This is really nice of you."

Bran squeezed her hand, but didn't let go of it. He rotated his coffee cup so he could pick it up with his left hand. Lina wondered if anyone else had noticed. She ought to tug her hand free, but couldn't make herself. How funny that she hadn't realized until this moment how alone *she* had felt, good friends notwithstanding.

The prospect of becoming a single mother was daunting. She'd have more support if she moved back home, but she hadn't seriously considered it. She loved her job and her coworkers, she liked Clear Creek, she didn't miss Minnesota winters and she hadn't felt close to her parents in a long while. She'd opened the distance because they hadn't liked David, and her mother, in particular, couldn't resist reminding her every single time they talked that she should have listened to them.

Yes, they'd been right and she'd been wrong, but she didn't need to hear it over and over and over. And now, an unplanned pregnancy and her being unmarried… Even though she *claimed* she was excited about her first grandchild, Mom would still be going on about the unmarried thing when Lina's daughter was accepting her college diploma.

Astonishingly, her baby had a father now. None of Lina's fears had materialized, at least not yet. The generosity of Bran's family astonished her. Tess, she thought, was genuine. Zach, Lina was less sure of, except that he'd been polite.

No, she couldn't entirely believe in all of this, but right now, at least…she didn't feel alone. And that was a gift.

CHRISTMAS HAD GONE WELL. Bran couldn't have planned it better if he'd been able to stage the whole thing. He'd seen Lina relax, minute by minute. Family was just what he'd needed to swing her to his point of view.

The twenty-sixth being a Saturday, Bran was at his desk. He'd gone in, hoping Novinski would have sent him the files she'd promised on the other robberies, but apparently she had taken the holiday off. Today, she'd loaded his inbox.

Warring had shown up today, too, as much a workaholic as Bran, and for the same reason. No wife, no live-in girlfriend, no kids. The thought drifted through Bran's head that he might change, but he shook it off. The threat to Lina, however improbable, had to be his priority.

"Good holiday?" Charlie asked, sitting down at the next desk with a cup of coffee.

"Yeah, it was." Surprisingly, he meant it. He had managed to buy Lina a present, which had both embarrassed and pleased her, if he was any judge. He'd stopped the afternoon of Christmas Eve at a jeweler and found a gold pendant that, with simple, almost abstract lines, depicted a man embracing a woman and baby. Bran's message wasn't subtle. "Had it with Zach and his wife," he said. And Lina. People would learn about the baby eventually, but he hoped to be engaged to her before then. "You?"

"My parents. They live in Seattle. My sister and her family were there, too." Charlie shrugged. "Her four-year-old thought Christmas morning was the greatest thing ever."

Bran's heart contracted hard, the sensation almost painful. Next Christmas, he'd have a kid of his own. Every once in a while, the reality of it hit him.

He forwarded some of the files to Charlie's email box, and they started to read. Bran, at least, was grimly determined.

It didn't take him half an hour to discover he concurred with the opinion of the feds: the same two men were responsible for at least five robberies besides the most recent. The first one, they'd made off with about $15,000, hastily gathered by a teller. The timing had been good enough after an armored car had arrived with cash at the Bank of America in Tacoma, they'd gotten away with nearly $100,000. The others were amounts in between, but altogether added up to damn near $300,000. Divided in half, though, that didn't make them rich men these days, which meant they were probably already planning their next job. The fact that they had killed people this time might make them nervous enough to take a longer than usual break—or getting away with it could have gone to their heads. They were already wanted not only for bank robbery but also for murder. What did they have to lose now?

His concentration wasn't as absolute as usual. Lina hadn't said what she would be doing today beyond her intention to swim laps at the high school pool. He didn't like the idea of her out and about even if common sense suggested that the last thing the two robbers would do was hang around Clear Creek. Unless they knew Lina's name, of course, but how could they? Even so, it wouldn't hurt for him to call and check in with her a couple of times.

He also couldn't forget that Mrs. Greaver, the neighbor from when he was a kid, had agreed to meet with Zach today. Talking to the woman on the phone, Zach, too, had sensed her reluctance. Were they about to catch a break?

Nothing about investigating their sister's murder had been pleasant. Zach, only nine years old when it happened, had been the one to discover Sheila's body. He would never be able to wipe that memory out of his head.

Their pretty, unfailingly happy sister had been raped and strangled when she was only six. The police had suspected Michael Murphy, Bran and Zach's father, if only because they had failed to come up with any other viable suspect. They had trouble believing that anyone could have sneaked into the house and taken Sheila out the back door without waking either of her parents, whose bedroom had been right next to Sheila's.

The marriage didn't last long after that. Bran had overheard enough of his parents' arguments to know they had thrown terrible accusations at each other. What marriage could survive that? Bran had already known that his mother was sleeping around, too. In the heated weeks following Sheila's murder, it became apparent that Bran's dad knew, as well, or had at least suspected.

In the end, a great divide opened. The boys had had to choose which parent they wanted to live with. Bran's bitterness about his mother's infidelity guaranteed he would choose Dad; Zach, who refused to believe Mom was anything but saintly, had chosen her. Turned out there was an added factor: he'd heard their father get up during the night of Sheila's death, although he told the police he'd never stirred.

Because of the lie, Zach had always believed their dad was the killer, too.

There'd been calls and letters and gifts at first, but contact slowed to a trickle by the end of the first year, then ended completely.

When the brothers had met up again this past spring, their divided loyalties had spilled over into their relationship. Mending it had meant keeping an open mind about who the killer could have been. Unfortunately, every trail they'd followed so far had dead-ended, however promising it initially seemed.

Most recently, they had been looking hard at men who'd been teenagers at the time of the murder.

"Crap," Bran said out loud. "I'm going to print

all this and take it home. The manager of the Bank of America agreed to meet me there today so I can watch more videos. I still have a couple days' worth to go."

Charlie stretched and groaned. "Sounds like a plan. Maybe I can do the same if I can get in touch with anyone to let me in." He'd taken Wells Fargo. "But damn, I keep thinking these assholes might have cased the banks two weeks ago. A month ago. Who knows? We could be wasting our time completely sticking to just the last week."

"But how practical is it for us to watch a month's worth of videos at every bank in town?" Bran countered. "And that's assuming they even have that far back. Why would they store more than a week or two?"

"Just saying."

"I don't like anything about this," Bran said shortly, and strode to the printer to start collecting the reams it was spitting out.

THE FIRST THING Mrs. Greaver said was, "It really is you." She looked shocked.

Zach laughed at that. "You thought I was lying about who I am?"

"I just don't understand why you're back in town." She let him inside. "You left a long time ago."

"Twenty-five years," he agreed, assessing the

small living room crammed with too much furniture. The drapes were closed, the light dim. He'd heard the television before he rang the doorbell.

As a kid, he'd been in and out of some of the other homes on the block, but not the Greavers' as far as he could remember. Their kids were older than the Murphy gang; they didn't play together. He'd known the daughter best, as she'd babysat them.

When he asked about Mary, Mrs. Greaver led him to the photos on the fireplace mantel. Studying them, he would have recognized his former babysitter anywhere. Like her mother, she had remained scrawny and short, with a foxy face and tight mouth. Mary hadn't loved babysitting, no secret about that. Or else she just hadn't liked the Murphy boys. She looked all buttoned up as an adult, too, though, so maybe that was just her.

The Greavers' son, Zach hardly recalled. Rob was a couple years younger than Mary, apparently, which would have made him around fifteen when Sheila was killed and Zach's family imploded. Bran, twelve then, remembered him better than Zach did, which was why their original plan had been for Bran to take this interview.

Mrs. Greaver asked about Bran, and Zach explained that he was the detective in charge of investigating the bank robbery, which was consuming his days. He didn't mention that the one witness was a woman who was pregnant with Bran's baby.

Zach learned more than he wanted to about Mary, who lived in Yakima now, on the eastern side of the mountains, was married and had two kids. Mary's oldest had joined the air force right out of high school. Momentarily stupefied, Zach thought, *Wait. Was that possible?* With a little calculating, he figured out that she must have had the kid right out of high school.

Funny thing, though, Mrs. Greaver didn't volunteer a word about Rob. Zach had to ask. He'd been married and divorced, his mother said. No children. Her mouth closed tightly. When prodded, she said he was in Seattle and drove trucks for a living.

Zach knew better than to push right out of the gate. Years as a cop had taught him how to get someone to open up. He told a funny story about Mary when she was taking care of him and Sheila. Bran must have been at a friend's, because he wasn't in that memory. Mrs. Greaver reminded Zach tartly of a few of his and Bran's more infamous escapades. Only gradually did he bring Sheila into the conversation. By that time, Mrs. Greaver seemed to have forgotten he'd ever moved away from the neighborhood.

"The reason we wanted to talk to you," he said at last, "is because your kids were older than Bran and me. We figured if anyone knew all the teenagers in the neighborhood, it would be you."

Instead of preening as he'd expected—people liked being considered an expert—she said grudgingly, "I suppose I did."

"I'm sure you'd have told the investigating officers at the time if you'd been aware of any older boys in the neighborhood who had seemed interested in Sheila," he said. "But it's possible you've remembered something since that might help us find out who killed her. Twenty-five years ago, the detectives probably didn't even consider a teenage boy could have done it. They were looking for an adult. But times have changed."

As he talked, her expression had become downright hostile. "From what *I* heard, the police believed your father killed that poor little girl. You may not believe that, but it doesn't excuse you wanting to shift the blame to people just because they lived nearby."

So much for softening her up.

"Mrs. Greaver, you must watch the news. There've been several ugly cases in the past year alone of boys who were only fourteen or fifteen years old sexually assaulting and murdering a younger girl. It happens. I'm hoping you can give me names of any boys who were around then. I'm not conducting a witch hunt, but one of them might have been arrested in the intervening years for something that will raise a red flag. None of them will ever even know I've run their names unless they become a person of interest."

Her spine stiffened. "Your sister is long gone. Why don't you let her rest in peace?"

He nodded and rose to his feet. "I'm sorry if I've upset you, Mrs. Greaver. I didn't want to do that. I can only remind you that Sheila was the victim. I loved my little sister. She was the sweetest kid in the world." Even after all this time, his throat tightened. "She didn't deserve what happened to her. Just think about this—how many other little girls has that man hurt in all the years since then?"

She didn't respond, or even stand to see him out. When he left, she was still sitting on her sofa, hands clasped tightly on her lap, looking straight ahead at the fireplace and all those family pictures—none of which included an adult Rob Greaver.

WHEN FIRST PROMOTED to detective, Bran had had no idea how much of his time would be spent watching piss-poor footage from surveillance cameras. Or how grateful he'd be that it existed at all, grainy and poorly lit or not. Half the time, it would turn out that the camera pointing right at a crime scene or escape vehicle hadn't worked in years. The business owner had been sure criminals would be scared off by the sight of a camera, functional or not.

Three hours after sitting in an office at the bank to watch the less than riveting action from two days before the robbery, Bran found his vision already blurring. He'd never given any thought to how busy banks were. The Bank of America didn't seem to have much in the way of lulls. Not many chances to fast-forward or let his mind wander. Thank God he didn't also have to watch footage from the camera outside that pointed at the ATM.

A fair number of the customers he saw coming and going appeared familiar to him. Clear Creek was the largest city in the county, but that wasn't saying much. In many ways, it functioned as a small town. Everyone knew everyone else.

He rewound a couple of times when someone behaved oddly, then shrugged and went on. The manager, who couldn't leave him alone in the bank, had gotten the coffee machine going and kept his cup filled, which he appreciated. So far, every bank officer in town had been completely cooperative. They were all but doing somersaults in their efforts to help. They knew damn well they'd dodged a bullet when the pair chose to rob a different bank. Outside urban areas, it was easy to get complacent about security. A whole bunch of people had just been awakened to frightening reality.

After rubbing his eyes, he watched as a woman with two toddlers came in, saw a line and turned right around to go out. A man politely held open the door for her and proceeded to one of the self-help counters. Beneath a parka he wore a gray, hooded sweatshirt. The fact that he didn't push the hood back had Bran sitting up. Then he stiffened as he saw how careful the guy was to keep his face averted from the cameras, the way he kept his chin tucked in to achieve maximum coverage from the hood. He took his time, filling out some kind of a deposit or withdrawal slip, but his head kept turning. Oh, yeah, he was looking around. After a minute, he ostentatiously patted his hip pocket but came up empty. Then the pockets in his parka. Nobody seemed to be paying any attention to him. He thrust the deposit slip in one of those pockets, then went to the display stand to grab a brochure. Finally, he strolled out, without once letting the camera capture his face full-on or even close to it.

Damn, Bran thought. They could, and should, use this video for training bank employees. *This is what you should watch for.*

From his size, this guy wasn't the one who'd shot Maya Lee. He was the partner, described by Lina as lean, wiry and not very tall. Bran went back several minutes to watch the same footage again in slow motion, freezing it a couple of times when he glimpsed the line of the guy's jaw or cheek. The IT people might be able to do something with this. The man had been wearing gloves when he opened the door, but stripped them off as soon as he was inside. It would have looked too odd if he hadn't. He didn't make a single slipup, though, using a pen he produced from his pocket and taking the only piece of paper he'd touched with him when he left, his back to the camera. Sure as hell, he had put his gloves back on before he pulled open the door.

It was frustrating, but more than they'd had. As Bran called Novinski, it occurred to him he'd be watching the camera positioned outside above the ATM after all. The guy probably hadn't parked in the bank lot, but everyone made a mistake eventually.

Of the two, he speculated, was this the brains of the outfit? The boss, responsible for making the decision on which bank was their best target? Or had they divided up the task of evaluating the possibilities and made the final decision democratically?

The FBI agent came on the line. "What's up?"

"I found one of them on camera at the Bank of America. No good look at the face, but someone with the skill might be able to do something with the video."

Another call came in before they finished talking. Charlie.

"Let me call you back in a minute," Bran said, and switched to his partner.

"Found him," Charlie said.

They compared dates and time. The visit to Bank of America had come first. An hour later, what had to be the same man had checked out Wells Fargo.

"Can't see his face," Charlie said in frustration, "but at least we know when they were in town. With only a few days in between, it's possible they stayed until the heist. I'm going to talk to bank personnel, just in case this guy caught someone's eye. If anyone saw him get in a vehicle..."

They both knew that was a pipe dream, but Bran would do the same. They had to try.

Calling Novinski back, Bran found himself wondering where Lina was right now. Then, irritated with himself, he made the effort to shove her out of his head. A distracted man could miss something important.

LINA MISSED BEING able to get in the hot tub after doing her laps, a no-no according to her doctor, but she felt wonderful anyway as she wrapped her wet suit in her towel and dropped both along with her goggles into her plastic-lined tote bag. Gotta love those endorphins. This was the most relaxed she'd felt since seeing her friend's murder, and the swim had revived her after a mostly sleepless night. Wow, she should definitely come every day until school started up again.

On her way out, she exchanged greetings with a few people. The mother of one of her students stopped her to ask her *exact* due date and say how much her daughter would miss Lina when she took maternity leave. She wasn't about to explain to anyone but a close friend how very *un*planned this pregnancy had been.

She stepped into the cold, crisp air as she left the phys ed complex and started toward her car. She didn't miss Minnesota's bitter winters. Here, she didn't have to wrap a muffler around her face to keep her nose from developing frostbite in ten minutes, but the seasons were still well defined.

With the gym and weight rooms open, too, the parking lot was surprisingly crowded considering school wasn't in session. Lina paused to orient herself, then spotted her landmark, a giant tan SUV. Yep, there it was. Naturally, her little car was hidden behind it.

Almost there, Lina had a moment of panic. Before going in the pool, she'd taken off the necklace that Bran had given her for Christmas and forgotten to put it back on. The gift had been so perfect, she'd never forgive herself if she lost it.

No, no, she'd tucked it safely in her coat pocket, she calmed herself, then remembered the peacoat had slipped off the hook and been crumpled on the bottom of the locker when she opened it. What if the necklace had fallen out and she hadn't noticed?

Relief flooded her when her delving hand found it immediately. She pulled it out, only then becoming aware a car was coming up behind her. Lina veered out of the way, seeing her car at the same moment.

Car keys. Darn it, she usually had them out already. She was about to grope for them with the same hand that already held the necklace...when she felt the fine gold chain slither out of her fingers. With a moan, she crouched to pick it up— at the exact moment she heard a strange popping sound and a metallic *ding*.

Still crouched, Lina started to swivel to see where the sounds came from, forgetting that her center of balance had altered. She was falling even as she heard a second *pop*...and felt a sharp sting on her upper arm.

Were those *gunshots*?

With a whimper, she flattened her hands on the pavement to push herself between the vehicles.

She heard raised voices followed by the pounding of running feet on pavement…and the roar of a vehicle accelerating away.

# CHAPTER SIX

THE BANK MANAGER had somehow sent the relevant minutes of digital images to the IT people at the Seattle FBI office. Bran had no idea how and wasn't sure he wanted to know. Probably he should strive to be more tech savvy, but the skills were rarely required for his investigations.

His phone rang when he was shaking the manager's hand, on the verge of leaving. Seeing Lina's name, Bran said, "Excuse me. I need to take this," and pushed through the exit to the parking lot. "Lina?"

"Somebody just, um, shot at me." She sounded shaky. "At least, we think…"

A fireball exploded in his chest. "Are you hurt?"

"Not really. I skinned my knees and my hands, and a bullet grazed my arm, but it's not much more than a scratch." She almost pulled off a laugh. "Who knew I'd ever get to say that."

"A scratch," he repeated, unable to move past what she'd just said. Someone had shot at her. She'd been grazed by a bullet.

"There's a deputy here," she added. "Do you want to talk to him?"

Already unlocking his car, he said, "Yes."

"Detective Murphy? This is Dan Elkins. Ms. Jurick thinks this incident may be related to your investigation."

Backing out of the parking slot, Bran asked, "Where are you?"

"What? Oh, the high school. She was walking out to her car after swimming laps."

He switched to hands-free, distantly surprised that he was functioning. A sort of autopilot had taken over. "I'm on my way," he said curtly. "Tell me what happened."

At least two shots had been fired, likely from a car. Lina said they sounded more like a pop than the crack that she expected from gunfire. By sheer chance, she had bent over suddenly to pick something up just as the first shot was fired. Startled, she had lost her balance and fallen, causing the second shot to miss, as well.

In other words, she'd been saved by a freakin' miracle. Two miracles.

Bran turned on the lights and siren, driving as fast as he dared. On the way, he heard more of the story.

Two men coming out of the gym had seen the car idling as well as Lina's tumble. Upon hearing what one of them recognized as shots, they had come running. The shooter had presumably seen them, because the car took off. One of the men was an off-duty firefighter, Elkins explained, the other a soldier home on leave.

Through the phone, Bran heard a siren cut off. "Paramedics are just arriving," the deputy said unnecessarily.

"Tell Lina I'll be there momentarily." Able to see the high school ahead, he ended the call. Fear and rage burned in him. Lina could have been killed, just like that. Gone. The thought was unendurable.

He shouldn't have bought into assumptions the FBI agents had made. He'd seen Lina's hesitation when he asked if she recognized the man who had killed her friend. He remembered what she'd said, word for word.

*He might just have had an ordinary face, but it's like, oh, if you see someone out of context and can't place them. They're a stranger, but not. You know?*

But the FBI didn't believe the two were local, so he'd gone with the ordinary-face explanation—and left Lina unprotected.

This was his fault.

He pulled in behind the ambulance, where a cluster of people stood. Lina sat on the tailgate. As he got out of his county car, he heard her protesting.

"Really, I'm fine. I can clean up at home—" Her gaze fastened desperately on his and she broke off. It was as if no one else was there. He saw no one but her. Completely unaware of people stepping aside, Bran went straight to her, taking in the sight of the thick gauze wrapping her upper arm and both her hands, the grit and blood mixed with tattered fabric at her knees. Her hair was falling out of whatever she'd used to confine it.

"No," he said softly, tipping her chin up with one hand.

"No what?"

"No, you're not cleaning up at home. You're going to the hospital." When her jaw set mulishly, he shook his head. "For my sake." Then he played dirty. "For the baby's sake."

"Oh." Bending her head, she touched her stomach with one bandaged hand. "I didn't fall that hard. I've felt her moving since." Lina met his eyes again. Whatever she saw must have been persuasive, because she nodded. "Yes. Okay. Only…"

"Only what?"

"Will you come?"

"I'll follow you there as soon as I get things started here."

She tried to smile and to thank him.

"Damn it, Lina!" The fear kept swelling inside

him, stinging his throat and sinuses. He bent forward and gently wrapped his arms around her.

With a funny little sound, she rested her forehead on his chest. He breathed in her scent and began to believe she was all right.

*But she might not have been*, a voice in his head persisted in reminding him. A few inches one way or the other and she'd be dead.

Even thinking that way was like stepping off a cliff. He couldn't let himself. Not now. He had a job to do.

"Okay, sweetheart," he murmured. "You need to go get checked out. I have to interview witnesses and start a search for the bullets."

Her head bobbed against him. She straightened and they looked into each other's eyes for one naked moment. Then Bran stepped back and let the pair of paramedics settle her in the back of the ambulance.

He was turning away when she suddenly called in alarm, "Wait!" Hand moving to his weapon, he spun in place to give the surroundings a swift, hard look. What had she seen?

But nothing had changed. A few more people were coming out of the gym, all gaping at the police cars and ambulance. He focused on the ambulance where she sat up on a gurney. "What?"

"My necklace!" She sounded on the verge of tears. "It slipped out of my hand. That's why I stooped in the first place. Please find it. Please. Oh, and my bag and my keys must be on the ground, too." Those were obviously an afterthought.

Jesus, this latest spike of adrenaline had him dangerously on edge. Without a word, he walked around the back of her car and saw a brightly colored, rubberized tote bag lying on its side. When he picked it up, he found the keys under it. The necklace took him longer. He scanned the ground until a glint of gold almost beneath her back tire caught his eye. An unfamiliar emotion gripping him, he picked it up, his gaze on the pendant.

When he returned her possessions to her, Lina had tears in her eyes. She snatched the necklace out of his hand, fumbling with the clasp until the female paramedic said kindly, "I'll put it on for you. That way you can't lose it."

"Okay now?" Bran asked hoarsely.

"Yes. Thank you." Lina's lips trembled before she managed to firm them. Her shimmering eyes were enormous. He wasn't sure he could have looked away.

The male paramedic slammed the back doors, cutting off Bran's sight of her, then went around to hop in behind the wheel.

Not until the ambulance pulled away was he able to make himself move.

Then at last he focused on the uniformed deputy and the two men who had saved Lina's life by their courageous decision to run toward the shots instead of away.

LINA HUDDLED BENEATH two thin blankets in the small exam room. She was freezing. Probably she was in shock, but did they have to keep it so cold in here? And what had happened to her coat?

The wound on her upper arm really was more of a burn. The doctor doubted it would even leave a scar. She had been unbelievably lucky.

Earlier, her hands had actually hurt the most, but they had been numbed so the nurse could clean them, picking out grit, before applying a salve and rewrapping them. Her knees stung, too, but she'd scraped them worse plenty of times as a kid on the playground.

She was waiting for the release papers and a prescription for a painkiller she doubted she'd take even if the doctor insisted it was safe for the baby.

Through the sliding glass doors of her cubicle, she could see the nurses' station and the tops of heads behind computer monitors. As she watched, the doctor who had taken care of her walked into a cubicle across the way and pulled a curtain for privacy.

Where was Bran? She couldn't leave until he got here. With no car, she was kind of stuck unless she called a friend. Maybe she should check with him. She'd bet Isabel or Sara, another teacher from her school, would come for her. Her phone should be in her tote bag. She turned her head until she spotted it, on the floor out of the way.

But at that moment her door slid open and Bran walked in, shrinking the small space in that way he had. She didn't know how he did it. At not much over six feet, he was a big man but not massive. What he had was presence. She didn't think she was the only person who'd look first at him in a crowd. Maybe it was a dominance thing, or that grim air.

His blue eyes homed in on her. "Lina."

"Hi." For the first time, she gave thought to her appearance. She could not possibly be at her best. "I think they're ready to release me," she said brightly. "Will you take me back to my car?"

He shook his head. "One of the bullets—we presume the one that grazed your arm—went into the front tire."

"You mean, I have a flat?"

"You do. But it's a little more than that. We jacked up your car and took the entire wheel. We're hoping that bullet is in better shape than the one that dinged the SUV. We found it, but it suffered some damage."

"But…when can I have my car back?" she asked in dismay.

He stood right beside the narrow bed, looking down at her, his eyes unsettlingly intense. Lina wasn't sure what his expression meant.

"Probably tomorrow, but you won't be driving it anyway until we catch these sons of bitches."

"You think...?" She couldn't make herself finish.

"We don't have a lot of drive-by shootings around here, Lina. I don't buy this was a coincidence."

She hadn't wanted to know, because if today's shooter was the man she'd seen kill Maya, that meant he *had* recognized her. He knew her name and where she lived. He must, because if he hadn't followed her to the high school, how had he found her?

"Then...when he looked familiar..."

"He was." He clenched his jaw so hard, it was a wonder his molars weren't cracking. "And I was stupid enough to disregard your gut feeling because the feds were so damn sure Pierce County was home ground for those two."

"But I don't really know him!" she cried. "At most, I've seen him somewhere. So how does *he* know who I am?"

Bran stepped even closer. She guessed he might have taken one of her hands in his if she hadn't had the blankets pulled up to her chin. "I'm going to walk you through your daily routines. We'll think about where you shop for groceries, prescription medications, shoes. Do you always go to the same gas station? You need to be thinking about parents of your students. School employees. He could be something like a janitor or bus driver. Those are the kind of people whose faces are familiar to you, even though you don't give much conscious thought to them. As a teacher, you're more visible. Once they let you out of here, that's what you and I are going to do if you feel up to it."

"I'm fine. Just..."

"Shaken up?"

"Cold," she snapped. "What did they do with my coat?"

"It was probably taken into evidence."

"Oh, wonderful." Her sudden grumpiness, Lina felt sure, was mere window-covering for the fear beneath. "It's keeping my car company."

Bran's grin took her breath away. "You should be glad neither of them are lonely."

The nurse returned then with the prescription and a couple pages of instructions for Lina to take with her. Once she'd clumsily signed her name with her gauze-wrapped hand, she was free to go.

Bran asked if they could take the blankets. He promised to return them. So it was that Lina walked out swaddled like a newborn, not much more than her nose and feet showing. It was a good thing, because the day felt a lot colder now than it had earlier. The temperature might have dropped—but she suspected shock was taking a toll, too.

Expecting a hike across the parking lot, she discovered a benefit of wearing a badge: his Camaro was parked only a few feet from the Emergency Room entrance in a spot marked For Official Vehicles Only.

"You changed cars," she said in surprise.

"I stopped by the station so I don't have to go back later."

She waited until he'd helped her ease into the passenger seat and gone around to get in himself before she asked if he was taking her home.

He paused in the act of buckling her seat belt. Of course his too-piercing blue eyes saw her every fear. "No. Lina, I'm putting you into hiding."

"But…" She stared at him. "What if you don't catch them right away? I have to go back to work a week from Monday."

"That's, what, nine days? We'll worry about it when it gets closer." He started the car, looked over his shoulder and backed out.

"Does the sheriff's department have a, well, a safe house? Or—oh, it would be the FBI, wouldn't it?" She couldn't imagine.

"Not the FBI. My call to Novinski was a waste

of time. They want to believe this shooting was random, because if it's not, that blows all their elaborate theories to shit." He sounded like he might be grinding his teeth. "Right now, we're going to my apartment so we can talk."

She felt…odd at the idea of encroaching on his personal space. Except, of course, eventually, if he chose to have visitation, she'd undoubtedly see where he lived.

She felt his occasional sidelong glance during the drive, but didn't meet it. He undermined her. Made her want something she doubted he could give. It was safer to remember that damn wedding invitation and wonder about the woman he had wanted to marry. How hurt had he been? Had he seen her since? Begged her to reconsider?

No, not that, Lina thought—it was impossible to imagine Bran Murphy begging for anything.

His apartment complex was about a mile from hers, but remarkably similar. It might even have the same owners. His unit was fourth floor, accessed via an elevator from the lobby. As soon as he let them into his apartment, she saw that the only personality in the living room came from the pair of bookcases that flanked a large-screen television. The leather sofa and recliner had to be expensive. But the plain white walls were undecorated, and being a man he hadn't bothered with knickknacks or throw pillows. *Decor* was probably not a word in his vocabulary. The living area had no windows. She'd noticed balconies; his must be accessed from one of the bedrooms.

She couldn't help noticing how spotlessly clean and orderly his place was, too. The kitchen counters were bare except for a coffee machine and a toaster. The small table was equally bare—no place mats for him. The spines of the books were perfectly aligned. Horrible man, he probably even dusted them.

"Have a seat," he said, turning the dead bolt and going straight to the thermostat, which he nudged upward. "I'll get you a sweater or something."

He disappeared down the short hall that led, she presumed, to one or maybe two bedrooms and a bathroom. He returned carrying a navy blue, hooded sweatshirt that zipped up the front.

Lina thanked him and shed the blankets. Of course she had to roll up the sleeves several times and the hem hung to midthigh, but it was cozy. She might be imagining it, but she was comforted to think his smell clung to the fabric. She heard a drawer open and close, and he came back from the kitchen with a notepad and pen. She couldn't decide whether she was relieved or sorry that he sat in the recliner instead of at the other end of the sofa.

"Damn," he said suddenly. "We forgot to fill your prescription."

"I wasn't planning to," she admitted. "Tylenol would be the best, if you have any."

He frowned, but nodded after a minute. "If you change your mind, I'll go out."

"I'll need clothes and stuff from home."

"Give me a list. That's the last place I want you to go."

"I'd really like to keep swimming every day." She sounded timid because she knew he was going to say no. "It's…really important I keep exercising."

The frown deepened. He hadn't liked the reminder that her health—and the baby's—was at risk. His "We'll see" was terse.

How could she not bow to his judgment? After seeing Maya killed and coming so close herself today, she'd be an idiot to insist on doing whatever she wanted. Except…what were her alternatives? An aerobics video? The ones aimed at pregnant women wouldn't give her anywhere near the workout she got from swimming half a mile.

"Are you hungry?" he asked.

"Not yet."

"You ready to start, then?"

"Yes." She really needed to feel proactive to combat the helplessness.

They discussed grocery stores. She most often went to Safeway because it was closest, but also shopped at Fred Meyer because of a few products only they sold. She couldn't absolutely swear the man she'd seen didn't work in the produce section or behind the customer service counter or in the pharmacy—she didn't fill prescriptions at either store—but shook her head decisively at the idea he was a checker.

"If all he's done is see me go by pushing a cart," she argued, "how did he find out my name? I might look familiar to him, but that's all."

"He could have asked around."

"But why would he?"

"You're a beautiful woman, Lina."

She only shook her head. "Then why didn't he ever call to ask me out?"

"This might have been a while ago," Bran reminded her. "Maybe he found out you were married."

She shook her head. "I only moved here a year ago, after my divorce."

"Why here?" He sounded genuinely curious.

"I wanted to get away. Finding a new job halfway through the school year wasn't easy. The opening here was perfect." She smiled a little. "Ironically, my predecessor quit because she'd just had a baby and decided not to come back to work."

"So you'd only been here six months when we—"

Her cheeks warmed. "Yes."

"Had you been dating?"

"No. I guess a few guys asked—" she had to think back "—but I wasn't ready."

"This guy wasn't one of them?"

"No. It was a couple of the male teachers, and a guy I got talking to one day at the library."

Bran gazed at her for a long minute. Finally, he said, "I have to ask you this. It doesn't have anything to do with the bank robbery or shooting."

Warily, she waited.

"I doubt you were ever much of a drinker. You know why I was at the tavern that night. Why were you?"

Of course he'd want to know. She looked down at her gauze-wrapped hands. "My ex-husband still lives in the same town as my parents. Every so often, my mother feels compelled to give me an update on him."

Bran didn't say anything.

"I really wanted to start a family. He didn't." She gave a one-shouldered shrug. "That should have been a clue, I guess. I mean, we'd talked about it before we got married. He'd wanted kids, too, eventually. Five years later, I thought the time had come. We started fighting about it." She still felt ashamed she'd been so oblivious. "I'm sure you can guess what happened."

"He was screwing around on you."

The kindness in his voice gave her the courage to lift her head and meet his eyes. "Yep. With a friend of mine, no less. A fellow teacher."

"I can see why staying on at the same school didn't sound very appealing."

"Yes." There was a point to this. "Um, the day you and I met? Mom had let me know Madison was pregnant. His new wife. *Really* pregnant. Due any minute." She grimaced. "He wanted kids. He just didn't want them with me. All those excuses he gave were bull. While I was dreaming about starting a family, he was already sleeping with her. Somehow, hearing that—"

Bran moved faster than she'd believed possible. He stepped right over the coffee table and sat on the cushion next to her. When she tried to hide her face, he turned it back so she had to look at him.

"Be glad you *didn't* have a kid with him," he said, his voice hard. "A guy like that doesn't have it in him to be any more committed to his children than he does to his wife."

"I know you're right, but…" She shook her head.

"It hurt."

This smile might have been a little better than the last one. "Finding out Wife Number Two might have already been knocked up even before he and I split was like…like an exclamation mark. He had everything I wanted, but me? Here I am, starting all over."

"Did you want to get pregnant that night? Is that why you went to the tavern?"

Shocked by what was really an accusation, Lina jerked her face from his hand and shrank into the corner of the sofa. Away from him. "Do you really think that? I went out to pick up some guy and trick him into having unprotected sex?"

"I'm asking," he said grimly.

"No!" Being on the verge of tears made her even madder. It had to be pregnancy hormones. "I don't want to be here anymore." Still hunching away from him, she swung her feet to the floor. "Find someplace else for me to go, or I will."

"Lina. I had to ask."

"No, you really didn't." She struggled with the zipper on his sweatshirt and, finally losing patience, tugged the whole thing over her head. When she threw it, Bran snatched the sweatshirt out of the air.

"Lina, please." He sounded hoarse. "You're right. I shouldn't have said that. I just didn't like to think—" He stopped abruptly.

Even through her anger, she got it. "That it was

you only because you happened to be the one who sat beside me and started a conversation."

"Yeah. Shit."

Her shoulders slumped. "Picking up a guy never crossed my mind. I don't *do* things like that. I just wanted to get drunk, something else I never do. Doing it in public seemed more—" God, this was humiliating to admit "—melodramatic." She scrunched up her face. "Stupid."

"Like me, a cop, deciding to get drunk, also in public and despite the fact I knew I'd have to drive myself home, that I'd risk my career if I got pulled over. All because the next day was supposed to be my wedding day."

"Now that you mention it."

The crease in one cheek deepened. "You didn't have to agree."

"You just accused me of being some kind of—"

He was still close enough to put a hand over her mouth. "Don't say it. I knew better."

"How can you?" Lina said honestly. "We *don't* know each other very well."

He opened his mouth, but then thought better of whatever he'd been going to say and closed it.

"What?" she asked, suspicious.

Bran only shook his head. "We'll fix that. We're going to be spending plenty of time together from here on out."

"Because of the baby."

"Because you're staying with me."

She should have realized that he hadn't brought her here just to talk. "But…do you have a spare room?"

He quirked an eyebrow. "Not like we haven't slept in the same bed before."

Lina glared at him.

Bran didn't react. "No, I turned the second bedroom into an office. I'll sleep out here on the couch. You can have the bedroom."

"I can't take your room. Anyway, I'm smaller. I'd be comfortable on the sofa."

"No." His tone shut down any further argument. "You're pregnant. You'll take the bed."

She hesitated. "Isn't there anywhere else I could go?"

His gaze was direct and unapologetic. "Where? Anywhere you go, you could endanger someone else. I thought about my brother's place, but Tess barely survived an attempt to kill her just this spring. I can't put them in that position." He shot to his feet. "In fact, let me give you a tour."

"What?" Was there a secret compartment? A Murphy bed that would be tricky to lower? A— But she saw from his face that he was serious, so without argument she trailed him down the short hall to the door on the right, which turned out to open into a bedroom with a big bed. As with the rest of the apartment, the room was bare except for plain furnishings: a bedside lamp and clock, and another bookcase.

He bent at the foot of the bed and pulled out a tangle of metal bars and chains.

Lina blinked. *Oh*. A ladder?

"That's right," he said levelly, and she realized she'd said that aloud. "Hooks over the balcony railing. And do you know why I have this?"

Obviously, because the apartment was four stories up. But she could tell that wasn't his point, so she shook her head.

He kicked the ladder back under the bed and straightened, his eyes boring into hers. "Because Tess almost died in a fire set by the asshole who intended to kill her. Made me think. It should make *you* think."

Any protest died unspoken. She'd seen the terror on Maya's face; seen her die. Watching someone else—someone *she* had put at risk? No. Bran had the skills to protect her. And he was right; they did need to get to know each other. She'd just have to live with the panic that made her want to run from him— the same panic that had kept her from telling him about the baby as soon as she should have.

She nodded. "I understand."

"You ready to get back to work?"

"Yes." She almost apologized for flipping out, but stopped herself. She was still angry at his accusation.

He held out the sweatshirt.

Subdued, she took it, turning it right side out before she put it on. It definitely did smell like him, she decided, as it went over her head.

He walked past her and, once again, she followed obediently. Without looking at her, he sank into his chair, picking up the notepad and pen on the way. "Where do you get gas?"

She understood his retreat. And this was important. Until she could remember where she'd seen that man, she couldn't go home.

"Usually Safeway. You know, because of the discounts. But sometimes Arco."

"Do you go inside to pay at Arco?"

"No. Lately I've been thinking about it, because the price is lower if you pay cash, but then I'd have to carry cash and I hardly ever do. So far, I've paid at the pump both places. If there's an attendant at Safeway…well…I've never noticed him."

"Prescriptions."

"We could go on like this forever without doing any good," she exclaimed in frustration. "I mean, what if I bumped into the guy on the sidewalk or in a parking lot?"

"How would he have known who you were?"

"Maybe he wrote down my license plate."

"Why?"

"He was pissed. Or attracted. Take your pick. *You're* the one who suggested—"

"Let's go with the odds," he suggested, unperturbed by her outburst. "Prescriptions."

Lina sighed. "I don't have any regular ones, but I'm getting my prenatal vitamins at Walgreens."

# CHAPTER SEVEN

BRAN HAD NO sooner poured himself a second cup of coffee the next morning when an irritating buzz startled him. He swore when he spilled coffee. Growling, he ran cold water over his hand before he grabbed a dish towel and finally went to the speaker.

"Yeah?"

"It's Zach. Buzz me in."

Without another word, he did. He cocked his head and heard the shower running. The knock on his door came seconds later.

Zach stomped in, scowling. "Do you ever answer your phone?"

"You know I do." He suddenly wasn't sure where it even was, an unusual state of affairs for him. Charging, that was it. "I slept in," he muttered.

"I left two messages yesterday. Texted."

Crap. He did vaguely recall ignoring his phone when it vibrated yesterday evening. He hadn't wanted to interrupt Lina or stop the flow of recollections.

"I was tied up."

His brother's gaze went to the pair of cereal bowls sitting in the sink. His eyebrows rose. "You have a woman here."

Annoyed, Bran said, "Not like you're thinking. It's Lina."

Zach smirked. "How'd you talk her into this?"

"She can't go home."

Zach frowned. "Because of the bank robbery? I thought you'd decided—"

"I decided wrong." And Bran really hated making mistakes. "Didn't you hear? Someone shot at her yesterday."

"What the—"

Bran told him what had happened as he poured them both coffee. The two men sat at the table.

"Man, she used up a lifetime of luck," his brother said, shaking his head.

Bran glared at him. "Don't say that."

"It was a figure of speech." Zach shook his head. "Was it the cargo van?"

"No. She saw only a blur as she dove for cover, but says it was gray. The two witnesses agreed it was a sedan, and kind of a beater. One of them looked for the license plate, and says it was covered. He thinks a white plastic grocery sack was tied around it."

"Which could be ripped off in about ten seconds as soon as they were out of sight of the high school."

"Yep. The driver was the shooter, too. He presumably already knew where Lina was parked, so he came up the aisle behind her so he could shoot out his driver-side window."

"He'd followed her," Zach said thoughtfully.

"Had to have."

"Not good."

"No. We talked to people using the gym and the pool, but nobody noticed a car fitting that description even though he had to be hovering somewhere."

"Most people don't pay any attention to their surroundings." Zach took a swallow of coffee. "You talk to the FBI agent?"

Bran told him what Novinski had said.

"I can see why she thinks that." Zach held up a hand before Bran could explode. "A coincidence like this might happen in a high crime neighborhood in Seattle, and that's her turf. Here, not so much. I agree you have to act on the belief that the shooter was the robber she saw."

Bran realized the shower had cut off a few minutes ago. Lina would be emerging any minute. He'd have felt compelled to warn her they weren't alone, except she wouldn't step out of the bathroom without being fully dressed down to shoes and socks anyway. Despite his optimism over the holiday, they were a long way from her relaxing that much around him.

"I'm going by her place this morning to pack

some stuff for her," he said. "I wanted to do it in full daylight so I can be damn sure no one follows me back here."

His brother scrutinized him. "What's your next step?"

Bran updated him on what he and Charlie had found from the security cameras, then went to get his notes from the night before. He handed his brother the notebook. "If you can think of anything I forgot…"

Zach flipped through the pages. "So far, you've come up with squat." He went back to the beginning and skimmed again. "Hairdresser," he said after a minute. "I know her hair is long, but she might still get it trimmed or, I don't know, lightened."

"The color is natural." Bran cleared his throat. Why did he have to say that? "But it's a good thought."

"And how about one of those places that does nails?"

Paige had gone for a mani-pedi more often than Bran washed his Camaro.

"What are the chances of her seeing a man there?"

Zach shrugged. "I guess men get theirs done, too."

A businessman or a salesman, maybe. But a bank robber?

The bathroom door opened and both men turned their heads. Lina stepped out, her eyes widening as she saw that Bran wasn't alone.

"Oh! Um, hi, Zach."

"Hey," he said. "I hear you had some more excitement yesterday."

She made a face and came toward them, wearing yesterday's maternity jeans and, he assumed, her own long-sleeve tee under the sweatshirt he'd loaned her. Her feet were bare, and her braided hair was wet. Swallowed by the oversize sweatshirt, she looked extraordinarily young and innocent, giving him a glimpse of the girl she'd been.

"I guess you need a hair dryer," he realized, hoping the huskiness in his voice went unnoticed.

"That will be on my list." She looked ruefully at their coffee. "My herbal teas, too."

"Really?" Zach sounded startled. "By *choice*?"

She chuckled. "No, I like my coffee. I *love* coffee. But I gave up caffeine for the duration."

His gaze flicked to her belly and he winced. "Pregnant women do that, huh?"

"If they're following their doctor's recommendations." She sighed and pulled out a chair. "Mine says the occasional caffeine is fine, but a good cup of coffee just makes me want more, so abstinence was easier."

"Man." Zach shook his head. "I'd better warn Tess about this."

This laugh of hers was more like a giggle, a ripple of sound that stirred Bran's body uncomfortably.

"I'm sure she knows," Lina said. "Women talk. Speaking of… If you want privacy…"

Zach shook his head. "He was telling me about your situation."

Bran frowned. "That's not why you came, though. What had you so hot and bothered?"

"I met with Mrs. Greaver yesterday, remember? I had to switch my days off with Badgley so I could do it. But you apparently don't give a—" He cleared his throat, clearly thinking better of his choice of words given Lina's presence.

"Don't accuse me of that. You offered to take my place because I'm tied up."

"Can't walk and chew gum at the same time?" his brother mocked.

Bran's jaw tightened. "Keeping Lina alive is my priority. Sheila has been dead a long time."

Zach slapped his hand on the table hard enough to make it jump. "Who are you kidding?" His tone was scathing. "I kept on with this even when Tess was threatened. Truth is, Sheila never was a priority for you. If she had been, you'd have done something a long time ago."

Bran had forgotten Lina was there, forgotten anything except his frustration with this brother who was unwilling to forgive. "You know why I didn't," he said through his teeth.

Zach's lip curled derisively. "Why did I bother to come over?"

"Goddamn it, you could just tell me what you learned—"

His brother pushed back his chair and stood. "You know what? I'll pursue this on my own." He slammed out of the apartment.

Bran tipped his head back, closed his eyes and let loose a few blistering words. Still steaming, he opened his eyes and grabbed his coffee cup. That's when he saw Lina, sitting right where she'd been, quietly watching him.

"Damn. I'm sorry."

She caught her lip in her teeth while she seemed to debate what she should say. She finally settled on, "I thought you were friends."

He grunted. "We are. Most of the time. These things just…blow up. I'd like to say it's always him, but he pushes my buttons, too."

"This isn't any of my business." She started to push her chair back.

Somehow, he clamped his mouth shut on what he wanted to say. *No, it isn't.* Because…that wasn't really true. She'd find out about Sheila and the damn investigation when—if—she married him.

Which meant he had to tell her something.

"You might as well hear about it now," he said brusquely. "We had a sister. When she was six years old, she was murdered."

Her hand still gripping the back of her chair, Lina gaped at him. It was a moment before she said softly, "Oh, no. I'm so sorry."

Bran shook his head. "It was a long time ago." Damned if he'd let this turn into a confessional. The basics were all she had to know.

Her forehead crinkled. "Sheila? That was your sister?"

"Yeah." To avoid her searching gaze, he swallowed his rapidly cooling coffee.

"But...who is Mrs. Greaver? What does that have to do with—"

"Does it matter?" he snapped.

After a long stare, she wiped all expression from her face. "Apparently not," she said coolly. "At least not to *you.*"

He ground his teeth. "What's that supposed to mean?"

"You managed to convince your brother you don't care." Lina pushed the chair in and walked away.

Bran thrust his own chair out of the way and stalked after her. "You want to know every goddamn detail? Is that it?"

Lina stopped with her back to him. "She would have been my daughter's aunt," she said with quiet dignity. "But, really, that will be between her and you someday, when she's old enough for you to tell her about your family. If you'll excuse me, I'll make that list of things I need from my apartment."

She might as well demand he peel a layer of skin off if he was to have a chance at talking her into a wedding, he thought, cornered. But he had to do it. Her walking away…that wasn't going to happen.

"Come and sit down," he said hoarsely to her back. "There isn't any reason not to tell you. It's just—" Damn, his throat was closing. He thought he'd gotten past that.

Lina turned, her expression grave, eyes dark and searching. "You have a right to say no."

Frustration flared. Yeah. Sure, he did. But all he did was shake his head. "It's hard for me to talk about. That's all."

Appearing less than thrilled about coming back to the table, she did. He was wound too tight to sit while he told her about the hideous day when Zach found their baby sister naked and dead in the backyard. Bran spread his arms and gripped the counter edge, seeing another time and place, even as he remained aware of Lina's muffled sounds of distress off to one side.

"My first sight of Zach—" Remembering his

brother's face, he bowed his head, eyes closed, and fought for control.

He didn't hear Lina coming, but suddenly she was rubbing the taut muscles in his back, giving him her silent support. Fighting the need to turn around and lunge for her, hold her until the wave of pain subsided, he clenched his teeth.

Thirty seconds later, the wave receded. He straightened, aware when Lina's hand dropped away. He gave himself another few seconds, then faced her.

"I'm okay."

She read his mood enough to retreat to the table. This time, Bran managed to sit, legs stretched out, in a pretense at relaxation. He told her matter-of-factly about his parents' ugly breakup and the choices he and Zach had to make. He had dedicated his life to never feeling so helpless again.

"Fast-forward twenty-four years," he said wryly.

"What? You mean—"

"We lost contact after about a year. After that, I never heard from him or my mother until this year, when I happened to run into the new deputy coming down the hall at headquarters. Now, there was a shock. As it turned out, for both of us."

"Wow. Neither of you looked for each other?"

"I thought about it, but..." He shrugged. "I figured he'd be a stranger to me." Which Zach was, in many ways, even as he sometimes seemed so familiar.

This tension with Zach was strictly between them. Except it no longer was, entirely, or maybe never had been, Bran realized; Tess had gotten involved early on, and now there was Lina. If she was going to be his wife—and he was determined she would be—he couldn't keep family secrets from her.

So he forced himself to go on, to tell her the rest: that Zach had always believed their father killed Sheila, because he knew Dad had lied to the police about not having gotten up during the night, and because the investigators had made it so obvious *they* thought Dad was guilty. In contrast, Bran had known by the time he turned twelve that their mother was taking one lover after another, right in the bed she shared at night with her husband. Some of those men must have seen Sheila; she'd had half-day kindergarten and stuck closer to home than Zach and Bran did.

Bran had passionately believed all these years that one of his mother's lovers had admired her pretty, delicate little girl and knew which bedroom was hers. Bran had wondered how many keys to the house Mom had given out.

"Dad was too stubborn to move away even though he might have had a better life if he had. He faced people down and stayed in the house.

Even when I made detective, he didn't want me to investigate Sheila's murder. I always thought it was because he believed, like I did, Mom shared a portion of the guilt, but he still loved her. He never remarried."

Bran fell silent, remembering the grief that had never left his father. He'd lost his daughter in the most horrible way, then his wife and one of his two sons. All those years, Bran hadn't been able to understand how a man could still love the woman who had betrayed him and maybe opened the door to the monster who did that to Sheila, but Dad wouldn't hear a bad word about Bran's mother, whatever bitter things he'd said to her himself.

"When Zach came back to town and realized I was a detective here and hadn't solved the crime, he'd been sure Dad had prevented me because he thought I'd come up with evidence proving his guilt." Bran huffed out a breath. "He claims to have changed his mind, but I'm not sure I buy it."

She had a way of looking at him that made him feel as if he was gazing into a crystal ball. It was damned uncomfortable.

He told her most of the rest anyway, because if she spent any time around him and Zach, she'd hear about it eventually.

Lina winced, hearing how he and Zach had tracked down as many of their mother's former lovers as they could identify and how they'd eliminated them as suspects one by one.

He'd just think he was done, thank God, and she'd ask a question. He talked until he was close to losing his voice, expressing his anger at the inadequate records that were all the Clear Creek PD could produce, and at the one original investigator who hadn't retired but had taken offense that the Murphy boys were stepping on his toes.

Forehead crinkling, she said, "But...what if it was someone passing through town, or even a local who didn't live near you but happened to drive down your street and see Sheila playing in the yard? At night, though..." she added lamely.

"Then we'll never know who did it."

That wouldn't happen. Bran looked down to see that he'd balled his hands into fists on his thighs. "How did a stranger get in the house? How did he know which bedroom was Sheila's? He'd have woken Mom and Dad if he opened their door, or us if he'd tried upstairs. No." He shook his head. "It had to be someone who'd been in our house, knew where we slept, knew the fence in back made the yard private."

Lina shivered. "That makes sense." She studied him with that same, grave expression. "So... who did Zach talk to yesterday?"

Of course they'd circled back around to the blowup with his brother. Bran felt the burn of resentment in his esophagus. He'd have gotten around to all this eventually, but she had to push. There was a really good reason he'd kept Paige at a distance.

*Which might be why she dumped me.*

That reminder failed to soothe his searing resentment.

"We've moved on to former neighbors. Mrs. Greaver's husband is dead, but she has a son who was, I don't know, two or three years older than me. He could have come by when his sister was babysitting Sheila."

"A neighborhood kid."

"The investigators settled on Dad right away, and didn't look closely at other possibilities."

She was quiet for a moment. "I think you should go after Zach. You two need to talk."

Bran stared at her incredulously, his resentment cresting. "I haven't talked enough to satisfy you? Is this some kind of test? If I don't go make nice, I fail?"

Lina shook her head and pushed back from the table. "Do what you want. I'll make you a list."

This time, he didn't try to stop her.

"You do that," he muttered, after she'd disappeared into the bedroom.

A sick feeling told him she was right; he did need to clear the air with his brother. But damned if he'd tell her that.

What he needed was a break from her, from the sexual tension that probably explained some of the frustration and anger that choked him. From the way she left him feeling like his guts were hanging out.

From his pitiful desire to tell her anything, if she'd just agree to marry him.

LINA HEARD THE sound of the key turning just as her stomach started to complain. Dread and hunger didn't mix well. She wished she'd eaten before Bran returned.

Unfortunately, the door opened while she was lying flat on her back on his living room floor. She hadn't managed to sit up when he appeared, arms laden and pulling her large suitcase behind him.

"Hey. Tipped over and couldn't get up?"

His expression was guarded. Or was that apprehensive?

Framed in the doorway, he was the sexiest man she'd ever seen. Disheveled hair—had he ever combed it today?—broad shoulders, sharp blue eyes. The awareness infuriated her, given the way he'd lashed out at her before leaving.

Weren't they supposed to be getting to know each other? His suggestion? Right. Sure.

It occurred to her that maybe they were. She'd

learned that having to acknowledge his own painful emotions turned Bran Murphy mean.

Flushing under his gaze now, she sat up with considerably less grace than she used to have. "Doing some exercises." Her eyes went to the white bag dangling from one of his hands. "You brought lunch?"

"Yep. Didn't know if you indulge in junk food, but it sounded good to me."

He had to do something nice *now*?

"I surrender occasionally." And, oh, it smelled good.

Lina waited until he'd detoured to the kitchen before rolling to her knees and using the coffee table as a crutch to help her get up.

"Cheeseburgers and fries," he said, setting the bag on the table. "Milk shakes."

While he took the suitcase into the bedroom, she explored the contents of the bags and distributed the food. Lina had already unwrapped her burger by the time he returned.

"Was my place okay?" she asked, before taking a big bite. Apparently, they were going to ignore the fight, if you could call it that when it had been one-sided. Which was probably better, given that she had no choice but to stay with him.

"Nobody had broken in, if that's what you mean. But why would they, if you're not there?"

He frowned. "Unless… Is there any chance this guy could be in a photo you've taken?"

"I can't imagine. I don't take many, and these days, only with my phone. So I post pictures on Facebook, or email them. I hardly ever print one."

She stuck the straw into her milk shake and ate a fry.

Sitting across from her, Bran didn't move. Lina picked up her burger again.

"I've never told anyone before," he said abruptly, voice gritty.

Startled, she looked up. "You mean, about your sister?"

He gave a single, hard nod.

"But…" Shaking her head in disbelief, she said, "How is that possible?"

His shoulders moved. "My father knew. We didn't talk about it. Neighbors and friends knew. Later, there was no reason to tell anyone."

"Not even Paige?" She couldn't help remembering what Tess had said about how closed off he was.

"No." He took a deep breath, his eyes never leaving hers. "I'd…put it out of my mind. As much as I could. Until Zach showed up out of the blue."

"And he knew, too."

"Yes."

Her heart had taken to beating fast. *I'm the first*

*person he has ever told.* He'd said it was difficult. She just hadn't had any idea how difficult.

"Why me?" she finally asked.

A nerve twitched in his cheek. "You're the mother of my baby."

Lina sighed. Not the explanation she wanted, but she'd accept it for now. She nodded and bent to her milk shake.

Bran took a couple bites before saying, "I stopped by Zach's."

"Seriously?"

"Yeah." He grimaced. "He apologized. I think he was embarrassed."

"Of course he was."

His eyebrows rose.

"Throwing a temper tantrum like that was childish."

"Tess was standing in the background, arms crossed, giving him the laser stare."

Lina laughed. "I don't believe that."

"She can be a tough broad, don't kid yourself." He sounded as if he admired his sister-in-law. "She was definitely giving him the look."

"The look?"

His mouth quirked. "The same one you gave me when you ordered me to go talk to him."

"I did not order you! I…suggested."

This was one of the first laughs she'd heard

from him. She could grow to love the sound and what it did to that hard, angular face.

"Uh-huh," was all he said.

She sucked on her straw, then reached for the fries. "So? Did he find out anything good?"

"Maybe. Mrs. Greaver was tight-lipped about her son. Sounds like he might be a disappointment to her, but Zach didn't think that was all of it. He said the fireplace mantel was crowded with pictures, but Rob was absent except for some family photos when he was a kid."

"That might not have anything to do with your sister."

"Maybe not, but Mama Greaver declined to be party to our investigation. If the police thought my father did it, that was good enough for her. Zach says she got uncomfortable when he asked about Rob, even just what he's doing these days."

"Guaranteeing that you two will consider him seriously as a possible suspect." Lina had mixed feelings. "The poor woman was trying to protect her son."

"The poor woman?" Bran's teeth showed when he leaned forward. "Is that any excuse if she suspects he likes little girls?"

"No, but…it would be hard. That's all I'm saying. Parents are, or should be, wired to protect their children, don't you think?" She saw where he was looking, and realized she had covered the firm mound that was now her waistline with both hands in an unconscious gesture of, yes, protection.

"Yeah." Bran's voice had softened, become gruff. He met her eyes again. "I do get that."

He was quiet, leaving her to wonder if he'd just been struck by the hard reality that he would soon be a parent himself.

Once so sure she could do this alone, Lina discovered at that moment how much she hoped Bran really would be in it with her for the long-term, and not only out of a rigid sense of duty and honor. This was a man willing to admit he'd been wrong. And while he hadn't exactly apologized, he'd come close enough for her.

She was bundling up the wrappings from their lunch when Bran said, in his usual, detached way, "I have a few more questions. Possibilities of where you might have seen the bank robber."

Lina could think about things she'd rather do, but she only nodded. She *needed* to remember.

WATCHING HER MOVING around the kitchen, Bran wished like hell they could take the rest of the day off. Pretend they were a normal couple.

Spend the afternoon in bed.

Not happening. But he should count his blessings. Lina was more forgiving than he deserved.

Even the act of pulling out a chair and sitting was graceful when she did it.

Seeing her expectant gaze, he asked, "Do you go to a salon or spa?"

"No, I haven't gone to any kind of spa since I moved here. I take care of my nails myself, and Maya—" her breath hitched "—always trimmed my hair."

"I'm sorry," he said gently. "You two were close, weren't you?"

Her reply was pained. "We met because I had a boy in my class last year whom she paid to mow her lawn. She saw some bruises on him and convinced him to talk to her. It was a bullying situation. He told her I was the coolest teacher, so we sat down to map out a strategy and I went with him to talk to the principal and counselor. After that, she invited me over for lunch and we just clicked. I'd already made friends here, mostly with other teachers, but they were all married, some of them had kids." This smile was small and crooked, reminding him of the jackass ex who'd hurt her. "Between work and family," she added, "they didn't have much time. Maya and I were both free to do things together."

He asked if she'd gotten involved in other situations like that. She might have barely seen an older brother, an uncle, a friend of the family at the house when she went to talk to a student's parents, but she shook her head even before he finished.

"I meet with parents at the school," she said firmly. "Always. Because this isn't that big a town, I've run into parents shopping or at the movie theater or whatever, but…" She stopped. "I don't remember meeting him that way. Truthfully—" she looked beseechingly at him "—I'm not convinced I ever did meet him. It feels more like the kind of encounter you dismiss right away."

"Car salesman?" he thought to ask.

"I already owned my Kia. I drove myself out here from Minnesota. It's sort of a stretch to think he's from back home and we just happened to end up in the same place, halfway across the country. And, no, I didn't have a stalker back home."

Bran fixated on part of what she'd said, his protective side kicking in. "You made that drive in the dead of winter by yourself? Didn't your parents object?"

She raised her eyebrows. "I wasn't eighteen and just leaving for college, you know. I was thirty-one years old. We have a lot more snow back there than we do here, so I'm experienced driving in it."

"Your parents didn't have anything to say about that?" Bran almost wished he and Lina weren't having a girl. He'd be scared shitless every time he had to take his eyes off her.

"My father wanted me to sell the car and buy a new one when I got here. Actually, he tried to convince me to live at home until I could find a job a whole lot closer to them. That made me all the more determined to get away."

Bran could understand that. A bigger mystery was why he had made a life here in Clear Creek after his sister's death, considering the attitude of people who should have been his father's friends. *And yet*, Bran thought uneasily, *here I am*.

It disturbed him to think Lina, in striking out on her own, had shown more independence than he had. Did she wonder why he'd stayed in this backwater county, or did she just assume it was all he knew and it felt safe and comfortable?

If so, she'd be wrong. He'd left for college, and then after the academy started his career with the Seattle PD. Originally he'd taken the job here because of Dad's declining health. But even after burying his father, he'd never considered moving away again. He had never really analyzed why, and *that* bothered him now.

He'd been having all kinds of unwelcome epiphanies since he met Lina Jurick, it occurred to him. And he thought he wanted to marry her?

But even this new sense of vulnerability couldn't shake his decision. She was right for him, and with her carrying his baby, they were already a family. He'd either learn to deflect her or he'd resign himself to having his hidden depths filtered until they became so crystal clear, even he'd be able to see right through them.

"We have the rest of the day," Lina said.

Crap. He knew what she was thinking. "You want to go swimming."

The hope in her eyes was timid, but there. "You said maybe."

He just hadn't said no. *Hell, no. Are you crazy? No.*

But, Jesus, what if *not* swimming endangered her and the baby? He frowned. The creep couldn't stake out the high school swimming pool ten hours a day. He wouldn't be looking for Lina in the Camaro.

Bran still wasn't happy about the idea, but…

"Yeah," he said gruffly. "We can go." Even though going to the high school, where she'd already been attacked once, went against his every instinct.

Her face lit up. "Really? Do you swim?"

"Not well enough to swim laps. I need to stay aware anyway. I'll watch."

Shadowed by the reminder, her expression dimmed. "You really think you need to be on guard while I'm in the pool?"

"Nah." He half smiled. "I was trying to get out of embarrassing myself."

Lina giggled. "Oh, for heaven's sake! Wouldn't it feel good?"

"The hot tub would," he admitted. Seeing her in a bathing suit. That would feel good.

"I'll go grab my stuff," she said eagerly.

"Aren't you supposed to give it an hour after a meal before you go in the water?"

Lina subsided, making a face at him. "I suppose. Fine. I'll go see what you brought for me."

"You mean, check to see what I forgot?"

She offered a saucy smile. "Now, what would make you think I'm that critical?"

Just like that, his body hardened. He needed to kiss her. *Now.*

She went still, her eyes dilating.

In silence, they stared at each other.

# CHAPTER EIGHT

BRAN FLAILED HIS way up and back half a dozen times, thankful he wasn't the only one in the pool whose strokes couldn't be mistaken for Michael Phelps's. He remembered Lina telling him she'd swam competitively, which explained why she sliced through the water with such effortless efficiency even with the extra weight she was hauling.

This was his second visit with her. She'd been so happy after swimming yesterday, so obviously invigorated, he'd agreed to this evening, too, even though he wasn't any happier about it than he had been yesterday.

Monday was one of his usual days off, as long as he wasn't tied up in a particularly intense investigation. This time, staying home hadn't been an option, between the double slaying during the bank robbery and the threat to Lina, never mind the rest of his caseload. And maybe that was just as well, given how hard it was to keep his hands off her. After yesterday's prolonged proximity, some distance today had seemed smart.

He stopped at the shallow end, shook his head, spraying water, and scanned the room. Two older women appeared from the locker room, the teenage lifeguard was flirting with a girl who didn't look more than about thirteen and a man who'd been in the lane next to Lina's had disappeared. No—that had to be the back of his dark head, appearing above the edge of the hot tub. All was well.

Bran had been disappointed to learn that, because of her pregnancy, Lina couldn't join him in the hot tub after her laps. Yesterday, he'd grabbed a few minutes in it when he thought she might be nearly done. If he sat so he could still see the pool, it seemed safe enough.

The added benefit was being able to watch her rise from the pool and walk across the deck toward him in a racing-style suit that fit her like a second skin. Yesterday, during the drive home, she'd ruefully confessed that it wasn't a maternity suit, and she was stretching out the fabric enough, she'd have to throw it away when she outgrew it. At the moment, it looked more than fine, however. Her body was everything he remembered and more.

Her legs and arms were still long and taut with a swimmer's muscles. The summer's tan was gone. Her already generous breasts were bigger, he thought, along with that ripe swell of belly.

Damned if she didn't turn him on as much now as she had before.

Time for the hot tub. He levered himself out of the pool, checked automatically to see where Lina was and strolled over to join the one other guy already lounging in the bubbling water.

He'd have liked to close his eyes and lay back, but couldn't let himself relax his vigilance. Lina was probably safe in here, but it wasn't in his nature to count on it. So even as the hot tub jets loosened his tight muscles, he scanned the deck, eyed the wall of glass looking for movement beyond it, automatically assessed everyone coming and going from the locker rooms.

He was glad to see Lina finally duck under lane ropes and take hold of the ladder. He doubted she bothered with a ladder normally, but her new bulk had to have changed how she did a lot of things.

Water streamed from her as she appeared, darkening her hair, confined in a single, fat braid. She gleamed, all that pale skin and rich curves. Her gaze went straight to him, which meant she'd noticed when he left the pool.

She stopped close enough he could have touched her pretty feet. "I so wish I could hop in there."

"Hop?" he teased.

That earned him a wrinkled nose. "Climb *carefully* in there." She sighed. "Take your time. I don't mind waiting if I get ready first."

He nodded, but had no intention of letting her emerge out front alone.

Like the day before, he had to take a minute to let his body's reaction to her near-nudity subside. Living with her and not making a move was killing him. He wondered if she had any idea how much he wanted her.

He wasn't 100 percent sure what was holding him back. Yeah, the fear of making her uncomfortable given that she had to depend on him contributed. He was chagrined to acknowledge that it was also his own fear of being rejected. From the way she looked at him sometimes—like yesterday—he believed she felt the attraction, too, as much as she had the night they met.

Trouble was, nothing between them was simple anymore. She'd had to deal with the shock of learning she was pregnant only to have him essentially accuse her of using him because she *wanted* to be pregnant. Not smart on his part. The damned wedding invitation and the timing of that night still stung when she thought about it, too, he knew without asking. Did she think he'd imagined she was Paige when they made love? Was he sure himself he hadn't been taking some subconscious form of revenge on Paige for dumping him?

Now, there'd be an irony, given how immensely grateful he now was that Paige hadn't gone through with the wedding. Which sent him back to yesterday's reflections on how poorly he understood his own deeper motives.

At least he could get out of the hot tub now, the depressing reflections having taken care of his problem. Bran showered quickly and wasted no time getting dressed. As a result, he had to wait a good ten minutes for her, no surprise given that she had to dry that mass of hair.

When she emerged from the locker room, for a moment he saw only her. Her glorious hair hung loose over a tunic that clung to her curves more than she probably imagined. As he watched, she shrugged on a parka that clearly would no longer meet in front.

"You're beautiful," he said roughly, catching her hand.

Her eyes widened. "I'm more than a little pregnant, in case you haven't noticed."

"I've noticed." He cleared his throat. "Got everything?"

"I…" Her gaze shied from his. "Yes."

"All right." He led her to the door, wishing the lighting was better in the parking lot. He had parked illegally as close to the entrance as he could, leaving a sign on the dashboard identifying the vehicle as law enforcement. "You know the drill."

Lina nodded. He tucked her close to his left

side, angling to keep her between him and the wall of the building until they reached the Camaro. There he unlocked and hustled her in before going around to the driver's side himself.

The arrival and departure were the part of the outing he had dreaded tonight. Yesterday, he'd had the advantage of daylight. Tonight, he was all too aware that someone could have waited for them to walk out, backlit through the glass doors, or have ducked between parked cars preparing to shoot as he drove past. But damn it, he'd swear no one had followed him, and how else could anyone know where she was?

In the rearview mirror, he saw movement.

"Take off the seat belt," he said suddenly. "Get down."

She fumbled for the release. With a hand on her back, he pushed her forward even as he accelerated with a squeal of tires. Lina hunched down, letting him use both hands on the wheel to circle the perimeter of the parking lot like a race car driver.

"What's wrong?" Her voice came out strangled. "Do you see someone?"

Christ—with only one road in and out, setting up an ambush would be a breeze. *What was I thinking?* Headlights came on behind him in the lot, somewhere midway down an aisle. Ahead... the beams of his own headlights found nothing.

He drove tensely, gaze switching from the road ahead to the rearview mirror to side mirrors. Only when they approached a major cross street did his muscles loosen. The light turned green as they approached, and he swung a right.

"Okay," he said. "You can sit up."

Lina groaned and straightened.

"Seat belt," he said.

She obeyed. "What happened?" Her voice was taut with anxiety. "Did you see something?"

"I thought I did." His fingers flexed on the leather-wrapped steering wheel. "Coming here is stupid. Open season."

"How can it be? They don't know where I'm staying, they don't know your car! What do you think, they're just staking out the high school?"

"It's possible." Pretty damned unlikely, but he wasn't about to admit as much.

"Really? Twenty-four/seven, on the off chance I show up?" Disbelief seemed to be warming up her temper.

"It's possible," he repeated. "The pool is the one place they know you've come. You're not home. Where else are they going to find you?"

"You're saying I can't go swimming again."

He hesitated, glancing at her profile under a passing headlight. The stakes were high either way—her health or her life. "I don't know. Let me think about it."

"What am I going to do if you can't find them?" She didn't look at him; he wasn't 100 percent sure she was even talking to him. "Maybe I should go home."

"To your apartment? The hell you're—"

"No. I mean home. Minnesota."

His hands tightened convulsively on the steering wheel until it creaked. He needed her to stay here, where he could protect her, where he'd *know* she was safe.

And, damn it, home should be here, where he was, not somewhere in the Midwest.

"If they know anything about you, they could find out where you came from. Where your parents live. What if they were to follow you, Lina?"

She clutched the belt in a fist where it crossed her torso above her belly. "Do you really believe they'd do that?"

"I don't know." That, at least, was honest. "As time passes, they may relax and decide you can't identify him. This soon… I'm guessing they're pretty focused on eliminating you as a threat."

Belatedly, he realized how brutally blunt that was. She didn't look at him.

"Maybe I'm being paranoid," he said, more quietly. "That goes with my job, too. But…"

"Better safe than sorry?"

"Yeah," he said regretfully. "Something like that."

She didn't say anything, which left him worrying about what she was thinking. Cops had a really high divorce rate, and there were good reasons. The unpredictable hours, the inability to talk about what they did, the high incidence of PTSD and alcoholism were all factors.

Paige hadn't seen Bran working except for their initial meeting, when he'd been at the hospital in Mount Vernon to talk to a gunshot victim. She didn't ask about what he did in any given day, he didn't offer to tell her. Long term, he thought now, they'd have been living together like two strangers.

That wouldn't fly with Lina, obviously. She had a way of seeing right through his defenses. If she didn't like what she saw…hell. How was he supposed to deal with that?

He took a couple of unnecessary turns in town to be absolutely sure no one was behind him before going home. After parking, he once again had her wait until he came around to help her out, then hustled her into the lobby and used his body to shield her from the wall of windows.

He hated when they had to wait for the damn elevator.

This wasn't the kind of place to raise a kid

anyway. He needed to start thinking about buying a house.

Once in the apartment, she went straight to the bathroom, undoubtedly to hang up her suit and towel. He hoped she wouldn't go straight to bed, although he wouldn't be surprised if she did. She obviously wasn't interested in talking to him.

Bran mumbled an expletive and scrubbed a hand over his face. He hated this uncertainty. Not knowing for sure how she felt about him. What she thought. He wanted everything tied up. A ring on her finger, the right to claim her as his. The idea of her, down the line, meeting some other man, starting to date, even marrying... The worry ate at the lining of his stomach like acid.

Lina emerged from the bathroom and came back to the living room, looking at him in surprise. "Is something wrong?"

"No."

"Do you want me to hang up your suit?"

"I can do it," he said grumpily.

"Okay." She went past him into the galley kitchen. "I'm going to make a cup of tea. Do you want something?"

Her. That was what he wanted.

"Coffee would keep me awake. I might have a beer."

When he came back from the bathroom, she had set a bottle of beer out on the table for him, and was pouring boiling water into a mug. Her herbal tea smelled okay; the box said it was orange-spice. She'd offered him a sip yesterday, though, and it tasted like barely-flavored hot water to him.

He had discovered that she was always cold. Her hands were almost always chilly when he held one. She rarely went barefoot around the apartment, which suggested her feet were cold, too. When he wore a sweatshirt or a long-sleeve T-shirt, she'd wear the same, add another layer and tug a fleece throw over herself, too, when she sat on the couch. He didn't own such a thing, but it had been on the list she'd given him: *Red fleece throw on back of couch.*

Everything on her list had been exactly where she'd said it was. His place was neat because he didn't own much, hers because she was organized. Hey, at least neither of them was a slob. They had something in common.

Along with a baby.

And he could warm her feet and hands at night. Volunteering would be no hardship.

He sat in his recliner, her in what had become her usual spot at the end of the couch. She kicked off her shoes and sat cross-legged, nursing the cup of tea.

"This can't go on forever," she said, her gaze direct.

Forever was exactly what he had in mind, but

he suspected she wasn't ready to hear that. And...
what exactly did she mean by *this*? Getting shot
at? Or living with him?

"I forgot to tell you that the artist can meet with
you tomorrow afternoon," he told her. *See? We're
doing something.* "I'll bring her here rather than
having you come into the station."

"Oh," Lina breathed in what sounded like dismay. "I'd almost forgotten." She reached for the
throw and pulled it over herself. "What if I don't
remember enough? It's been days now, and I only
caught the one glimpse anyway. It's not like I
have any kind of artist's eye." Anxiety seeped
from her every word.

"Do your best. I think you're going to be surprised. This artist has a gift. I've only had occasion to use her a couple of times, but I've seen
other sketches of hers. She's a genius with traumatized children, some of whom are barely old
enough to speak. Somehow she worms enough
out of them to come up with a portrait so accurate, the sight of it throws them back into terror."
Which, come to think of it, might not be the note
he'd meant to strike.

"You're saying I might scare myself?"

"I'm saying this could be the break we need."

Her forehead wrinkled. "Will you hand it out
to the media?"

"Let's wait and see how good it is." He had

other reservations, but decided not to share those. He hesitated before saying what else he was thinking, but then went ahead. "My hope is that when you see the face looking back at you, it might spark your memory."

"Of why he looked familiar," she said slowly.

"Right."

"Okay. I'll do my best." Her expression seemed to suddenly turn inward. "I don't know if you'd be interested, but...well...the baby is being really active right now." She regarded him shyly. "You could, well, feel her move, if you'd like."

"Yeah." Clearing his throat did nothing to unclog the emotions crowding him. He circled the coffee table, set down his mug and held out his hand, not quite sure where he ought to place it.

Lina lowered the fleece throw to her lap, then lifted her shirt, baring the pale swell. She took his hand and opened it, placing it over her belly. Surprised at how hard her stomach was, he waited, not breathing.

Something squirmed beneath his palm. Blinking, he lifted his head to meet her eyes. She smiled. Her whole belly bobbed, as if the baby had done a somersault.

Good God, Bran thought, in a kind of awe; maybe it had.

No, maybe *she* had.

"Having this happen inside you must feel really strange."

That soft, incredibly gentle smile still curved her mouth. "Yes and no. It makes me very aware there's a whole separate person in there. I don't suppose it's all that different from carrying a baby in a snuggly against your body."

"No, but—" He shook his head. Probably he should remove his hand, but he couldn't make himself. The next movement was more subtle, something passing beneath the surface of the water. His awareness that this was a baby, *his* baby, made the sensation incredible. "How do you sleep?"

"She does get active when I'm relaxed. I think my walking around rocks her, so she goes to sleep. I'm told sleep for me gets to be more of a challenge the bigger she gets. Eventually, she'll be punching and kicking me. I haven't felt hiccups yet, either, which happens."

"You have three more months."

"Not quite." She paused. "Unlike most people, I know exactly when I got pregnant."

Yeah, she did.

"I keep track. Tomorrow, I'll be at exactly twenty-seven weeks. So I do have ten or eleven weeks to go, if I make it full term."

Jolted, he said, "You might not?"

"Well…if my blood pressure becomes a real

issue, the doctor might decide at some point to induce labor." While he was still reeling from that, she gave him a small lecture on pregnancy and what was still to come. He was blown away to learn that the fetus was already fourteen or fifteen inches long.

"She probably only weighs a couple of pounds, though. Maybe a little more." Lina looked ruefully down at herself. "She takes up more space than she should."

Since he hadn't felt any more movement, Bran reluctantly removed his hand. Lina immediately tugged her shirt down and lifted the throw back up to her chin.

"Thank you," he said huskily.

"Yes, well…" She drew the last word out as she sneaked a glance at him, her shyness resurfacing.

That bothered him until he reminded himself how very intimate they'd become on one level, while having spent so little time together. She'd only come back into his life…five days ago? Was that all?

"Well?" he prompted. Probably he should go back to his chair, but he liked sitting close enough to see the fine texture of her skin, the way her lashes curled, the striations of color in her eyes.

"I was leading into an invitation," she said.

He sat back. Was she actually…

"I don't know if you're interested or…or can

get away, but I have a doctor's appointment on Wednesday at ten. You could hear the baby's heartbeat."

Ah. A doctor's appointment.

"You're not driving yourself," he reminded her, ignoring the flare of mutiny on her face. "But I'd like to come anyway." He stared halfway down the fleece throw to where he decided the swell of her pregnancy had to be. *A heartbeat. Damn.* "How often do you go?"

"Monthly, at this stage. I think weekly the last month, at least."

"Okay." And he'd be at every one of them with her.

"I'll be taking childbirth classes, too. The session lasts six weeks, and they have evening classes."

Was that an invitation, too? "Are they just for mothers?"

She shook her head. "We're encouraged to bring a partner to be a coach. The father, or…or a friend. I'd asked Maya, but—" Her voice broke. "If you do it, you'd have to stay for the birth. If you think—"

"Yeah." God, now he sounded hoarse. "Of course I want to do it. You couldn't keep me away."

"Well, good. I mean, we haven't talked about

how involved you'll want to be once she's born, but—"

Bran didn't let her finish. "Very. This is my child. Did you think I'd just write checks?"

She scrutinized him as if this was the first time she'd ever had the chance. Maybe, in a way, it was. Finally, slowly, Lina shook her head.

"No, you'd never turn your back on your own child. From the minute you asked me to trust you, I suppose I knew."

"Knew?"

"You'd…take responsibility." She offered a small, crooked smile. "Look at how far you've gone to keep me safe, just because of the baby. It's not as if we're—"

Abruptly pissed, he cut her off. "We are, Lina. I told you, I'd have called you right away if you hadn't run out on me. Every time since I've seen a woman with hair close to the color of yours, or who walks like you do, I looked. I'd catch a voice, and turn. Don't pretend we're strangers."

Her eyes widened before she ducked her head. "Okay."

"That's it? Okay?"

She looked up again. "Isn't that enough?"

No. It wouldn't be enough until she agreed to marry him, but he knew she wouldn't believe he really wanted her and not only the baby if he asked this soon. And…was that even the truth?

Bran was shaken by his lack of doubt. There was a reason he'd been celibate for six long months, and counting. Until that night six months ago, when Lina had stepped into his arms as if it were the most natural place in the world for her, Bran hadn't understood the punch Zach had felt the first time he set eyes on Tess. Not that he was inclined to slap a label on how he'd felt. Whatever love was, he didn't want to feel it, not after witnessing firsthand the damage *love* had done to his father.

Lina…felt right, that's all. They fit. Sooner or later, she'd see that. And, although he didn't like the threat to her, this proximity was a fortunate side benefit. Because he voted for sooner rather than later.

He *really* wanted her in his bed.

Prudently, he withdrew to the recliner. "I'll stick around in the morning until the artist shows. I can make calls without going in. Novinski dodged me today, which I don't appreciate." Annoyance killed some of the sexual tension. "We're doing most of the legwork, and she can't even keep me informed?"

"She might have had the day off," Lina suggested.

"In the middle of an investigation like this?"

"She may always be in the middle of this kind

of investigation. A bank robbery is a rarity for us, but it's probably not for her."

"You're right." In fact, Novinski was a specialist in bank robbery. He let his irritation subside, if reluctantly. "Still. They're looking at footage at Snoqualmie Community Bank. One of those two *had* to pay it a visit. Hard to get through two sets of doors without looking straight ahead into a camera."

"I've been praying you'd find a clear picture of his face. Of either of their faces," she corrected herself.

"It would take the pressure off you," he agreed. "Although not until we find a way to let *them* know we have it."

"Which would mean publishing it."

Bran moved restlessly. "Maybe."

Lina didn't call him on the equivocation, assuming she recognized it as such. She only nodded. "What time did you say the artist will be here?"

"She's coming from north Seattle, aiming for nine thirty or ten, depending on traffic."

"Oh, in that case, I think I'll go to bed now." She sounded elaborately casual. "Or at least read in bed for a while." She slid forward, putting her stocking feet on the floor.

He would be better entertainment than her

book. Take her to the heights, let her down softly. Rock her to sleep.

His fingers bit into the upholstered arms of the recliner. "Good night, then. I'll need to use the bathroom once you're out."

She nodded, for no real reason. This was inevitably an awkward moment. Their toothbrushes now sat side by side in a ceramic holder. She'd made apologies, but some of her toiletries cluttered the counter. He had assured her he didn't mind. In the morning, after she'd showered, her much smaller feet left an imprint on his bath mat. The bathroom had taken to smelling like her, as if he brushed against mint leaves every time he stepped in. The bedroom…well…he still had to go in there in the mornings to collect clean clothes.

He hadn't lived with anyone else for a long time. Paige had spent the night occasionally, or he had gone to her apartment, but not often because of their working schedules. Of course he'd had roommates in college and after. Living with Lina did not feel the same.

She admitted to needing a book to settle down once she went to bed. He'd be staring at a dark ceiling for hours—and not only because the damn sofa wasn't quite long enough.

They said their good-nights. Bran listened grimly to the quiet sounds she made brushing her teeth, braiding her hair and doing whatever else it was women did getting ready for bed.

Could it be she was waiting for him to make a move? He stifled a groan. He wished. *Five days*, he reminded himself. The next time he took her to bed, it would really mean something, and they both knew it. *Let her know you*, he thought, and wanted it to happen faster.

He heard the soft sound of the bedroom door closing and sighed, rising to gather his bedding from the small linen closet where he stuffed it every morning.

# CHAPTER NINE

"I THINK...THE HAIRLINE was higher." Lina closed her eyes, trying to freeze that one instant when the bank robber and she had stared at each other. "It came to a sort of widow's peak. He's balding," she realized. "That's why he shaves his head."

She heard the soft sound of the artist brushing charcoal off the pad, subtly altering lines. When the artist showed her the change, she murmured, "Yes. Did I say there was an earring?"

"Hoop or post?"

"Post. I caught a glint, as if it was a stone, not just gold."

Hannah Austin had arrived at a little before ten, and within minutes had assembled her drawing board on the dining room table. It turned out she was pregnant, too. At not quite three months, undetectably so thus far. Her warmth and gentleness had made Lina more optimistic before they started.

"I prefer to work alone with the witness," Hannah had told Bran. He hadn't replied, just looked implacable. That was something he did well.

Apparently resigned, the artist settled for banishing Bran to someplace out of Lina's sight, saying in a steely voice, "You will not intrude."

If he was impatient with Lina's many hesitations and corrections, she thought thankfully, at least she couldn't see him. And he had managed to keep his mouth shut.

She studied the drawing again, still not satisfied. "The jaw doesn't look quite right," she decided. "Although I'm not sure why."

With a few lines, some blurring, the jaw in the portrait became square, which had her now decisively shaking her head. "No, the other way around, I think. Leaner, more—"

The artist deftly made changes.

Lina's eyes widened as she took in the face, not just one detail at a time. Her heart raced and she felt like hyperventilating. "Oh, God. It's him."

Hannah smiled. "Nothing you want to change?"

"No. Oh, God," she said again, stunned to see *him* looking back at her, and this time without thick glass between them.

"Lina?" It was Bran, sounding closer than she'd realized he was, the very deepness of his voice calming to her.

Shivering, she couldn't tear her eyes from the

picture. "I didn't think it was possible, but…there he is."

His big hands closed over her shoulders. She could feel his heat at her back. There was silence as he studied the drawing.

"Do you know him, Lina?"

"Yes." She shook her head. "No."

"Only from that day?"

She expected him to be frustrated, but heard his understanding.

"No," she whispered. "No, I've seen him somewhere else. I can almost picture it…"

The artist murmured, "Close your eyes, Lina. Tell me what he was wearing. A T-shirt, or one with a collar? A coat?"

As if she was in a trance, she heard herself say, "Collar. Blue, like chambray, but dirty. There's a smear of dirt on his face, too." But she hit a wall. His surroundings eluded her. Had he been talking to someone else? What was he *doing*? What was *she* doing? Lina made a strangled sound that was almost a scream and shot to her feet, pushing the straight-backed chair aside.

"Hey." Bran tugged her back against him, until his entire body supported and reassured her. "It'll come. Forcing…rarely works."

"No, but…it's so close. Why do I have this snapshot that's so…ungrounded?"

"It's more interesting that you remember him

at all," Bran commented. "If you've seen him before, there had to be a reason you concentrated on him, if only for a moment before you were distracted."

"It's true," Hannah put in. "I think the context will float into your mind at some unexpected moment. Worrying at it won't make it come any faster."

Within minutes, Hannah had packed up and, after a last, comforting hug, was gone, taking the drawing with her. She still had work to do on it, she said, and had been promised the use of a room at the station. She would send a copy later today or tomorrow.

Lina sank down on the sofa. "I'm sorry."

"Sorry?" Bran raised his eyebrows. "You and Hannah recreated his face. Even if we don't go public with it right away, we'll show it to bank employees, for starters. The FBI must have a whole pool of other potential witnesses from the previous robberies to show it to. And we'll share it with other law-enforcement agencies. Somebody capable of shooting an innocent woman in cold blood can't have been a saint before he took up bank robbery as a profession. What do you want to bet he has a record somewhere?"

"I didn't think of that."

He sat on the coffee table, his knees bumping hers, his craggy face lined with worry. "I hate to leave you. I know you must be bored out of your skull."

She wrinkled her nose. "To tell you the truth, I think I've had about as much excitement for one day as I can take. I know you won't like this, but…is there any chance we could go to the pool this evening?"

Lina could see the refusal forming, but then he blew out a breath.

"Probably. If we're careful. Maybe I'll see if Zach and Tess want to come. He could provide some added security."

She had a mental picture of his Camaro sandwiched in a presidential-style convoy, but wasn't about to argue if it meant she could swim her laps and let go of some of this seemingly unending tension. Which must be doing wonders for her blood pressure, still in the "watch and wait" category at her last doctor's appointment.

Of course, there might be another way…

No. Sex would complicate everything unbearably. Whether she liked it or not, they were locked in a relationship that would last a lifetime. Sex now, for no better reason than because it would release stress, would be foolish.

Bran had risen to his feet. In that way he had, he stood looking down at her for longer than was comfortable. His expression wasn't quite a frown, but it was something near. She didn't dare quite let her eyes meet his, in case he could tell what she'd been thinking. Or…in case he was thinking the same thing.

"All right," he said abruptly. "I'll see you later. I can bring dinner again."

"Why don't I cook?" she suggested. It would fill a little of her time. "You have chicken and hamburgers in the freezer, and most staples. I can come up with something."

"Call if you need me to pick up anything at the store," he said promptly. How like a man.

She smiled vaguely in his general direction and he left. She heard the dead bolt slide home, turned by a key from the outside. Whatever else Bran felt, he was very committed to keeping her safe.

"Did you take a few days off?" he growled. Bran had had his feet stacked on his desk, but when Novinski actually answered her phone, he swung them to the floor and sat up.

At the desk across from him, Charlie set down his own phone in favor of eavesdropping.

"I *am* working on other cases," the agent told him.

"More important than this one?"

She sighed. "No. Listen, I'm forwarding you the best close-ups our tech came up with from what you provided. None of them are any better than what we already had."

Which was, to use Zach's word, squat. Five previous robberies, and, in every case, both of those sons of bitches had managed to keep their faces from appearing on camera while visiting multiple banks on their way to choosing a target.

"What did you find from Snoqualmie Community's footage?" This was what had infuriated him most. He was supposed to share, but the FBI didn't? His willingness to cooperate was leaking away.

"Nothing," she said, to his stupefaction. "Not a damn thing. I'd swear neither one of them set foot in that bank in advance."

To Charlie, waiting impatiently, Bran shook his head. Aloud, he said, "Crap," although he was thinking something more profane.

"I think it's safe to say one or both of them was already familiar with Snoqualmie Community Bank," the FBI agent said, which was exactly what Bran was thinking. "They waffled enough to check out a couple other possibilities in town, but went with their first choice."

"The artist met with Ms. Jurick this morning," he said. "She's confident they nailed his face. As soon as I get the final from Hannah, I'll send it to you. Somebody, somewhere, knows this piece of scum."

"Ms. Jurick doesn't?"

"She's convinced she's seen him, but not that

they'd ever met. He caught her eye, that's all. But it suggests he is local, or at least has a connection that has brought him to Clear Creek before."

"She could easily be convincing herself she's seen him before."

"The face was pretty damn vivid in her mind."

"Not surprising, given the circumstances in which she saw him." When he stayed silent, she added, "It sounds as if you've got her locked down well, even if you're right and I'm wrong."

"That's not possible." Teeth bared, he didn't know whether to be glad Special Agent Novinski couldn't see him, or wish she could. "I'm one man. She should have round-the-clock coverage."

"You know our resources are limited. We deal with potential witnesses all the time. It's rare for a perp to risk going back to silence someone."

"But he seems to have done just that."

"Or she got in the middle of a local gang shooting. You do have gangs?"

"We have gangs," he growled.

"A face puts us a quantum leap ahead of where we were." Novinski suddenly sounded a lot more cheerful.

Bran was glad one of them was, especially since he knew she wasn't going to like the next thing he had to say.

"I don't want to publish this."

"Why?"

"First, because he'll take off if he sees his face on the news. Right now, he's *here*. I know he is. He has no idea we're as close to getting him as we are."

"All right," she said. "What else?"

"This asshole is dangerous. What if he's in a convenience store and sees his face on the front page of the newspaper right by the checkout stand? He turns around and the person behind him in line looks from the drawing to his face. You think he's going to just walk out? Or is he going to kill everyone in there?"

Novinski argued, but not very hard. They were dealing with a ruthless bastard. The risk was real, whether he was living in Bran's county or somewhere else. Finally, she said, "I'm okay with giving it some time. If we don't get anywhere, we may need to put this out there."

"Don't do it without talking to me first."

She didn't like being challenged, but, as he'd already noted, she didn't have ego problems. "I'll give you fair warning," she conceded.

He couldn't ask for more. Bran only hoped like hell his caution didn't tie their hands.

BRAN'S BED WAS huge and amazingly comfortable. She closed her eyes, remembering how it felt to have his big body wrapped around hers. Smiling, she fell into a deep, luxurious sleep.

Abruptly, she came awake. Holding herself very still, Lina listened.

Oh, God. Had she heard a key in the door? Because…she'd swear the entry door was opening and somebody was coming in. Bran hadn't been gone that long. Why would he be back so soon?

Heart pounding, she slipped out of bed, taking a second to pull on her elastic-waisted maternity pants. Bran might not have called out if he'd guessed she was sleeping…

She tiptoed to where she could see down the short hall, through the living room to the entry, where somebody was indeed coming into the apartment. Only…it wasn't Bran.

Lina clapped a hand over her mouth to stifle a cry. She was mostly looking at a substantial rear end and polyester-clad legs. She thought it was a woman backing in, pulling…something.

Lina dashed to where she'd left her phone on the bedside stand and dialed Bran.

He answered on the second ring. "What's wrong?"

"Somebody is here," she said, keeping her voice low. "Inside."

*"What?"*

"She had a key—"

"Oh, hell," he groaned. "I completely forgot. This is Tuesday. A woman comes in for a couple hours once a week to clean. Middle-aged, a little plump?"

Oh, thank goodness. "Yes." Lina tried not to sound shaky, although she felt it. "That seems about right. What's her name? I'd better go introduce myself so I don't scare her, too. Unless she knows I'm here?"

"No, I didn't think to tell her, either. Andrea Young. Damn, I'm sorry, Lina."

She reassured him and made a production of swinging the bedroom door farther open before she went out into the hall and said, "Hello?"

The woman who had just plugged in a vacuum cleaner jumped, as startled as Lina had been. She might have just as good reason, too; letting herself into other people's theoretically empty homes must be a little unnerving.

Lina approached. "Bran forgot to tell me you were coming, and apparently to tell you he has a houseguest. I apologize for surprising you."

The woman, fortyish with many-times-dyed blond hair, smiled. "Well, we hardly ever talk. He mostly leaves notes and checks on the refrigerator. I'm Andrea Young."

"Lina Jurick."

"Would you rather I didn't stay today?"

She wouldn't go back to sleep anyway, not with so much adrenaline flooding her bloodstream.

"No, this is fine. I feel a little guilty lazing around while you clean, but I'll just stay out of your way."

Lina went to the kitchen to survey possibilities for dinner, leaving Andrea to vacuum the living room, bedroom and Bran's rather bare office, which Lina had yet to see him use. Then she retreated to the sofa while Andrea cleaned the kitchen, finally mopping. Bathroom next, then she dusted. Yes, even running her duster over Bran's books.

They barely exchanged a word, although the woman thanked Lina for holding the door for her when she left.

After locking behind her, Lina leaned her back against it and wondered why she still felt so unsettled. It only took her a minute to understand. She had felt safe here, as if the locks on the door and the bar securing the sliding glass door made Bran's apartment impregnable. But who else might have a key? He'd probably given Paige one, maybe friends. Zach? People were careless with their keys. Copies could be made so easily.

Her faith in locks had just been shaken.

HARD AS IT was to focus on anything but the threat to Lina, Bran still had a job to do. He caught a break on an assault case he'd had to put on the back burner. Finally having a believable witness testimony, he took another detective along, per procedure, and made an arrest. Booking and his report took a good part of the afternoon. When he was done, he considered skipping out early, but instead swore under his breath and set to doing background searches to keep his promise to Zach.

Zach had been determined to research Rob Greaver's history himself. Most of the names of other neighbors' boys from their childhood that he had passed on to Bran came up clean. A few had sounded only vaguely familiar, but others evoked memories, faces. One girl Bran had looked up only out of curiosity after searching for her brother, who now worked construction and lived in eastern Washington. The sister he remembered better. Zoe Tacher had become a physical therapist? Well, she'd been good with her hands and mouth, as half the boys who'd attended Clear Creek High School with her could attest. Bran grinned before moving on.

Derek Brooks, now... Bran scanned his record, then deepened the search. Derek had been part of the neighborhood gang, but not a friend of Bran's even though they were close in age.

Good old Derek had been arrested twice, once for rape, once for statutory rape. The first time, he got off. His attorney had probably succeeded in persuading the jury that the sex had been consensual. He'd been twenty-six at that point, the girl...barely eighteen. After the second arrest, he wasn't so lucky. He insisted the girl had said she was eighteen, when in fact she was only fifteen. By then, he was thirty-three. He served a ridiculously short term and got out no doubt to prey on other young women.

Bran called the Bellingham PD and counted his blessings to find the arresting detective was still with the department and willing to talk to him. Detective Sanchez had to look up the case, but then said, "Oh, yeah, I remember that one. He up to his old tricks?"

"This isn't a current matter. His name actually came up regarding a very cold case." He explained, having to admit his relationship to Sheila since they shared the same last name. "He lived about a block from us at the time. Neither of his arrests involved young girls, but he'd have only been thirteen when Sheila was killed. Seems like women his own age intimidate him. Maybe girls his age did, too, back then."

"I don't know," the detective said. "He may not be able to handle women his own age, but I will say the girl could have passed for a college kid. Really buxom for a fifteen-year-old. Would he go for that if he preferred little girls?"

Probably not. All Bran could do was thank him and cross Brooks off his list. As, so far, they'd eliminated every other possibility, with the exception of Rob Greaver. And Zach wouldn't like to hear him say so, but Bran couldn't help thinking they were jumping to some major conclusions there. There were a lot of reasons Mama Greaver might be proud of her daughter and not her son.

His mood sour, Bran shut down his computer. He had to get going if he and Lina were to eat early enough for her to swim.

Yes, once more he'd be driving her straight into the perfect location for an ambush. He was acutely aware that Lina was never more vulnerable than she was at the high school, where she'd already been attacked once. Tonight, at least, he'd have backup from Zach, who hadn't even hesitated about agreeing to help.

Having family still felt strange, Bran reflected. And, yeah, good, too.

ZACH WAS SHOCKED to find Tess had never learned how to swim. How had he not known? In part, he realized, because his days off this summer had been spent working on the house, not going rafting or to the nearest lake for a dip.

"I can float on my back, but the idea of putting my face in the water gives me the creeps." She had almost drowned when she was three. She admitted to remembering the terror, rather than what had actually happened, but her parents had told the story often. It involved a company potluck at a lakeshore park, and her mother and father each thinking the other was keeping an eye on her. Apparently she had ventured out onto a dock, watching the big kids splashing in the water. Nobody knew whether she'd jumped in or gotten too close to the edge.

"You know how murky lake water can be. In my memory, it's black. I'm sinking and I can't breathe."

"God, I'm so sorry. Who pulled you out?"

"Several kids saw me go in and my father came racing down the dock. One of the boys had managed to pull me to the ladder by the time he got there, though." She shuddered, her expression unusually vulnerable. "I've tried taking lessons a couple times, but I always panic."

"Then forget tonight," he said roughly.

But, gutsy woman that she was, she refused. In swimming pools, she said, at least the water was clear and she could see the bottom. She could paddle around, and she liked hot tubs.

Paddling was about what she did once they got there. He was a better swimmer than his brother, he discovered, but he took it easy so he could keep an eye on Tess. When Lina offered to give her a lesson, Tess accepted despite her deep fears.

Relieved to see that the lesson was very basic, Zach hoisted himself out of the pool to join Bran in the hot tub, which they had to themselves. He groaned with pleasure as a jet of bubbling water hit a sore muscle in his lower back.

Bran took advantage of the chance to tell him which names he'd run background checks on that day, and Zach managed to keep his mouth shut. It would have been easy to say, *Really? You found the time?*

He knew the accusation would have been unfair anyway. No, his brother wasn't as driven as he was to pursue this, but Zach regretted the scene he'd made last time this came up. Bran really was slammed right now, with the double murder at the bank, the rest of his caseload and the threat to Lina. And he'd been right—after twenty-five years, what did a few more days or weeks matter?

Zach stood, craning his neck to see how the lesson was going and saw the two women's backs. Lina appeared to be demonstrating a stroke, Tess watching carefully. Each wore a single, fat braid down her back.

"How's it going?" Bran asked lazily.

"Looks okay." He told Bran her story, which made his brother wince.

"That would do it." He watched Zach lay back and close his eyes. "You done anything about Greaver?"

"Called. Left messages. He's not returning them."

"Mama probably warned him about you."

Zach grunted. "I know where he works. I'll lie in wait for him when he gets off."

"Monday?"

It was one of Zach's days off. "Yeah."

"I can come if you want."

Zach opened his eyes. "You're serious?"

Bran scowled. "Of course I'm serious. You know this guy isn't going to be very happy to see you."

Zach grinned. "You're worried about me."

A smile might have twitched one corner of Bran's mouth. "In your dreams."

He sank lower again, utterly relaxed. Finally, he said, "Sure."

The next time he opened his eyes, it was to find a pregnant woman standing above him in a wet bathing suit. He couldn't help thinking how he'd really like to see Tess carrying their baby.

"Your wife wants you to come watch," Lina said.

"Really?" Zach levered himself out of the hot tub. Just as well; he'd been about to fall asleep. Some security he was proving to be. He followed Lina to the pool, where Tess was waiting.

"Courage in action," she told him, sounding flip to hide the fact that she was completely serious, he suspected. Lina, who had sat on the side of the pool, gave her a nod of encouragement. Tess took a deep breath, bent forward, put her face in the water—and lifted her feet off the bottom. She floated, unaided, for a count of ten or so before standing up again in a rush. Her eyes found his.

He applauded, and realized Bran was beside him doing the same.

Zach crouched, and waited until Tess came to the edge, looking up at him. "I have never, for a moment, doubted your courage," he murmured, just for her.

Her smile lit her face.

HEARING THE BABY'S heartbeat was the damnedest thing. It wasn't as if Bran hadn't believed she was in there; he'd felt her move. But he was mesmerized by that quick, light beat. It made him want to say, *I'm here.* When she was born, would she know his voice?

She wouldn't if Lina moved back into her apartment.

It was all he could do to make himself take off the stethoscope, tearing his gaze from Lina's stomach to meet her eyes. He had a bad feeling he looked as stupefied as he felt, but her smile was soft and understanding.

"It's amazing, isn't it?"

"Yeah," he said hoarsely. "She's really in there."

The doctor chuckled. "And we're getting closer to when she needs to come out."

Childbirth terrified him. As a patrolman, he'd helped deliver a couple babies, and had nightmares about the experiences long afterward.

He didn't know what his face showed, but her hand found his. To reassure him? Or because she needed the connection?

He couldn't tell, because the doctor had whisked Lina's shirt back down and was talking.

"Everything looks good so far. Your blood pressure is about the same, which is a real positive. I'm glad you're able to stay active. Swimming is an excellent choice, although you may find you have to give it up toward the end."

In other words, she might not be able to make it up to take a breath, not with a rock dragging her down. And, damn, Bran wished the doc had ordered Lina to change exercise plans *now*.

"I've noticed I swim a little lower in the water," Lina admitted.

"Make an appointment on your way out," the doctor added briskly. "I think we can safely go four weeks again." She nodded at Bran. "Glad to see you here."

The door closed behind her. Bran let go of Lina's hand to slip an arm behind her and help her sit up. When she turned her head to smile her thanks, her lips were only inches from his.

He kissed her, feeling her inrush of breath. But then her lips softened and parted, and he deepened the kiss. Only briefly, because, damn, this wasn't the place, but his body was hardening at even so brief a taste. With a last nip on her lower lip, he straightened.

Her dazed expression was an ego-booster. "I... What was that for?"

"You were there," he said, truthfully.

"Oh."

He held open the exam room door and she slipped past him. While she made her next appointment, he went to get the car, pulling up directly in front of the clinic door. He didn't see anything to alarm him, but hurried her into the Camaro anyway.

During the drive, he kept an eye out for pursuit, but also on her since she appeared subdued. "Are you worried?" he asked, at last.

"Worried?" She looked at him. "Well, of course I'm worried! Why else do you think I'm spending all day twiddling my thumbs in your apartment?"

"Ah... I actually meant about the baby being born." He gestured vaguely. "You know."

"Oh." Her shoulders relaxed. "A little. I haven't thought about it too much yet, I guess. I kind of hope they don't show really explicit videos in the childbirth class."

"It's pretty freaky-looking. When the head crowns."

Lina gaped at him.

He told her about his experiences, not uncommon for patrol officers. "One woman hadn't even noticed she was *in* labor until something like forty-five minutes before she gave birth. The baby just...fell out."

Into his partner's hands, thank God, not his. Bran thought he might have been twenty-three or twenty-four then.

"The other birth was during a blizzard. On the way to the hospital, the car went into a snowbank. Seems the wife was having a really bad contraction and the husband got distracted."

*Bad*, he thought belatedly, might not have been the best choice of words.

Lina was silent until he pulled into his complex and put on the signal as they neared his assigned spot. "Now I'm glad I'm due in the spring instead of winter," she said.

He came to a stop, set the emergency brake and turned off the engine. Neither of them moved right away. "You won't be alone," he said.

She sneaked a sidelong look at him. "We'll probably be meeting at the hospital."

"No."

"What do you mean, *no*?" Her voice rose. "That's months away! It's not like you'll still be stuck with me."

Her attitude was getting to him. "Damn it, I'm not *stuck* with you. This is where you should be."

Her "What?" was almost silent.

"You're having our baby. I don't want to be a weekend father, Lina." He yanked out the keys, unfastened his seat belt and opened the door. "You might try getting used to living with me."

Her mouth was still hanging open when he got out.

## CHAPTER TEN

LINA COULD NOT believe it when Bran slammed his car door before she could so much as get a word out. Her hand shook as she unlatched her own seat belt and grabbed her swim bag. The minute Bran opened the passenger door to let her out, she said, "You *cannot* be serious."

"I'm serious about getting you safely into the apartment," he snapped. "Pay attention."

Fuming, she let him hustle her into the building and up to the fourth floor. His relentless concentration didn't ease up until they were inside the apartment and he was locking the door behind them.

Lina stalked as far as the kitchen table, dropped her bag and turned to confront him, arms crossed. "What, you think you own the baby now? And, gosh, better keep the brood mare close to the barn to be sure she doesn't wander off?"

Muscles knotted in his jaw, he flung his wet towel and suit toward the counter. "You're pregnant. I want us to get married."

She laughed in disbelief, even though boiling

up underneath was…something else. "You're crazy. This is not the 1950s. Single motherhood isn't scandalous anymore, in case you haven't noticed."

"Is single motherhood what you really want?"

Her mouth opened and closed.

"You really think people don't still get married because they're having a baby together?"

"Want to bet on how many of those marriages make it? Or what the kids go through with the divorce?"

"You mean, divided custody? Isn't that what you're suggesting?"

"But this is different!" She struggled to calm herself. "We don't have to be hostile."

"You're yelling. That sounds pretty damn hostile to me."

He, of course, wasn't yelling. Instead, his expression had become remote. That stone face was probably useful on the job. When Bran's brother lost his temper the other night, he probably hadn't liked that cool stare any better than Lina did.

She'd quit believing Bran was just unemotional. She'd almost cried at what she saw on his face while he listened to their baby's heartbeat. He'd just become good at putting a lid on all those things he didn't want to feel.

She had the strange thought that his anger the night she'd got him to spill all the stuff about his sister was hopeful. His emotions had swung wildly. In reliving an awful part of his life, he had gone to an emotional place he hated. For her.

Still, she tried logic again now. "It makes no sense to tie ourselves together just because we're having a baby. We can be good parents without—"

Blue eyes glittering, he paced toward her; she retreated, without daring to look over her shoulder to make sure she didn't run into anything.

"When I make a promise, I keep it," he said softly, which did not make what he said sound any less menacing. "I want a family."

She quit backing away and stood her ground. "As a replacement to the one you thought you had lined up? And, oh so conveniently, this one comes with a baby already on the way?"

He was smart enough to look wary.

"A baby—" her voice began to rise "—conceived on *your wedding day*?"

It was as if all the tumult created when she set her eyes on that invitation, swirled with bitterness when she did the first pregnancy test, had turned into a poison that flooded her now. Her hands knotted into fists. Her skin burned. She wanted to hurt him for thinking an "Oh, sorry, I screwed up, but let's tie the knot now" would be good enough. She was *glad* to see his shock.

Only…she didn't just see shock. Was that…

*grief* deepening the lines on his face, aging him before her eyes?

"So that's it?" he said after a minute. "You can't get past the timing?"

Her fingernails bit into her palms. "I don't know."

"You dislike me."

She had to swallow at that. "No," she whispered.

"But you can't imagine living with me, sharing a bed with me." He didn't say, *a life*, but he might as well have.

Her retreating anger left her feeling shaky. Lina wanted to clutch at it, but it felt as if it was leaving her for good.

"It's not that," she mumbled.

He tipped his head. "Then what is it?"

*You don't love me.* The one thing she couldn't say, because it sounded too much like begging.

"You're trying to make a family like, I don't know, picking out blocks and trying to nail them together even if they don't line up. That's not how it's done. If you loved Paige, I won't be any kind of substitute. Don't you understand?"

He stared at her, as if she was speaking a foreign language. "I didn't love Paige," he said.

"Ever?" she whispered in shock.

His mouth tightened. "I'm almost thirty-eight years old. I wanted a wife, a family."

"So you did try to assemble one, no emotional attachment required?" Oh, God—that was even worse than she'd imagined.

His face went blank again. Only his mouth tightened. "I suppose I did."

"Didn't you learn your lesson?"

Was he even blinking? "Yes."

"What's that supposed to mean?"

"It means this isn't the same."

"Because I'm pregnant?"

"Not…only that."

"I don't understand," Lina had to admit.

Bran thrust his fingers into his damp hair, making it stand up in spikes. "Does it matter? If you've made up your mind?"

"Made up my mind about what?" she asked in bewilderment.

Those muscles in his jaw pulsed again. "Me. What else?"

"Bran…we've known each other for exactly one week. Plus an evening…and a night," she added hastily. "So we'll call it eight days. If I weren't pregnant, would you have even begun to think about me and marriage in the same scenario?"

Lina wished she could read his expression.

"Yeah," he said slowly. "I think I would have."

Because he was stubbornly determined to have that family. But Lina only shook her head.

Whatever he saw on her face made him close down. "I'm sorry I can't let you go home yet," he said in a distant tone. He snatched up his towel, dangling from the counter, and the wet suit that had dropped on the floor, and started past Lina.

She had a strange vision: Tess letting herself fall forward in the pool, trusting, despite her darkest fears, that the water would hold her up.

Lina spoke to his back. "I didn't say no, never."

He went still, his back rigid.

"Just...that I won't marry you so fast. Or only because of the baby. That's not enough for me." *Tell me you love me.*

But no, it was too soon. She knew it was, even though she had a very bad feeling *she* was falling in love with him. Why else would it hurt her so much to see his pain?

Bran turned, very, very slowly. His eyes were a dark navy. "I've been trying to let you know me," he said gruffly.

Lina bit her lip and nodded. He had. Not always gracefully, but she couldn't deny he'd pushed himself out of his comfort zone.

"Living with you, though..." He cleared his throat. "I want you more than I've wanted anything in a very long time."

Behind the intensity, his phrasing was so careful. Knowing as much as she did now about his childhood, Lina understood. He must have wanted, with all a boy's heart, for his sister not to have been killed. For his family not to shatter. To not lose his mother forever, and, maybe even more, his brother.

She wouldn't have believed him if he'd insisted he wanted her more than he'd ever wanted anything. This…she believed.

Smiling tremulously, Lina said, "I suppose that's another way we need to get to know each other."

HAD HE HEARD RIGHT? Muscles locked, Bran stared at her. She was giving him a chance. *Another* chance. That should have been enough. He was appalled to discover it wasn't.

"Do you want me?" he asked harshly.

Her lips parted in surprise. "Of course I do! How could you not know?"

"I wanted to think I did." He started toward her. When he stopped, inches away, he noticed the damn wet towel and suit in his hand. An easy problem to solve—he tossed them sidelong, not caring where they landed, leaving his hand free to slide beneath her damp hair. When he squeezed her nape, she made a tiny sound that shot right to his groin. He remembered that sound.

"You did just issue an invitation." This time, he had to be absolutely sure.

Lina nodded, then flung her arms around his

neck, bringing her breasts and the swell of her pregnancy into contact with his aroused body. Rising on tiptoe, she pressed her lips to his.

Bran groaned and made the kiss into something more. She was in his arms. She wanted him. She'd said, *I didn't say no, never.*

He devoured her mouth before checking himself. Desperate as he was, her belly was a distraction. He kept kissing her, his hands searching restlessly over her body, but he hunched slightly, afraid of crushing the baby.

"Bed," he managed, when he came up for air. Lying down, he could figure out how to get as close to her as he needed to be.

He had her shirt off before they'd reached the hall, her bra a few steps later. Her already generous breasts were definitely larger, the areolae darker. "You're so beautiful," he said, unable to tear his gaze from those breasts. He cupped them, and finally bent to nuzzle them. But when she whimpered, Bran needed more.

He tore off his own shirt before he had her backed up to the bed.

"I'm so…" Lina seemed to be trying to cover her stomach with her hands.

"Gorgeous. Ripe." He had to grit his teeth at how fitting and erotic that word was. Gently, he took her hands and set them on his shoulders, after which he crouched to remove her shoes and socks and peel off her stretchy jeans and panties. Looking up at her naked body, he thought he'd never seen anything so glorious. Her hair was like sunshine tumbling free over her breasts. Her eyes were wide, locked on his. Didn't she *know* how beautiful she was?

He spread his own hands over her stomach, rubbing gently, then laid his cheek against it. A soft touch told him Lina was stroking his hair.

Painfully erect, he grimaced as he rose from the crouch. She smiled and reached for the fly of his jeans.

Once he had her in bed, he wallowed in those amazing breasts, teased her with a hand between her legs until she moved restlessly and whimpered, trying to pull him even closer. Finally, he positioned her the way he'd imagined, her legs over his thighs, and pressed against her slick opening. She felt good, so good—

"Don't stop," Lina moaned, and he slid home.

IT WAS AS if she'd been ultrasensitized. Lina hadn't even dreamed making love could be better than it was that one night, with him. But now, his mouth on her breasts, every touch of his hand, the sense of fullness, combined into a tsunami. Before she knew it, she was tumbling. Bran was all she had to hold on to. And when she came, it was as if her expanded womb served as an echo chamber. She cried out.

At nearly the same instant, Bran went rigid above her, throbbing deep inside her. His groan vibrated in his chest. He started to collapse forward, but caught himself on stiff arms, and rolled to the side instead. His chest heaved as he struggled for breath, but he finally recovered enough to gather her into his arms, her head on his shoulder. She didn't fit quite the way she had six months ago, but they found a new fit. She could so easily have said, *I love you*, but restrained herself. For one thing…*eight days, remember?* She had to be sure. Anyway, no matter how she felt about him, could she marry a man who either refused to let himself love, or who just plain didn't love *her*? Lina didn't know.

"That was a damn good reason to get married," he said suddenly.

It was, but she shook her head anyway. "Time. Getting to know each other, remember?"

"We'll be doing that." He sounded smug.

Because he thought he had a sure thing now?

"Give me a few minutes," he added.

Lina snickered. "We could talk."

"I think I'm a little too drunk with pleasure to talk." He was quiet for a minute. "What do you suppose that felt like? For the baby, I mean?"

"I suspect not that much different from when

I'm housecleaning or swimming. Anything reasonably vigorous. She's well-cushioned, you know."

"Hmm."

Lina could feel him thinking.

"Have you thought of a name yet?" he asked cautiously, as if he was afraid of intruding somewhere he didn't belong.

"No. I've looked through baby name books. We do have a while." She explored the contours of his chest with her fingertips. "Were you thinking you'd like to name her after your mother?"

"God, no!" he said explosively. After a pause, he asked, "Yours?"

"No." She loved her mother, but... "For one thing, her name is Shari, which is okay, but I don't love it."

"Grandmother?"

"Well...maybe as a middle name, although probably not my maternal grandmother's. She's Lorraine Mildred—named after *her* mother, I think. Dad's mother is Ellen, which is better. I don't remember her middle name." She pushed herself up enough so she could see him and shook back her hair. "What about your grandmother's?"

"We'd have to go further back if we wanted Irish." His expression became more guarded. "That's if she's going to be a Murphy."

Lina had thought about this, and already decided. She might not feel close to her family right now, but she had the advantage of having grown up with a stable, essentially loving family. She already felt powerfully connected to her baby. Given Bran's broken family, she sensed that having any children sharing his name would be important to him, which made it no contest. Maybe she, too, wanted the link to Bran. *Because I love him.*

"I like Murphy," she said simply.

He reared up enough to kiss her. "Dad's grandmother was Siobhan," he said, spelling it for her. "She'd spend the rest of her life telling people how to pronounce her name."

Tentatively, Lina said, "Were you thinking of your sister? Sheila is pretty."

He lay staring up at the ceiling for a long moment before shaking his head. "I think it would always make me sad."

"That makes sense." She thought about it for a minute. "Then let's start afresh. No relative's name, just something we like."

"Good." He kissed her again, with more intent this time. "I think we've talked enough."

She slid a hand down his hard belly, following the downy line of hair, and murmured against his mouth, "Oh, I think so, too."

"Yeah, I've seen him, but I don't know who he is," the deputy said plaintively, handing the poster Lina and the artist had created back to Zach.

Bran sat back in his chair, aware that all movement around him had ceased. Warring half turned from his desk, while the other two detectives and the clerk had stopped speaking.

Bran groped for the deputy's name. He knew everyone in the department, but some not as well as others. He might never have worked the same shift with the guy, and if none of his investigations had so far involved... His gaze dropped to the badge. Karl Ingebretsen. Yeah.

"Do you remember the circumstances?" Bran asked, with more patience than he felt. "And how long ago?"

Ingebretsen was in his early forties, at a guess, and still fit. His brow furrowed in thought. "Had to be a year ago." He shrugged. "A year and a half?"

"I take it you didn't arrest him?"

The other man shook his head. "He was a bystander, really. It was a domestic, I remember that. The usual, a neighbor called, heard yelling and a woman scream. I knock on the door, the wife says nonsense, they had the television on too loud. See, they had company. *He* was the company. Just a guy standing behind the couple, listening. He didn't say anything. My gut told me the woman was lying, but what can you do? I apologized for disturbing them and left."

There wasn't anything else the guy could have

done. Bran had been on too many calls like that. If there was no visible sign of injury and everybody insisted everything was okay, you did your best to shrug off the fear that the next time you came to this address, somebody would be badly hurt or even dead, and you'd think *if only*.

For once, nobody's phone rang. Everyone in the bullpen held their silence, gripped by the possibility of an ID on the perpetrator of one of the worst crimes ever committed in their jurisdiction.

"Could you find the house?"

The deputy shook his head decisively. "Not a chance. You have to know how many of those calls I answer. Nothing stood out about that one. I'm surprised the guy even looked familiar, and I could recall when I'd seen him. I can't picture the woman's face, or her husband's. I know I'd never been there before."

"I understand." Bran didn't let his frustration show. Warring knew enough to keep his mouth shut. "There has to be a reason you do remember a man who wasn't doing anything but standing in the background."

He earned a shrug. "If you'd stuck a picture of the woman in front of me, she might have looked familiar, too."

"Maybe. But maybe there was an odd vibe. Could it have been a setup, and he was really the husband or boyfriend?"

Bran's casual, let's-think-about-it tone served its purpose. Ingebretsen frowned. "Unlikely. He was younger than they were."

He remembered more than he knew. "So he seemed out of place?" Bran prodded. "Dressed differently than the husband and wife? Not young enough to be their kid, but you wondered in the back of your mind why he was there?"

"No, it wasn't that. I see all types. You must, too."

Bran dipped his head in concession, letting the silence draw out. Ingebretson's frown had deepened, and his eyes had an unfocused look Bran found hopeful.

"He was smirking, like he thought it was funny I was there," the deputy said suddenly. "Rubbed me the wrong way, but you can't haul someone in for being a prick."

"Unfortunately," someone in the room muttered.

With an expression of regret, Ingebretsen said, "I wish I could tell you different, but I think that must be why he stuck out and the other two people didn't." He promised to skim his reports to see if anything rang a bell, but his lack of optimism was contagious. Bran let him go.

Zach lingered long enough to say, "I dragged him in here because he was so sure he didn't know anything useful, he wasn't going to come to you. But, if nothing else, he's confirmed that this creep is either local or has friends or family here."

"And more may come back to him now that he's started thinking." *I wish.* But it was possible, just as he was convinced Lina would remember more, too.

"Thanks," he said.

Zach nodded and went on his way.

Bran and Charlie threw out a few useless ideas, after which Bran scowled at the wall and brooded. Was it a bad decision not to have put this guy's face in every newspaper and newscast?

But his gut feeling hadn't changed. This bastard had proved himself to be ruthless, violent and lacking a conscience. What would he do if he was surprised by his face on a telecast in a bar, when everyone turned to look at him? What if he was buying a six-pack at a 7-Eleven and saw the clerk looking at him funny, right before he discovered his picture staring up at him from the local paper?

The guy had to have a record. Somewhere, for something. If only the right cop would see the drawing.

*If only.* Not the most helpful words in the English language.

NO SWIMMING THAT EVENING, it being New Year's Eve, or the next day, either, of course. Tess had invited Bran and Lina to join her to count down the New Year, since she'd otherwise be alone with just her father. Zach had to pull a double shift. As many deputies as possible would be on the road. Law-enforcement agencies did not love this particular holiday.

When Bran passed on the invitation to Lina, he seemed bemused, a reminder of how little family he had in his life. "A couple of friends have asked me to parties, too, if you'd rather," he added. "They're people you'd like, although…"

"They're Paige's friends, too?"

"It's not that," he said, not quite answering her.

Right now, she realized, his friends would either assume the baby wasn't his, or they'd be counting on their fingers and come up with a date that was damn close to his non-wedding day. Nobody would come right out and ask *her* for an explanation, but she'd know what they were thinking. And they would, eventually, ask him.

If she and he didn't become a couple—well, didn't stay a couple—she wouldn't have to deal with any of the whispers.

"I'd prefer Tess's," she admitted, "unless you'd really like to go to a party."

"No. I'm not much for big groups."

"Oh, good," she said with relief.

On the drive over to his brother's house, Lina

asked when his father died. Getting him talking about their relationship was like opening a rusty umbrella, but he told her a little.

There was no question he had loved his father, Lina concluded, but it sounded as if the missing pieces of their family had a sort of ghostly presence that created long silences neither of them chose to fill. She was left to wonder if he missed his father, but she knew better than to ask.

She'd insisted they get there early so that she could help with dinner instead of leaving it all to poor Tess. Upon arrival, she discovered his quick agreement to aim for five o'clock instead of dinnertime didn't represent any sacrifice on Bran's part. Turned out there had been two earlier college football bowl games he'd missed because of work, but the Orange Bowl started at five.

"No, he doesn't care which team wins," Lina told Tess once they were alone in the kitchen, "but apparently that doesn't matter—a game's a game."

Tess rolled her eyes. "You do know there are *five* bowl games tomorrow, don't you?"

Lina set down the can opener. "You have to be kidding."

"Nope. Two are at the same time. Since we don't have a split screen, that means really the menfolk will only be able to watch four. Back to back."

"Won't Zach need to sleep?"

"You'd think," his wife said drily.

"My dad and brothers watch some college football, but they save their obsession for the Vikings."

"Live and learn."

Except it turned out to be fun. Even Lina got sucked into the night's game. Tess proved to be more enthusiastic than she'd sounded, too.

They ate at halftime, and saved dessert and coffee for post-game. Lina might have thought the four of them would run out of things to talk about, but that didn't prove to be the case. For one thing, Tess and her dad were both readers, too. His politics were considerably more liberal than Bran's, giving them the chance to have spirited debates that stayed civil. Lina's were more liberal, too, but she began to see why working in law enforcement would skew someone to the right.

Jaded, cynical, sick of human failings, Bran seemed to have lost the ability to trust that people would do the right thing on their own—if he'd ever had it.

When midnight neared, Tess produced a bottle of champagne, and even Lina had a few sips. The television showed the countdown at the Space Needle in Seattle. At midnight, fireworks exploded into the night above the city.

At the first *crack* outside, Lina flinched and automatically turned her head in search of a hiding place. But then the racket continued throughout the neighborhood, and she closed her eyes. That hadn't been a gunshot. Not a gunshot.

Bran put his arm around her. "Flashback?"

"Kind of," she admitted quietly. "Except… I don't think I *heard* the shot when Maya was killed, so I don't know why—"

"Your mind knows that what you saw should have come with sound. It's filled in any blanks. Plus, the guy shot at *you*, too." He searched her face. "Hey. This is a celebration." He bent his head and kissed her, not holding back. If Tess or her dad were watching…

Lina's cheeks felt hot by the time Bran lifted his head. Before she could wonder whether he was establishing a public claim, he smiled, and she saw that his eyes were heavy-lidded. "Happy New Year," he said softly, for her ears only, and he spread a hand over her stomach.

Tears formed in her eyes. Happy ones, because she wouldn't have wanted to be with anyone else, but the tears stung, too. Hormones, she tried to convince herself, but she knew better.

However much she tried to believe they had a future together, her fears stayed with her.

"Happy New Year," she said, too, then hugged Tess and her father both.

## CHAPTER ELEVEN

THE MOMENT SHE stepped foot in her apartment, Lina saw that the needles on her Christmas tree had turned brown and also littered the tree skirt. The ornaments Lina had hung seemed pathetic.

"Oh, no." She hurried to it. "I forgot about it. The only thing sadder than a Christmas tree after the holidays is a dead one."

"It was going to be thrown out sooner or later," Bran reminded her.

Mr. Sentimental.

She made a face at him. "Let me put the ornaments away and then you can bag the tree and take it down to the Dumpster."

"No, why don't you pack and I'll take down the ornaments?" he suggested.

That made sense, since she'd be back at work Monday. The casual clothes he'd grabbed for her wouldn't be enough.

So she brought out the bright red box that had space for way more decorations than she owned yet. The ornaments she'd bought during her marriage had stayed with David, as had all the furniture and household goods.

"What are you thinking?" Bran surprised her by saying. He had proved to be unsettlingly good at sensing when her mood turned dark. Nice to know she gave him a chance to practice his interrogation skills. But there wasn't any reason not to tell him.

"Oh, just remembering all the ornaments I started collecting when I got my first apartment. I bought the basics—you know, lights, and red and green and gold balls—then had fun every year buying a really special ornament or two. I had to start over this year, and then what did I do but abandon my poor little tree."

He frowned. "If the ornaments were yours, why didn't you take them?"

"I was fleeing to my childhood bedroom," she said wryly. "What would I have done with a bunch of stuff? Fill my parents' garage? I left almost everything with him, which is probably a good thing considering I then moved across the country. To tell you the truth, I never gave a thought to the ornaments until last Christmas at Mom and Dad's, and by then my creep of a not-quite ex and his floozy had probably hung mine on their tree."

"Contaminating them," Bran said straight-faced. "Of course you wouldn't want them after that."

"No, I wouldn't!" She eyed him in suspicion. "Are you laughing at me?"

His mouth was twitching, but he said promptly, "Wouldn't think of it."

She sniffed. "I just hope they did use my ornaments, and every single one of them makes her think of *me*."

Bran lifted an eyebrow. "Doesn't he deserve a guilt trip, too?"

Lina wrinkled her nose. "He totally does, but Christmas ornaments wouldn't do it. I doubt he'd know one from another."

Bran gently set the glass reindeer into one of the slots in the box, then patted her butt. "Go get what you need."

Using her biggest suitcase, she began to lay out clothes. By the time she had enough to get through a couple weeks of classes, both the closet and her dresser looked empty. Even the few pairs of shoes left on the floor of the closet appeared forlorn. With most of her toiletries gone, the bathroom had reverted to rental basic.

Lina took one last scan for anything she might have forgotten, then stood just looking around for a minute. She'd taken pleasure in creating a home here. She'd been gone such a short time—only nine days. But this place didn't feel like home anymore. Because Bran's apartment did now?

But that wasn't quite true. It was Bran, she realized with a small shock. Not a place, a man.

*I have to be careful.* He had a goal, and she wasn't resisting his efforts to move her that way. It was hard to, when she *had* to stay with him. Her biggest trouble was that she was tempted to accept what he was offering, even if that wasn't what she really needed from him.

She touched her stomach. *We need more.* She couldn't let herself forget it.

She pulled the suitcase out to the living room. "I'm all set."

NEITHER MAN MOVED to get out of the pickup, parked outside the trucking company where Rob Greaver worked. This south end of Seattle was entirely industrial.

Both gazed at the blank facade of the building broken only by a front entrance and, around the corner from it, a side door. At the back were a couple of maintenance bays for company-owned trucks. Otherwise, the fleet was parked in a gravel yard enclosed by a tall, chain-link fence topped with barbed wire.

Bran was keeping an eye on his watch. Today had been Lina's first back at the middle school. He hadn't relaxed his guard despite the passing days with no second attack. He *hated* that he couldn't protect her where she worked.

Since he had today off, he drove her to the school and walked her to the main doors.

"Like a father insisting on seeing his kid to the classroom door," she'd mumbled. "This is almost as embarrassing."

He resisted reminding her that she was a killer's target.

Since she'd been stuck attending meetings after the last bell, the plan was for her friend Isabel to drop her off at Tess's business. By now, she should be safe at Fabulous Interiors, where she would stay holed up until closing.

"You told Tess to keep an eye out driving home?" he said.

Zach looked exasperated. "You already asked me that. Yes."

Bran rolled his shoulders in hopes of releasing the tension. "I don't like her going back to work. If that piece of shit knows who she is, finding out she's a teacher wouldn't be hard."

"There's no reason to think he has sniper creds, and he's not going to walk armed into the school."

"It's been known to happen."

His brother conceded the point with a grimace, but said, "It would be really high-risk."

"But he could lie in wait outside."

Zach didn't say anything, and for good reason, because that was the logical course for someone determined to kill Lina. Ambush her in the parking lot if he could, or follow her to wherever she was going. Bran's shoulders and neck tightened again as he pictured the guy walking into the home store, maybe taking out Tess, too, then either escaping through the back or strolling out the front. If he had a silencer…

Bran tried hard not to let his thoughts show on his face. If Tess was killed, too, Zach would never forgive him.

His brother's rage wouldn't touch him, not if Lina was dead.

Shit. He should have stayed home to protect her, rather than wasting his time in this insane quest to find the monster who'd killed their sister. What were the odds, after all this time?

Zach stiffened. "That might be him."

They'd watched several trucks return, the drivers, one by one, entering the building, then coming out a few minutes later to go to their cars.

Bran had seen Rob Greaver's driver's license photo. The face didn't bear much resemblance to the boy he vaguely remembered. He didn't get a good look until this guy wearing the tan company uniform emerged and headed straight for a pickup truck parked not far from Zach's. Bran would have sworn his memory of Mr. Greaver was even hazier; parents just weren't that interesting to a kid. But man, there he was, big and good-looking, striding across the parking lot toward them. Even the dark blond hair had come from his father, although the son's was shaggier.

"Oh, yeah," Zach murmured, and they both got out.

Greaver's head turned when he saw the two of them approaching. "Well, if it ain't the Murphy boys," he said with a sneer. "I thought Mom was making it up."

So Mom hadn't cut her son off, after all.

"We just wanted to ask you a few questions," Zach said, seemingly relaxed and even friendly.

Bran kept his mouth shut. He didn't feel either relaxed or friendly.

Shaking his head, Greaver unlocked his truck and tossed a small, insulated container inside. Then he turned back. "You really do think you're going to find out who killed your sister twenty-five years ago."

"Why not?" Zach said. "Cold cases are closed all the time. DNA is magic, you know."

Something flickered in Rob Greaver's eyes. Alarm?

"You know, what happened was really lousy," Rob said, sounding like he meant it. "I don't blame you for wanting to see someone fry for doing that to a child. But I can't tell you anything. I never even talked to your sister. She was just another little kid."

"Your sister babysat her."

"Then why aren't you talking to her?" His mouth curled in an unpleasant facsimile of a smile. "My sister was known to have boyfriends hang around when she was babysitting. You might ask her about *them*."

"You never dropped by when Mary was at our house?"

His expression hardened. "Mary and I were not friends."

"There a reason for that?" Bran put in.

His gaze switched from Zach to Bran. "Yeah. She was a little princess and a bitch. Probably still is. Pity the idiot who married her."

"I understand your nephew just enlisted in the air force," Zach commented.

"So Mom says." Rob couldn't have sounded more indifferent. When another truck rumbled in, he lifted a hand in greeting, then looked back at the brothers. "Are we done?"

Still pleasantly, Zach said, "Your mother didn't want to talk about other teenage boys in the neighborhood. Can you give us the names of any you remember?"

He scrutinized them, as if they were something peculiar he was about to scrape off his boot. "*You* were a teenager," he said to Bran. "You know who was around."

"I was a lot younger than you."

"And why are you looking at teenagers? Are you trying to find a scapegoat besides dear old Dad?"

Bran's hackles rose and he let Zach respond.

"It happens we have inside knowledge. That's why we were interested in talking to you." He laid just the slightest emphasis on the *you*.

Rob snarled and took a step forward to crowd them. "You can take your questions and shove 'em!"

"How about one more?" Zach cocked an eyebrow, wordless indication he wasn't intimidated.

Rob gave them the bird and turned to his open pickup door.

"Why is it your mother didn't want to talk about you?" Zach said to his back. "Why doesn't she have any proud pictures of you on that mantel along with the ones of your sister and her family?"

Greaver stopped, his back and shoulders rigid. Bran braced himself, but the guy kept going. He got in his truck, slammed the door and fired up the engine. A moment later, he backed out without so much as checking his mirrors to make sure he didn't run one of the Murphy boys down. He never looked at them again as he drove away.

Zach scratched his chin. "Interesting."

Bran grunted.

Zach waited until they were both seat belted in

before he raised his brows and said, "You can't watch her 24/7, you know."

"You took your eyes off Tess, and look what happened." Bran felt like a shit the minute the words were out, even before he saw his brother's expression close. Zach and Tess had had some kind of fight—neither had ever admitted what it had been about—and she told Zach to get lost. That was the night Deputy Andy Hayes decided to get rid of the more vulnerable of the two witnesses to a crime he had committed. Zach barely came to his senses and returned to her house in time to save her. "I'm sorry. I shouldn't have said that."

"No, you were right." Tone flat, Zach backed the pickup out of the slot and aimed them toward the street. "You should have left this to me today."

Bran squeezed the back of his neck. "No. I'm... on edge."

"Scared shitless, you mean."

After a minute, he pushed a single word past a constricted throat. "Yeah."

"Then don't worry about it," his brother said, his glance friendlier than Bran deserved.

Lina was smart and careful. So was Tess. And...Bran found a sense of urgency driving his outrage. This mattered. With Dad gone, he wanted to see Sheila's killer pay.

This was where Bran had needed to be.

LINA CAME SCREAMING out of a nightmare. She was trying frantically to scramble out of bed when Bran's hard arm caught her.

"Where are you going?"

She strained against his grip, quivering with a desperate need to escape, before the peaceful darkness of the bedroom and his presence became real. She heard herself whimper as the hideous images receded.

"Come here, honey." Bran pulled her back, helping her turn to rest her head on his shoulder. Then he began kneading her neck and shoulder while holding her close. "Bad one?"

"I keep seeing it—" She shuddered. "I don't want to!"

"I know," he murmured. "It'll fade with time, I promise. It's…hard when you've never seen anything like that before."

She absorbed that, then tilted her head even though she could barely make out his face in the minimal light seeping through the slats in the blinds. "Have you?"

"It's different for me."

She waited, but that was it. God forbid he admit his ironclad control had ever been shaken.

Chilled by his silence, she rolled away to face the wall.

After a long pause, he started talking. "The first time was a suicide." His voice came out so scratchy, he cleared his throat. "Happened right in front of me. I was begging him not to do it when he pulled the trigger. I've never forgotten." He paused. "This was worse for you."

Lina turned over and fit herself beneath his arm again, head on his shoulder. "Because we were friends."

"Right."

"I wish…" She stopped.

He waited, displaying the patience she suspected was another technique used in interviews.

Of course it worked. "Oh," she mumbled, "that Maya was being buried here. So I could go."

"Her body is being released tomorrow."

"I know. Her…her mother called to tell me."

"Have you ever met the parents?"

"Yes, they came for a visit last summer. Um, not long after we—"

He let that go. "I don't remember where they live."

"Reno. And I know it's not that far. She'd like me to come. She said Maya talked about me a lot. I could get time off to go…"

His stillness this time had nothing to do with patience. It was resistance. But even though she gave him time to open his big mouth, he didn't. The restraint must be all but killing him.

Lina sighed. "I know it's not safe. You don't have to tell me."

"You said you didn't want to fly because of your pregnancy, either."

She made a face he wouldn't be able to see. "It's perfectly fine for pregnant women to fly, you know. What I told my parents at Christmas was an excuse."

"I figured that." His tension didn't ease. "I hate funerals."

Curiosity piqued, she tried to make out his face again. "Have you been to so many?"

"Sometimes for the job."

"Oh. You really do go to the funeral after someone's murdered?"

"You mean to catch the killer red-handed?" There might have been a hint of amusement in his voice this time. "Hasn't worked that way for me." He paused before adding, "I go for the families. I…get to know them."

The halting admission caused her eyes to burn from unshed tears. Rubbing her cheek over hard muscle, she wondered how he could be so compassionate and sensitive in so many ways, yet so resistant to acknowledging his own deeper emotions. Of course, she thought with renewed depression, it was also possible he couldn't acknowledge what wasn't there.

He'd admitted to getting engaged once to a woman he didn't love because she fulfilled some criteria he hadn't shared with Lina. He claimed Lina was different, but couldn't or wouldn't describe what he felt for her. It was entirely possible the only thing different about her was his powerful sense of responsibility. He needed to protect her because she was a witness to murder. He needed to take care of her because she carried his baby. Did love even register with him, compared to imperatives far more basic?

He abruptly flipped onto his side to face her, shifting her head to rest on his biceps. "What are you thinking?

"That you're a good man," she said honestly. The rest…she couldn't tell him.

Bran rubbed his cheek against her head, snagging strands of hair on his bristles.

"Ouch," she complained, without much force.

"You're thoroughly awake now."

At the husky note in his voice, she slid her hand upward over the bunched muscles in his back and his strong neck until she could curl her fingers into his hair. "So I am." Surprised she could sound sultry, she pushed herself up onto her elbow so she could nuzzle his neck. "Want to talk some more?"

"Not what I was thinking." He grasped her hips and lifted her to straddle him, startling a squeak from her before she laughed.

She wriggled, loving his powerful response. He reared up to kiss her, which signaled the end of the conversation.

"ARE YOU GOING to let me drive myself today?" Lina asked as she poured boiling water over her herbal tea bag.

Bran, the rat, was leaning back against the counter, sipping his first cup of what smelled like strong coffee. "Nope."

She frowned at him. "You can't keep taking the time—"

"I can." He shook his head when she opened her mouth to argue. "Even if I thought the drive was safe, the walk across the parking lot isn't."

That, she knew, was that. And…she had to admit the memory of falling between cars outside the high school was still more vivid than she liked. It would take a lot longer than a couple weeks to fade. Thinking about how defenseless she'd been…she shivered.

His gaze sharpened. "You haven't said how it went, being back at work."

"I'd have been happier if I hadn't become famous." She busied herself slicing a bagel and popping it in the toaster. "It's all anyone wants to talk about. The teachers and staff are bad enough. The kids are worse. When I said we needed to focus on our material, Jamie Peters told me I *am* current events now."

Bran's mouth twisted. "He's right. But you know damn well what they really want to hear about is the bloodshed. Little ghouls."

"Little? A couple of the more annoying teachers have this avid glitter in their eyes every time they see me. It gives me the creeps."

Voice flinty, he said, "Tell them all you're part of an ongoing police investigation, and you've been asked not to discuss anything. That ought to hold them off."

"That's sort of what I've said, but your way is better." Lina set the tub of margarine on the counter and went to him, wrapping her arms around his waist and letting herself lean. Even with her belly forming a hard lump between them, it felt so good.

She heard the clink as he set his mug down, before his arms closed securely around her. "My way is always better," he murmured.

Lina was able to straighten with a laugh. "Keep telling yourself that."

"Your bagel popped up," he said helpfully.

"And I would never have noticed."

There was that rusty laugh again, a sound she could hug to herself all day, the memory as good as one of those bean-filled bags you heated to relax sore muscles.

But…did she have any sore muscles?

*Of course I do,* she thought in bemusement as she put jam on her half of the bagel. The heart was a muscle, wasn't it? Hers seemed to ache constantly these days. Because of the baby, Maya, Bran. The fear she was having to live under, and the threat to her unborn child.

As an automatic addendum, she started to add her ex-husband and his new wife to the list, but stopped. Was there even the slightest twinge? No. And she knew why. David had been thoroughly supplanted by the man who had just playfully snatched half her bagel and was slathering it with peanut butter, which as far as she was concerned ruined it. Lina couldn't summon even a smidgen of regret about her divorce.

The idea that Bran could both hurt her and heal her was odd, but she thought, true.

"Do you have plans today?" she asked.

"Agent Novinski has assigned me the task of showing your drawing to the teller who hasn't seen it yet."

"I thought they all had," she said in surprise.

"This one is young and had fallen apart. Novinski and her partner interviewed her the day after the robbery, then gave her permission to go home to Walla Walla. Tomorrow is her first day back to work. Her supervisor isn't so sure she'll be able to handle it."

"Being in the bank had to be terrifying." The huddled employees would have *heard* the gunshot that had been silent to her. Suddenly feeling cold, Lina said, "I wonder if any of them turned around after...after Maya was shot."

"So far, they all say they didn't." Bran nodded to the half bagel that still sat on the plate. "Eat."

She had lost her appetite, but nodded and picked it up. She couldn't afford to end up starved midmorning. Between bites, she said, "I can't believe the bank reopened so quickly."

"What were they going to do, tell people they couldn't sign loan papers that had already been prepared or cash in a CD?" He hesitated. "The FBI evidence team pulled out the carpet behind the teller counter the day after the robbery. The bank had new carpet installed over the weekend. They painted, too."

When she shuddered, he made a gruff sound and tugged her toward him again. "Damn, I'm sorry. I shouldn't have said anything."

"No, I was wondering. I'd rather know."

"Okay," he murmured against her temple, his warm breath stirring her hair.

After a minute, she thanked him and made herself straighten. While she finished the bagel, Bran disappeared to the bedroom, wearing his holstered weapon and badge on his belt when he returned. As if it was part of dressing for the job, his expression had become guarded, too. He was all cop now.

"Have you ever lived with anyone before?" she blurted. She'd been itching to know, but her timing sucked. "I mean, a woman?"

His eyebrows twitched. "No." More cautiously, he said, "I've had women spend the night, if that's what you mean. Does it matter?"

"No, I was just thinking how nice this is. You know. Talking about our day."

The ghost of some emotion crossed his face. "I've been telling you more than I probably should about this particular investigation only because of your involvement. Most of the time, I won't be able to talk about open cases."

"I understand." She hoped she could deal with it. Lina dropped a couple of energy bars into her purse before saying, "I just meant, in general."

"Guess that's a benefit of marriage." His voice had become utterly expressionless. "One you must have missed."

Scrutinizing him, she grappled with the possibility that he was jealous.

"If so, I've missed it for a long time," she told him frankly. "I can't remember when David and I really talked in the morning." Or any other time? And she'd been stupid enough not to notice.

Bran held out her parka and helped her into it.

With a sigh, she said, "Probably I was always

the one doing the prattling. This morning, too," she added ruefully, stepping out into the hall and waiting while he verified the door was locked. "You're just being nice."

He swung to face her. "No."

Her echoed "No?" was barely more than a whisper.

His fierce blue eyes held hers. "I like it when you talk to me. Don't stop." Then he took her arm and started her forward. "We're going to be late."

The drive was mostly quiet, his attention on the traffic and their surroundings. They were behind enough to arrive during the rush he liked to avoid. The parking lot was rapidly filling with employees' vehicles, along with those of parents who had some reason to deliver their kids personally. The first school bus was just pulling up in the bus lane; in minutes, kids would be straggling off it with their usual, crack-of-dawn lack of enthusiasm.

Bran pulled up right in front of the main entrance despite the red-painted curb, left his car in neutral and walked her to the doors, keeping his body between her and the crowded parking lot. She knew he saw, evaluated and dismissed every single person streaming in as well as the cars arriving.

Bran's long arm reached past her to open one of the two glass doors. She turned to issue her usual polite, "Thank you." This time, she didn't have a chance. Bran bent his head, murmured, "Three o'clock," and kissed her cheek, throwing in a tiny nuzzle at the end.

He issued the same, crisp reminder every day. The kiss was new.

Barbara Ervin, one of the science teachers, caught her eye and grinned. Given the audience, by lunchtime half the teachers would have heard she had something going with a detective. Everyone would be in the know by the end of the day, and speculation about whether he might be the father of her baby was bound to be rife, too.

Despite her discomfiture, Lina couldn't resist stopping just inside to watch Bran walk back to his car with his long, purposeful stride. She wondered if he even noticed the way people steered out of his way so he never had to deviate from his path, or whether he took it for granted.

On a sudden thought, her eyes narrowed and her temper sparked. Would he have been calculating enough to have kissed her when and where he did to *start* talk? As in, thinking a public claiming would push her a little closer to giving in and agreeing to marry him?

But, exasperated or not, she also remembered fleeting expressions on his face this morning. She'd already known she was pushing him out of his comfort zone. It was obvious he didn't know if he liked it or not.

Because she had the power to both heal and hurt him, too? Was that possible?

His car pulled away from the curb, and she turned to head for her classroom. Why was it that hope felt so delicate?

## CHAPTER TWELVE

BRAN SETTLED THE young teller in a comfortable chair in front of a currently unoccupied desk in the bank proper rather than in the small break room. Not, he hoped belatedly, Maya Lee's. Here they were out of earshot of any other employees, while the meeting felt casual rather than official.

Makayla Lander was a pretty little thing, a red-head with freckles and chocolate-brown eyes. If he'd seen her in the grocery store, he'd have guessed she was about sixteen, but assumed she had to be older than that. Surely the bank didn't hire anyone without at least a high school diploma.

"I stayed only 'cuz I had to talk to you." She pouted, as if he'd been mean to her, when he'd done his damnedest to be kind and soft-spoken thus far. "I *can't* come back to work." Her voice shook. "I told Mrs. Chainey as soon as I got here. I feel bad not giving notice, but…I just can't."

"What will you do?" Bran asked, with the goal of making her want to be helpful.

"I'm moving home again. I only came here because of a guy I'm not seeing anymore. So I don't have any reason to stay."

"A piece of advice, Ms. Lander," he said calmly, feeling like a parent determined to speak common sense even knowing it would go in one ear and out the other. "The trauma you feel can't be left behind. Whether you like it or not, you'll be packing it and taking it with you. You're feeling pretty shaken up. I'd recommend you see a counselor in Walla Walla."

Tears welled in her big brown eyes. "I don't understand how *anyone* can just keep working here like nothing happened! I will never forget!"

"I doubt a single person who was here that day will ever forget." He knew damn well Lina wouldn't. "People handle grief and fear in different ways, that's all."

With the exception of this very young woman, the surviving employees projected an air of admirable determination and what he could only call defiance. He'd seen it in other victims of crime. However unconsciously, they wanted whoever had hurt them to know they refused to be broken. He was charitable enough to decide this girl might just be too young to be capable of that kind of strength. It didn't hurt that she could run home to mommy and daddy, too, instead of having a family of her own dependent on her paycheck.

A tear trickled down her cheek. "I didn't really see anything. I already told those FBI agents."

"What I'd like is for you to take a look at a picture. Tell me if this man looks at all familiar to you."

"Why would the picture mean anything to me?"

"There's the possibility he lives locally," Bran explained. "He might have been in the bank doing business at some point, or you could have seen him somewhere else."

"Oh." Her face cleared. "Okay."

Not having a lot of hope, he opened the folder and handed her the copy of the drawing. So far, all he'd gotten were blank stares and a headshake.

Makayla Lander stared, all right, but tiny crinkles formed on her forehead. His attention sharpened.

"I don't *know*," she said finally, "but, um, he looks kind of like this guy who hit on a girl I know at a bar."

A bar? Good God, was she over twenty-one?

"Did you talk to him yourself?"

She shook her head. "I thought he was kind of old, and his head was shaved, but Pippa said he was hot."

Bran shared her doubt, but what did he know? "Do you recall when this was?"

Her face scrunched in thought. "Like…six months ago, maybe?"

"And where was this bar?"

"Well, it's more of a tavern. The Creek. Do you know it?"

"Yeah." He did. When he and Zach first reconnected, that was where they'd gone.

It took some effort to extract the friend's full name and phone number. Then Bran let her go. Makayla hurried out as if this was school and today had been the last day before summer.

This might be the break they'd been waiting for.

Lina had learned not to be chatty while Bran transported her. He'd said, "I have to stay alert." She could respect that.

Today, they were barely inside the apartment when he told her he wouldn't be able to pick her up tomorrow after work. "I'll call Zach and see if he can do it."

She plunked down her tote, filled with essays she needed to read and grade. "He can't do that without taking time off. Bran, there's no reason I can't drive. You know, it's been long enough. I'm wondering if the shooting really could have been random. Anyway, I promise I'll be careful. I'll time it so I arrive and leave when everyone else does, and make sure I'm in a crowd going to and from the parking lot."

He frowned. "Let me think about it."

It was everything she could do not to vent the rebellion she felt. Under any other circumstances, she wouldn't have put up for a minute with a man thinking he had the right to tell her what to do. Lina kept her mouth shut because of the chill she felt at the thought of scuttling across the parking lot knowing she might as well have a bull's-eye pinned to her back. Bran might be domineering—okay, *was* domineering—but he had been putting himself between her and danger whenever he could. He deserved some slack.

"Do you have an appointment tomorrow afternoon?" she thought to ask.

He did, with a young woman who had supposedly been hit up at a noisy bar by a guy who might be the bank robber. Only, when he had called her, she hadn't actually remembered the particular occasion or guy, but if Makayla said, it must have happened. Anyway, she went out with a lot of guys, and maybe he'd been one of them. She was currently a student at Western Washington State in Bellingham.

"God, I feel old," he grumbled.

Lina leaned back against the counter, watching as Bran opened the refrigerator, stared into it, then closed it without taking anything out. "What brought that on?"

"The teller I interviewed today." He shook his head, half-disgusted and half-bemused, if she was reading him right. "She pouted and whimpered like a thirteen-year-old, and her friend doesn't sound a lot better."

"You must deal with kids and teenagers all the time."

"Yeah, but—shit." His shoulders slumped. "What if I'm too old to become a father?"

Bran Murphy, plaintive? Lina blinked. "Um… it's a little late for that."

"Yeah, I know. I just…got to worrying today."

"Do you think you'll be impatient with her?" She laid her hand on her stomach in silent reassurance and saw that his gaze had followed her hand.

"Something like that," he muttered. "At least she'll have you."

"Oh, Bran." It was a funny moment to feel a sting of tears in her eyes. She crossed the small kitchen and slid her arms around his waist, laying her cheek on his shoulder.

He was still for a moment before his arms closed around her, too.

Lina sniffed and wiped her cheeks on his white dress shirt, then backed up, hating the moment when his hands fell away. "Hormones," she mumbled, turning almost blindly in search of a paper towel.

She heard a *rip*, and Bran thrust one in her hand. "This what you're looking for?"

Lina blew her nose without trying to be delicate.

"What inspired that?" He yanked off his tie and dropped it on the counter, then started on the buttons at his cuffs.

"Just that you've showed me every quality you need to be an amazing father." She had no doubt he would love his child. "Although you might want to think twice about snapping orders and expecting them to be followed *this instant*."

He had a funny look on his face she didn't understand until he said, "Change isn't easy."

She had to hug him again. "You don't have to change." Deciding not to overwhelm him with more emotion, she said, "How about tacos tonight? I can make them quick."

"That sounds good."

She sensed he was grateful for the chance to retreat, physically and emotionally. In fact, he was backing toward the living room when his phone rang. He took it from his belt and saw the number. The intensity in his eyes shook her. He muttered something under his breath and silenced the phone, setting it on the counter and walking away.

Lina looked from the phone to his broad back.

What had just happened? Did she dare ask who the caller was?

More disturbed than she'd like, she opened the refrigerator and took out the hamburgers. Could Paige have been calling? He might not have been entirely honest about how he felt about his former fiancée. They'd never really talked about her, and no wonder, given what had happened the night before the canceled wedding. And the consequences, she thought, looking down at the bump pushing out her shirt.

No. She wouldn't mention the call.

The hamburger and onion were sizzling and she was on tiptoe searching for spices by the time Bran came back.

"Chili powder okay?" he asked, finding it easily.

"Sure."

She accepted his offer to grate the cheese while she opened the can of tomato sauce and dumped it in the frying pan.

He set the essentials on the table and found the sour cream while she chopped a tomato and shredded lettuce. The evening domestic dance was becoming natural, it occurred to her. It was going to feel strange when she was back in her own apartment, cooking alone for herself.

She didn't love the idea, but also knew, whatever happened with her and Bran, it would be smart of her to go back to her own place when it was safe. Thinking clearly didn't come easily when she shared most of her waking minutes away from work with him.

She suppressed a sigh and began putting together her first taco. "I should have made a vegetable, too."

"Lettuce is a vegetable."

"Well…at least this isn't iceberg." Which was what he'd had in his refrigerator when she first moved in.

Both were quiet for a few minutes. Lina could feel his all-too perceptive gaze on her. He had a way of watching her more than was comfortable.

"That was my mother," he said abruptly.

She looked up. "What?"

"If you were wondering."

"Then…why didn't you answer? I wouldn't have minded." Although she could understand why talks with her were difficult. After the years of estrangement, their relationship couldn't be easy. Or…had he ever met with her, even after reconnecting with his brother?

"I was nice when she came to Zach's wedding," he said shortly. "We did not have a heartfelt reunion, if that's what you're thinking."

"But…" She should shut up, she knew she should. He was waiting, however, eyes only slightly narrowed, so she finished what she'd begun. "She's your mother. The only parent you have left. I know you don't approve of some of her behavior—"

His lips took on a nasty curl. With an air of finality, he said, "She's nobody I want to know."

Lina was stupid enough to open her mouth again. "But—"

"No more," he said curtly.

They finished their meal in silence. Leaving him to clean up the kitchen, Lina retreated to the sofa with her pile of essays. Pretending to be absorbed, she didn't so much as look up. When he was done, he disappeared into his little-used home office.

Concentrating took a supreme effort for her, and she was far more relieved than usual to scrawl a *B-* in red pen on the final essay. She still had to record the grades, but she could do that in the morning before the first bell rang.

She and Bran spoke politely when she came and went from the bathroom, but somehow Lina wasn't at all surprised that he still hadn't come to bed before sleep dragged her down.

LINA HAD BEEN polite but distant this morning. Bran couldn't blame her. He'd been a jackass last night. Thinking about his mother had a way of doing that.

What he couldn't figure out was why she was

being so damn persistent. Some persistence when he was a stunned, angry twelve-year-old boy might have meant something. Yes, he'd been angry with her, but he'd also still loved her, his mom. But she'd given up on him all too quickly. As he'd told Zach, any effort she made now was too little, too late.

As he and Lina got ready to go out the door, he had tried to apologize for the way he had shut her down, but she glanced at him without interest and said, "You have nothing to be sorry for. I was sticking my nose into something that wasn't any of my business."

"That's not how—"

Digging in her purse, she wasn't even listening. "I must have car keys in here *somewhere*."

The cap on his mood came with the reminder that she was driving herself today, the first time she'd be behind the wheel in—he had to count back—almost three weeks. He'd make sure she got into work safely this morning, but she'd be on her own coming home.

He felt confident that he hadn't been followed when he drove her anywhere. If the man who wanted her dead had done his research, though, he'd have been watching for her at the middle school. He'd have seen who was dropping her off and picking her up. From the Camaro, he had likely figured out she was staying with Bran and had found his address listed somewhere on the internet. Now the asshole would finally have a chance to catch her alone.

"Find them?" he said finally.

"Yes, thank goodness." Lina brandished a set of keys.

He walked her to her car, parked in a visitor spot, waited until she had to adjust her seat slightly to accommodate her changed girth and buckled in, then said, "I'll be behind you."

She rolled her eyes but didn't protest.

"Lina…" Her pleasant, impersonal gaze choked off what he'd meant to say.

"Shouldn't we be going?"

"Yeah. Be careful today."

"I said I would."

He nodded and headed for his Camaro. He maintained his vigilance until they arrived and she was safely inside, then stayed at the curb in front of the school while he called his brother.

Zach answered right away. "Bran?"

"I'm wondering if you can do a favor for me." Man, that was harder than it should have been to say. Because he rarely needed help? Because he was supposed to be the big brother?

"Anything," his brother said immediately and with a seriousness that surprised Bran.

"I have business in Bellingham this afternoon."

"To do with the bank robbery?"

"Yeah."

"You want me to pick up Lina from school."

"Actually, she drove." He hesitated. "I followed her and saw her in. I'm hoping you can break away from your patrol long enough to follow her home."

"You know I can," his brother said. "But did you tell her to expect me?"

"Uh…no."

Zach laughed. "Is she going to be pissed?"

"Maybe. But alive."

"Gotcha. Hey, you two want to come to dinner Saturday night?"

"I'll ask Lina. She'll probably say it's our turn to have you, though."

"Yeah, but you don't need a helping hand. I do."

Bran laughed. "Should have figured. Doing what?"

"Hauling the new shower, toilet and vanity upstairs."

"That I can do." He thought about mentioning the call from their mother he hadn't taken, but decided it could wait. Or maybe Zach already knew. *He* took Mom's calls. If she'd been whining to him that Bran was ignoring her, he'd been smart enough not to say anything.

Unlike Lina. Bran winced at the thought.

"I'll leave you a message when she's at your place, safe and sound."

He resented the reminder that his place wasn't her home, but said only, "Thanks."

For the rest of the morning, he succeeded in doing his job, making phone calls in pursuit of a suspect in an unusual home-invasion robbery, even eating at his desk to allow himself no time to brood before he set out at two for Bellingham, almost an hour north toward the Canadian border. Pippa Marks had one and two o'clock classes, apparently, but had agreed to meet him fifteen minutes after her last class at a coffee shop near the campus.

Unfortunately, the near-hour drive on a freeway little-traveled at this time of day gave him the opening he didn't want to think about the sometimes explosive, always bewildering, emotions he'd been hit with since Lina came back into his life.

No—longer than that, if he was to be honest. A lot of this had been brewing since he'd come face-to-face with the brother he'd never expected to see again and started the investigation into Sheila's murder. As if all that wasn't enough, then there was Lina. Beautiful, stubborn, balking at the idea of accepting a sensible marriage. She made him feel more than he wanted to—but she expected still more. She hadn't directly said as much, but Bran knew damn well she was waiting for a declaration of true love, him on his knees.

She was determined to shatter the self-control that defined him.

Paige had wanted the same thing. When she didn't get it, she walked. Logically, the pregnancy should make a difference to Lina, but he had a feeling it wouldn't.

Bran's fingers tightened and loosened repeatedly on his leather-wrapped steering wheel as he remained caught up in his disturbing reflections, the Camaro eating up the winding miles through country that became increasingly mountainous.

He could give Lina everything important, but not that. Even if he had been in love with her—whatever that meant—he couldn't say the words. They put too much power in her hands. *His* commitment to her and the baby would be absolute, but how could he trust that hers to him would be anything he could rely on?

Hell, she should be as wary as he was! Her creep of an ex had given her a harsh lesson: nobody can be trusted, not even people you love. Maybe in both of their cases, *especially* people they loved. If love was what he felt for his family.

It had been, once upon a time, he knew. He'd been a regular kid, with a regular family, until he'd walked in on his mother in bed with his father's best friend and discovered what betrayal meant. Then, a matter of months later, Sheila was gone in the most hideous way.

As the miles rolled by, traffic grew heavier and freeway exits crowded with businesses closer together, making Bran aware he was coming into town. Time to focus—and thank God he had an excuse to quit brooding.

From previous investigations that had brought him up here, Bran had no trouble finding the coffee shop. So close to the campus, parking spaces were at a premium and the sidewalks crowded. He felt lucky to find a parking place several blocks away.

Walking toward the meet, he glanced back to see some young guys had stopped to look at his car. Nice to know however old he felt, at least his car was cool.

A heart-stopping thought erased his smile between one step and the next. He was about to become a family man. Babies were vulnerable. They were supposed to ride in the backseat, which the Camaro didn't have. In fact, he could carry his wife or the baby in the sports car—but not both. Which meant he'd need a bigger vehicle, one with a backseat. Did that mean *selling* the Camaro?

He almost walked right past the coffee shop, but out of the corner of his eye saw the logo painted on the window. *Do your damn job.*

Bran turned in, searching the jammed-together tables for a woman meeting the description Pippa

Marks had given him. Brown hair streaked with hot pink, and she'd wear her favorite feather earrings.

The clientele was typical of a college town—a mix of young students, some older ones who might be in grad school and a guy with a scruffy gray beard, absorbed in a book, who had to be a professor. Everyone seemed to have a smartphone in hand. His weapon and badge earned him some curious looks, but no one caught his eye.

From behind, a woman said tentatively, "Are you Detective Murphy?"

He swung around. She must have walked in the door thirty seconds behind him. Hot pink streaks—check. Feather earrings that reached her shoulders. Eyebrow hoop she hadn't mentioned. Black knit shirt that formed a second skin. Butt-shaping skirt over lacy stockings that disappeared into what appeared to be combat boots. Probably tattoos he couldn't see.

God. Someday his daughter might dress like this. He felt not only old, but old-fashioned, too.

"Miss Marks," he said. "Thanks for meeting me. Let me buy you a cup of coffee."

A small, round table in the back corner opened at the right time, and they were soon seated with their drinks. Upon questioning disguised as general conversation, Pippa admitted to being from

Clear Creek, and said she and Makayla had met at a party.

When he asked, she told him she was majoring in chemistry with the intention of going on to grad school to become a chemical engineer. No airhead, here.

He was tempted to ask what she and Makayla had had in common, but it didn't really matter. Instead, he opened the folder he'd brought and turned it so Pippa could see the drawing.

She scrutinized it for a long time, then looked up. "Yeah, I'm pretty sure that's the guy. I remember him. He did ask me out. The thing is, I said no. He seemed too old, for one thing, and… there was something about him." She cradled both hands on her paper cup as if she was suddenly chilled. "I don't know what it was. I mean, he's okay-looking, and he was nice. He liked my singing."

"Karaoke," Bran remembered.

"Yeah." She grinned at his tone. "Not your thing, huh?"

"For many reasons," he agreed.

Her gaze dropped to the drawing again. "This is…really eerie."

"Is it accurate?"

She shivered. "Yeah. What if I'd gone out with him?"

"He might have seemed like a decent guy. He

must be lacking in conscience, but that doesn't usually show on the surface."

"No. I've read about the Ted Bundy kind of guys, super charming."

Bran nodded at the face looking up at them. "Was he?"

"No-oo. I mean, I don't remember that well. I don't think we talked for that long. When I turned him down, he shrugged and moved on."

"Any chance you remember what you talked about?"

Pippa wasn't pretty in the same way as her friend had been, the two sides of her face not quite lining up, but there was an appealing quirkiness about her.

"Mostly, he asked about me. And we had to practically shout, you know." She shrugged. "I think he said he was staying around there."

"Staying," Bran repeated thoughtfully.

"Like, with friends?"

He remembered the deputy telling him about the odd scene during the domestic disturbance call. He should have asked more about the husband.

But first, he had the fifty-million-dollar question for her. "Did he tell you his name?"

## CHAPTER THIRTEEN

BRAN GROANED AND STRETCHED. "Damn. I'm glad you didn't want to put in a cast-iron bathtub upstairs."

Zach laughed. "The weight might have deterred me. The worst thing about fiberglass showers is the sheer bulk."

"Let's take care of the vanity next," his brother suggested.

"Don't forget the toilet."

Bran complained some more when he saw the solid maple vanity in the bed of Zach's pickup truck, backed as close to the porch stairs as Zach had been able to get it. The day had started out chilly—hovering around freezing—and, once the early, winter darkness descended, the temperature dropped into the low twenties. Zach didn't even feel it and he doubted Bran did, either. Sweating the way they were, who needed a coat?

The yard was lit garishly with porch- and floodlights. After the spring attacks on him and Tess at both of their houses, he'd gone overboard with the night lighting.

The frozen grass crackled underfoot, and he stepped extra carefully on the porch steps in case of ice. At the top, they took a break for the sake of their backs and to catch their breath, then heaved the thing up again and through the front door. Lina and Tess came out of the kitchen to form an anxious audience.

"Careful," Zach exclaimed, as a minute later the two men maneuvered to make the turn at the top of the narrow staircase. He was the one to groan when they set the blasted thing down carefully on the already sanded bedroom floor. Grinding the heel of his hand into his lower back, he muttered, "I sure hope having a bathroom up here is worth the money and work I'm pouring into it."

"We really wanted one when we were kids," Bran surprised him by saying. They didn't talk much about the years before Sheila's murder. Which was too bad, since they'd been good years. Zach had idolized his older brother.

He cleared his throat. "That's occurred to me. Anyway. When we sell the place, people go for a classic master bedroom."

Bran looked askance. "I thought you two had decided to stay in the house."

"For now. We might want a bigger one once we have kids."

"Kids." Bran shook his head, not in disbelief so

much as bemusement, if Zach was reading him right. "You're the one who didn't want them."

Zach slapped him on the back. "Times change."

"You mean, passing time ages you."

"You're in a mood." He looked more carefully, and saw how set his brother's expression was. "Not being able to find this guy getting to you?"

"Yeah. Shit." Bran took a few steps away, then turned back. "Among other things."

"The toilet can wait. Let's get a beer and go out on the front porch." Where the women in the kitchen wouldn't be able to hear them talk, assuming it was Lina Bran needed to talk about.

He grunted, which Zach took for acquiescence. When they appeared in the kitchen, Tess teased them about needing to recover after a whole half hour of hard labor, but also gave him a quick kiss. Lina smiled politely, but without looking at Bran.

Outside, Zach half sat on the railing and let his brother have the new porch swing. The cold penetrated his jeans in seconds, but what did a numb butt matter? Anyway, the way his breath was hanging on the air, he figured they had fifteen minutes tops before their sweat froze. Both opened their cans of beer. Bran took a long drink.

"Problems with Lina?" Zach asked casually.

"There's been some tension." He gazed out at what he could see of the neighborhood in the dark, finally sighing. "Mom has been calling."

"So she said."

Bran's eyes met Zach's. "What does she want?"

"To get to know you. I made the mistake of telling her about Lina."

Bran growled an obscenity.

"She'd find out sooner or later anyway." Zach paused. "She just wants to talk."

Bran set the beer on the porch floor, braced his elbows on his knees and let his head hang. "That's what Lina wanted, too."

"To talk?" Poor woman. Getting Bran to strip bare his emotions when he didn't want to was akin to trying to crack open a geode using a toothbrush. Not much chance of ever finding the glitter inside. Zach knew he wasn't much better. Tess would say it was the blind leading the lame, he thought in amusement. "About what?" he prodded, giving it a try anyway.

His brother looked up with a grimace. "Mom."

"Ah. So Lina's sulking because you clammed up?"

The lines furrowing Bran's forehead suggested the problem was more complicated than that, but apparently he was done sharing. No surprise there. Instead, he changed the subject. "I didn't get anywhere with the name."

He didn't have to explain what name he meant, given that the threat to Lina was foremost in Bran's mind.

"It's tough with a partial like that," Zach said.

"He probably made it up," said Mr. Doom and Gloom.

Not that Zach could fault his brother for the attitude. Three and a half weeks had passed since the bank robbery without them so much as having developed a suspect. The only significant lead had been the drawing, but despite initial excitement, Bran and Charlie Warring weren't any further ahead. Of course, there might be something the typically closemouthed feds weren't saying, but Bran had bitched that their strategy was to wait for the pair of robbers to strike again.

Bran had to be especially discouraged about the most recent hope, a girl who'd actually *met* the creep, but wouldn't you know she'd only remembered a first name. Or it could be a nickname. Or…? Tag. Short for Taggart? Or, who knew? Turned out, there were exactly two county residents with the last name of Taggart, and both had been eliminated immediately.

Bran only shook his head when Zach asked about his next step.

Both men turned their heads to watch some neighborhood boys shoot down the street, appearing in the pool of light from a streetlamp, becoming indistinct once they left it. Two were on bikes, one on a skateboard. The kid could really move on it. None of them wore coats, either.

Zach's mouth quirked. Mom used to get so mad when she discovered they'd left for school without their jackets even after she'd reminded them.

"Funny thing, us both hooking up with women who needed our protection," he commented.

"The parallel has occurred to me. Usually when I'm remembering how close that shit Hayes came to killing Tess."

Trust Bran to focus on the near-tragedy.

Finding Tess collapsed with her bedroom burning around her was a memory Zach still relived too often. Having Bran sitting beside him in the hospital while he had to wait for the doctor to tell him whether she'd make it or not had transformed their sometimes-testy relationship. They might still quarrel, but they had each other's backs.

"You know, while I'm here, why don't you call Mary Greaver?" Bran suggested. "She and her husband might be out on a Saturday night, but it's worth a try."

Zach had to go find his cell phone. On the way back, he grabbed a down vest and Bran's parka. As he let the screen door bang behind him coming back out, he saw his brother straighten his shoulders and wipe a morose expression from his face. Without comment, Bran snagged the parka and shrugged it on, then added leather gloves from the pocket.

Zach scrolled to the number he'd tried a couple

of times already this week, and waited while it rang. This time, a girl answered.

"Just a minute, please," she said politely, then bellowed, "Mom!"

When he identified himself to Mary, she said disagreeably, "Mom told me about you being around."

"Good to hear your voice, too," he said mildly.

A huff of air might have been a snort. "What do you want?" Her rudeness was balanced by curiosity, at a guess.

"You know I'm a cop."

"Mom said you and your brother both are."

Zach's eyes met his brother's. "That's right. Your mother didn't much want to talk to me, but I was hoping you would. You were more our age. Between your friends and your babysitting, you probably knew more people in the neighborhood than anyone."

"That's true." As he'd hoped, she sounded pleased.

He leaned against the porch railing again, keeping his eyes on Bran, who was listening alertly. "I guess I was hoping you'd tell me what you remember about that night. Were you home?"

"By the middle of the night? Of course I was. Earlier…" She hesitated. "I was babysitting. The Swanson brats."

Normally, he wouldn't have expected her to

have the slightest idea what she'd been doing on a particular evening twenty-five years ago, but everyone in this neighborhood would remember that night. On a smaller scale, it was like 9/11. As Bran had once put it to him, a Before and After. Innocence lost.

"I suppose you didn't hear anything during the night."

"No-o." But she said that slowly.

"I heard our back door open or close," Zach told her. "But I was a kid. I thought Dad might be going out for a smoke. I went back to sleep."

"That must eat at you," she said with more sympathy than he'd expected.

He had to look away from his brother and clear his throat before he could admit, "It does."

"In the morning, I thought—" She put on the brakes. "Nothing important. There were police cars outside your house, and word flew up and down the street. People went out in their bathrobes to stare."

He hadn't seen any of that. Bran had kept him inside, protecting him from anyone but the police officers who insisted on asking him questions. *God, how I missed him.* Having his brother here now, working together, that meant more than he had let himself admit.

"Your sister—everybody loved her." Mary sounded softer than the girl he'd remembered.

She'd had a family of her own since, he reminded himself, which had probably changed her perspective. "Mostly I hated babysitting, but not when it came to Sheila."

"Just me."

"You and your brother were butts."

Smiling despite himself, he said, "We probably were."

"After that, things were never the same in the neighborhood, you know. It was like..." She was obviously groping for the right words. "It set things off," was what she settled on. "Nobody felt safe. Parents all came down harder on their kids. Mom didn't want me babysitting anymore, especially late. Dad and Rob fought even more than they had before, which made Mom quiet and tense. I could hardly wait to get away. But it wasn't just our family. Do you remember Joann Erwin? Her parents got so strict, she ran away from home. They dragged her back, but it was all so weird."

Listening to this took Zach aback. Sheila's murder had destroyed his family. Nothing existed for him beyond the four walls of his own home. It wouldn't have occurred to him that the murder had reverberations throughout the neighborhood, although as an adult he understood. As a cop, he'd seen it happen.

Bran's intense stare pushed him to focus on

one thing she'd said. "I didn't know Rob and your dad butted heads."

This quiet, he guessed, stemmed from reluctance. "Well, they always did, kind of, but it got way worse after that night. Mom tried to get between them, and then they were both mad at her."

"Did you ever ask Rob what was going on?"

"He said what did I care, because I'd be out of there." He heard an echo of her brother's sneer in her voice. "We never got along. He was crude, and he said I was snooty."

He and Bran had thought she was, too.

"Did they ever make up?" he asked. "Rob and your dad, I mean, before your dad died?"

"Rob wouldn't even come to the funeral. Mom's never forgiven him." After a brief pause, she said, "Why am I telling you all this?" Her voice had changed, as if she'd been snapped out of a trance.

"Because there were mysteries in your own home you never solved," he suggested.

"I guess there were," she said grudgingly. "But no one in *my* family got murdered."

"That's true. But someone came into *our* home and murdered my little sister." He no longer cared if he alienated this woman. "That *someone* had seen her, had been in the house before and knew which bedroom was hers. He wasn't a stranger, Mary. He was a friend or a neighbor."

"Or your own father." Now she sounded like

the bitch her brother had described. "That's what everyone thought, you know."

"Did you?"

Silence.

"Or did you always wonder, because *you* heard a door opening or closing that night, too?"

"This is what I get for trying to be helpful? Good*bye*, Mr. Murphy." She was gone, not having to slam a phone down to make her point.

"That's the first time I've been called Mr. Murphy." Zach set the phone on the railing and shoved his frozen hand into the vest pocket.

Bran set the swing to moving. "We're tarred with the same brush."

Zach grimaced. "How much of that did you hear?"

"Not much of her side."

So he recapped, then waited to hear Bran's thoughts.

"Wish I'd known Rob better then," he said finally.

"You didn't later, after I was gone?"

"He went wild. I knew there was a lot of conflict at the Greaver house. You could hear shouting sometimes." Faint humor curved Bran's mouth. "Rob went goth, got some piercings, had a jacked-up car with a hole in the muffler he probably put there himself. Rumor had it he was into drugs."

"Did whatever he could to enrage his dad."

"That's...not unusual. Fathers and sons." Bran shrugged, but his eyes were unfocused, as if he was looking back.

"You didn't rebel." Zach had never even had to ask.

"No. I was a badass, too, but that's because I had to defend Dad from all comers."

"That is truly touching." Smiling, Zach pulled his left hand from his pocket and lifted his beer in a salute.

Bran hoisted his own can. The ensuing silence was almost peaceful.

Until Bran flattened his foot on the porch boards to stop rocking. "Mr. Greaver might have known Rob went out that night."

"That would shake a father up," Zach agreed.

"But there's another possibility, you know. What if it was the other way around? What if Rob heard his father leave the house?"

The possibility exploded in Zach's head. However shaken, would a teenage boy tell anyone something like that? For all these years, Zach had held his silence about hearing Dad get up during the night. And there was what Bran had just said: *I had to defend him from all comers.* Rob might well have done the same, but anger and doubt would have made him even more volatile than he'd already been. Never sure whether his father could have done something so monstrous...

Yeah. It worked.

"But Mrs. Greaver is mad at Rob."

"Because he made wild accusations she couldn't let herself believe?"

"Jesus," he said, then thought back to her odd tone. "What if her father molested *Mary*?"

"Who was conditioned not to tell anyone," Bran said slowly. "Not Mom, not her brother. Maybe did her best to block the memory. Mary stood by her parents—for her mother's sake?— but with her dad gone now, those memories could have crept out of hiding. What if tonight she connected some dots? She talked to you because she wanted to help, but she still can't bring herself to admit what happened to her."

"All logical, but it could as well be fictional," Zach pointed out.

"I can't argue."

"Did you run Mr. Greaver?"

"Yeah. No arrests popped. But we both know a lot of pedophiles never get caught."

"No. We could try Mrs. Greaver again," Zach said, but doubtfully. He thought she was too entrenched in the way she'd framed the family history to admit to any crack in it.

Bran shook his head. "Rob. If there's any

chance we're right, Rob is seriously conflicted. A part of him has to want to spill what he knows."

"Would you?" It was risky to ask this, but Zach felt compelled. "If you'd had a suspicion about Dad?"

A few months ago, that would have been enough to light the fuse of his brother's temper, but now Bran only shook his head. "If I'd had a suspicion... I don't know. But I never questioned whether Dad could have done it. Not for a minute."

After a pause, Zach said, "I shouldn't have, either. I wish—" He couldn't get it out.

"He never quit loving you," he said quietly.

"Damn." Zach turned his back, not wanting anyone, even his brother, to see him with tears in his eyes.

"We can't go back."

No one knew that better than him. But, *God*, sometimes he wished he could.

"You know, I'm freezing my ass off here. What I suggest we do is get that toilet upstairs before my joints lock."

"Yeah." If he sounded a little hoarse...Bran was unlikely to comment. Zach used his shirt-sleeve to take a surreptitious swipe at his face. "There's a plan."

SUNDAY WAS A strange but good day. Except for grocery shopping, which he insisted on doing,

Bran stayed home with Lina, displaying little of his usual restlessness. The effort he was making was painfully obvious, but…sweet.

Last night, while the two men had been out talking in sub-zero temperatures on the front porch, she and Tess had done some talking of their own while they lurked in the kitchen, ostensibly working on dinner. Until Bran, Lina had never known a cop, and she'd been wondering how typical he was.

Bran was so controlled—too controlled. Too protective. It might be refreshing to have him yell at her.

"I wouldn't call myself an expert," Tess demurred. "On Zach, maybe, and he and Bran do have some traits in common… Overbearing and dictatorial, come to mind." Tess grinned. "Zach tries."

"Overbearing is definitely one word to describe Bran," Lina agreed. "And with him so determined to keep me safe, I've had to give way more often than can possibly be good for him."

"What is it you're worried about?" Tess asked bluntly.

She'd always disapproved when friends or women at work complained about their boyfriends or husbands, and didn't want to be like that. On the other hand, she had to talk to someone. Tess not only had insider knowledge, she was becoming a good friend.

Lina bit her lip, then said, "He's so closed off a lot of the time. So…unemotional. Remote."

Tess made a sympathetic face. "That probably is part of what happens to them with the job. I mean, they'd have to distance themselves."

"Yes, but I look at Zach, and then I look at Bran…"

"I know what you mean," Tess conceded. "How well he hides emotion is actually the first thing I noticed about Bran. Along with the fact that he's as sexy as Zach."

Lina laughed. The brothers did look an awful lot alike.

Frowning now, as if determined to find the right way to say this, Tess went on, "He was being polite to me, and yet it was all I could do not to shiver. I thought it was probably just me until… um, he was still engaged at the time."

Reluctantly curious about the fiancée, Lina nodded.

"He'd have to be different with her, right? But when Paige walked up, even when he smiled his eyes were cold. I wondered how she couldn't have noticed."

"She did call off the wedding."

"Well, that's true. But my point is, he's not like that when he looks at you," Tess said slowly.

"Sometimes I think you scare him a little, but he feels a whole lot."

*Please, God.* "If he'd just *talk* to me," Lina exclaimed in frustration.

"Patience, patience."

In explanation, Tess had told Lina a lot of what she'd figured out about how the two brothers' background had affected them in the same and different ways. Some of it Lina already understood.

Remembering that conversation today, she made patience her watchword. Bran was relatively relaxed. He'd done some pretty amazing things for her, after all. Plus—except for the night when they first met—they'd known each other not even quite four weeks. Maybe she was expecting too much.

At lunch and after, he made it plain he was open to talking, although predictably not about himself.

Because he seemed to really want to know, she did tell him more about her family. It was his pointed questions that had her analyzing for the first time why she had to pretend to her parents that her marriage was fabulous even when she'd begun to see fissures opening. And why the humiliation of having to turn to her parents at the end and admit he'd been cheating on her had been almost as bad as finding out he had been in the first place.

"Mom's...critical," she finally said. "She calls it honest. I mean, I've never doubted she loves me, but she says things without thinking. Or maybe doesn't believe in little white lies. I don't know. You're taking your ego in your hands to ask her if she likes your new haircut."

Bran nodded, eyes steady on her face and... warm. As if he'd meant it when he asked her not to quit talking to him. If only he understood it had to be reciprocal, she thought wistfully.

"I think Mom and Dad love each other, but she's sharp with him, too. I suppose she eroded my confidence. The guy you marry—that's big. I took him home to meet my parents. After he left, Mom snapped, 'What on earth do you see in him?'"

Bran grimaced. "Makes me eager to meet her."

"Something tells me she'll approve of you." She should feel happier about that than she did, a bothersome thought she pushed away. "If I don't marry you, she'll tell me I should grab what I can and quit imagining life's a fairy tale. It's as if *she* was disappointed, but if so, it's not anything she's ever talked about." Lina sighed. "I'm making her sound worse than she is. Mostly, we're friends. But...she has this way of puncturing my mood when I'm feeling good about something. If I buy a dress I think is a little daring, she'll say, 'You don't really plan to wear *that*, do you?'"

"What did she think was wrong with David?"

"He tried too hard to be likeable. 'Doesn't he have any confidence in himself?'" She found herself mimicking her mother's voice. "'Any substance?'"

Bran gave a rough laugh. "I'd feel sorry for him if he hadn't turned out to be such a loser."

*That* topic ended with her sticking out her tongue at him and saying, "Thank you." Although she did manage, later, to say, "Looking back sometimes helps."

Come late afternoon, they went swimming— his idea—albeit he persuaded Zach and Tess to join them again. She felt sure both men had gone armed into the dressing room. Lina might have minded Bran calling for backup if she hadn't liked Tess so much. Plus, after another lesson it was obvious Tess was at least slightly less terrified of trusting herself to the water, which made Lina feel good.

And then there was the raw hunger in how Bran looked at her when she got out of the water and walked toward him, lounging in the hot tub. And with her being seven months pregnant. Muscles knotted in his jaw and his eyes glittered. His gaze lowered, slid over her as tangibly as a touch. If her nipples hadn't already been hard, they were by then. She'd had to swallow twice before she could say, "I'm ready to go shower."

He made a sound and let his head fall back. "Yeah," he said huskily. "You do that."

Neither talked on the drive home. As usual, his attention was on their surroundings as he rushed her upstairs to his apartment, but they were barely inside when he had her backed up to the door.

"God, I want you."

"Yes," she whispered, wrapped her arms around his neck and rose on tiptoe to meet his kiss.

They made it to the bedroom barely, and only, she thought, because he worried about hurting the baby. She'd been ready for him from the moment she saw that expression on his face at the pool. Bran seemed desperate. He kissed her, touched her, sucked on her breasts, then flipped her over and took her from behind with near-frantic lunges.

Lina's body seemed to implode. A guttural sound escaped him, and he drove one more time, going rigid.

Lina was shaking, stunned by the power of what they'd just done. Bran had to help her lie down on her side, his powerful body spooning her. It helped that he was breathing as hard as she was and that she felt his heart hammering against her back.

She wanted to say something—Wow? What

was that?—but didn't. She waited for him to speak, to express his tenderness in more than the way he stroked the curves of her body or pushed her braid aside to press his lips to her nape, but he didn't. In fact, five minutes later, he stirred.

"I'll go start dinner."

As a mood killer, it didn't get much better than that.

# *CHAPTER FOURTEEN*

COME MORNING, BRAN was his usual guarded self. Instead of putting in some hours at work as he often did on Mondays, he'd volunteered to help his brother work on that new upstairs bathroom. Later, once he had her safely locked down at the apartment, he and Zach planned to drive back to Seattle to confront Rob Greaver again, she knew.

Lina eyed the shoulder holster he wore with jeans and T-shirt. "I suppose you plan to follow me to school?" she asked, knowing the answer. Why else would he be armed now?

In the act of pouring himself a second cup of coffee, he barely glanced at her. "I'll drive you."

"It's been a while," she said. "Nothing's happened. Even if the shooting at the high school was him, he may have—"

He cocked an eyebrow. "Given up? Would you, if you were him?"

That momentarily silenced her as she tried to imagine being someone who was willing to hold a gun to a woman's head and pull the trigger just because he was being denied something he wanted. "The drawing is out there," she said finally. "I'm not so important anymore." Her "Am I?" came out more timid than she liked.

"Yeah." His darkened eyes seemed to show both regret and the caring he was unable or unwilling to acknowledge. His voice deepened as he gripped her arm. "You're important. You're—" He shook his head rather than finish the thought.

"Do you mean...to you?"

"Unfortunately, I think you are to him, too. Even if he knows about it, the drawing is merely suggestive. You on a witness stand in court saying, 'That man right there' as you point at him will send him away. You're the *only* witness, Lina."

"So you think..."

Bran's voice was hard as he said, "He's watching. Waiting. After his screwup, I've had you under wraps. That doesn't mean he's given up."

She didn't say again, *I'm sorry you're stuck with me*, because she knew better than that. However much of an enigma he was, she had no doubt he wanted her, or that he was determined to marry her. And that he'd keep her safe even if he had to die to do it.

Could that *be* his way of saying I love you? But Bran, she suspected, would throw himself between any woman or child and danger. His protective instinct was that powerful.

So…was she really special to him, or just his current focus?

She nodded and said, "Okay," which seemed to satisfy him. As usual, on the way down to the car he let her carry her own tote, packed lunch and handbag, she presumed to leave him free to reach for his gun if he had to.

During the drive, Lina thought about her day. She was starting a new unit in her seventh grade social studies classes, this one focused on civil rights. Beyond the framework of the required textbook, she brought color to any topic by using other sources and by encouraging questions and discussion.

As they neared the school, she noticed how heavy traffic was. They must have gotten a late start.

It really would have helped if she could have gone to the library this weekend—

"Son of a bitch!" Bran said sharply, accelerating while swerving at the same time to avoid rear-ending the car in front of them. From behind came the screech of brakes and tires skidding on pavement.

Heart pounding, Lina turned, craning her neck to look behind them. She met the driver's wide, shocked eyes. He was a kid, and the car was packed full of other boys, presumably on their way to the high school, just ahead.

Lina's teeth chattered, adrenaline flooding her. "They almost hit us, didn't they?"

"Yeah." Bran's gaze took her in. "It didn't happen, Lina. We weren't moving fast enough for anyone to be seriously hurt even if it had."

"Your car—"

"I'd have been mad as hell about that," he admitted.

Still shaking, she dug her fingernails into her palms. "I was hit…oh, not that long after I moved here. March or April, I think. A boy came down a driveway on a bicycle. I didn't see him sooner because of a parked car. He shot right out in front of me. I slammed on the brakes and *wham!* I'd vaguely known a car was behind me, but I'd slowed down and I guess he hadn't. It…was really frightening."

Bran put on his turn signal and whipped around the next corner into an apartment complex.

"What are you doing?"

He circled and pulled to a stop facing the entrance, then set the emergency brake. Looking fully at her, he said, "I want to know what happened. Were you hurt?"

"Bruises from my seat belt and some whiplash. Fortunately, the boy was pedaling away fast enough, I didn't hit him even though my car was knocked forward."

"No airbag?"

"Getting rear-ended doesn't set one off. Since I missed the parked cars… There was some major damage to my poor car, though. At first, my insurance agent seemed to think they were going to total it. Instead, I ended up taking it to an auto body shop." A picture formed in her mind. Her car on the lift, the men looking at the crumpled metal. All turning when she stepped into the garage.

She might as well have touched a bare electrical wire. Lina clapped a hand to her mouth as she turned to look at him. It took an effort to make herself pull her hand away. "It was there." Her voice rose. "Bran, that's where I saw him! Oh, my God. It wasn't dirt smearing his face and the shirt. It was *grease*."

BRAN HAD BEEN living for weeks with the knowledge that he could fail, that everything he could do to protect Lina might not be good enough. A bullet could shatter the windshield of his Camaro. She could die, sitting right there beside him. She could be a target in her classroom with the windows looking out on the playfield. No lock could keep out someone who was determined enough. He sweated every minute he wasn't with her, and some of them when he was.

If that scum got to her, if she was killed…

Usually he faced what had to be faced and went on. This…was different.

But now, at last! There was nothing like the feeling when an investigation cracked open, when he knew he was finally closing in on the creep he'd been hunting. After leaving Lina at the middle school, Bran expected to feel the same thrill. Instead…he was charged, sure, but the relief and deep-down anger overpowered any sense of triumph. This wasn't a job; it was deeply personal.

He'd driven straight to the autobody shop that fixed her car, confident this was the kind of business that would be open by eight.

When he pulled into the parking lot, the doors were up, exposing both bays of The Car Doc. Had to be half a dozen guys working on the two vehicles currently on lifts. All wore the same blue uniform pants and shirts, names embroidered on the pockets. That matched Lina's recollection. He got out of his car to the sound of ringing metal. Unfortunately, none of the men's faces matched the drawing. If Tag had been here… Bran hoped he'd have had the self-control to cuff him rather than kill him.

Unfortunately, Tag was earning big bucks in his new occupation. Why would he hold on to a job laboring for someone else?

Aware that his arrival had been noticed, Bran

walked into the cramped front office. The buttery smell of popcorn made him glance into the small waiting room. Currently unoccupied, a few vinyl and metal chairs were squeezed in, all aimed at a wall-hung television playing a raucous talk show.

The pop machine was in the office, along with a short counter and a calendar featuring vintage cars. As tense as he was, Bran smiled at that, remembering a similar picture he'd mooned over when he was a kid. Zach had called it his pinup.

A skinny, older man appeared from the garage. "Carlos Avila. That's quite a car you have out there. It been damaged?"

"No." Bran introduced himself and showed his badge.

Avila's eyebrows went up. "What can I do for you?"

Bran handed him the drawing. "I have reason to believe this man may have worked for you."

Avila studied the face. "He wasn't here long. I had to let him go."

"Why?"

The shop owner shrugged. "Bad attitude. Always thought he knew better than anyone else. Came on to any pretty woman bringing her car in, too. I gave him a trial month, let him go. He didn't appreciate it." He handed back the drawing.

"Can't say I'm surprised a cop's looking for him. He was the kind that felt entitled. You know?"

Bran saw plenty of those. "Do you recall his name?"

Avila scratched his head. "Something a little different. I'll have to look through my files." But instead he stepped to the doorway leading into the first bay. "Howard? Got a question for you."

A well-built, graying man about the same age as his employer separated himself from the others and came to the office, nodding at Bran.

"You remember that guy from this spring who only lasted a month? Had an earring." He touched his lobe.

"Tag?"

"Yeah, yeah, that was it. Don't suppose you remember his last name, too? Detective Murphy here is looking for him."

Howard pondered the question. "Something real ordinary. Figured that's why his parents gave him such a different first name. Not Smith." He stared into space, finally saying, "I want to say Jones."

Avila's expression cleared. "That was it. Thanks, Howard."

He nodded, looking at Bran. "What year is that Camaro?"

"'73."

"Nice. Do the work yourself?"

"I did."

It became apparent that Howard was a vintage car enthusiast. His baby was a '55 Chevy Bel Air. The gleam of a fanatic in his eyes, he encouraged Bran to consider entering the Camaro in a classic car show being held in June. Bran took the information even as he was thinking how much his life would have changed by then. He'd be a father.

Unreal.

Carlos Avila had disappeared into a tiny office as the two men talked. He emerged with a tattered file folder covered in greasy fingerprints.

"Hope to see you there," Howard said and went back to work.

Avila handed over the file. "Here's what I have. There's not much."

"Anything is more than we've got."

From Bran's perspective, it was all gold. The application had to have been filled out by Tag himself. It would have his fingerprints on it. He'd supplied not only an address and phone number, but a social security number and previous employers.

"Did you check his references?" Bran asked, glancing up.

"The most recent." The shop owner nodded at the application. "I made a note there. See?" He pointed to a scribble that had to be some kind of personal shorthand. "Means I talked to someone there. Wouldn't have hired the guy if they'd had anything bad to say about him. Can't say I remember what I *was* told, though." He looked apologetic. "I hire a lot of young guys, which means turnover. It gets old."

"I understand." Bran picked up the folder. "Can I take this?"

"It's all yours."

Fifteen minutes later, Bran was behind his desk in the bullpen. His first call was to his brother, who had been expecting him. Zach didn't argue about priorities.

"I'll have to let you know whether I can get away to go talk to Greaver," Bran added.

"Good enough. If you need me to, I can pick up Lina."

This was a different kind of backup from what he was used to on the job. He wondered if he would ever learn to take it for granted.

Charged with energy, Bran went online, looking for a driver's license—and found one for a John Taggart Jones. It felt unreal, seeing that face, photographed by someone at the DMV. He was younger than he had appeared to Lina, for good reason. The license was due to expire in a year, which meant he'd gotten it six years ago.

Bran shook his head. He didn't know how the artist created such realistic likenesses, but this wasn't the first time she'd been dead-on.

From there, he searched for the two companies that had previously employed Tag Jones.

The first one, an autobody shop in Puyallup, not far outside Tacoma, was legit. A manager who remembered Jones came to the phone and said without much enthusiasm, "He was all right." Like Carlos Avila, he had to pull Jones's personnel file for details while Bran waited. "He worked here a little over a year. Tell you the truth, I was glad when he quit. Competent enough, but he kind of wore on the nerves. I guess I'd have given him an okay reference, but I don't remember ever getting a call." The address he had for Jones matched the one on the driver's license.

He'd left the job in September of the previous year and gone to work at The Car Doc here in Clear Creek in March. He must not have lasted long in the intervening job.

Bran took down the references Jones had given to the shop in Puyallup, although he didn't have a lot of hope for them.

The most recent employer turned out to be fictitious. No such business had ever been licensed by the state, had a website or advertised in the yellow pages. When Bran looked up the address, he found it belonged to a Tesoro gas station that had been on that corner for years. The phone number was no longer in service. That raised the question: what had Tag been doing in those six months between jobs? Getting fired from someplace he didn't dare give as a reference? Likely a friend of his had provided that recommendation to Avila.

Over the next hour, Bran discovered that the address in Puyallup had been for an apartment that, no surprise, had another tenant now. More interesting, the manager said Tag Jones's name had never been on the lease. The name of the tenant at the time proved to be another dead end.

The phone number Jones had given Carlos Avila now belonged to a church. The address was for a rental house managed by a local real estate company. The woman Bran spoke to on the property management side told him the owner lived in Texas and did nothing but cash checks. The previous tenants had moved out in May of that year. It was a couple, she said, a Derrick and Melissa Cobb. She had no forwarding information for them.

"They had the house for almost two years and paid their rent on time. The house wasn't as clean as I'd have liked when they moved out, but there was no significant damage."

"Did you meet the Cobbs?" he asked. He was already running the name.

"Mr. Cobb. He dropped the check by a couple of times."

"Can you describe him?"

"I…well." Starting to get flustered, she said, "It's been a while. He wasn't very tall, I do recall that. Thin and…to tell you the truth… I'm not even sure I'd recognize him again."

Having pulled up the Washington State driver's license photo for Derrick Cobb, Bran had no doubt he was looking into the face of the man he'd seen on surveillance video casing two banks. "Did Mr. Cobb have anyone with him either time he came into your office?"

"Not that I recall." She hesitated. "Should I be concerned if he reappeared?"

"I think it's safe to say you won't see him again, Ms. Rowman. However, if you do, please call me immediately."

He'd just ended that call when Charlie walked in, chafing his cold hands together, his nose red and running. He left his parka on and headed straight for the coffeepot, despite his usual preference for a Coke.

"Damn, it's cold out there!" He gave all three detectives present an obscenity-laced story about staking out a house in hopes the resident's boyfriend would show, and freezing his ass off because if he'd started his car to run the heater, thanks to the cold snap the exhaust would have billowed. "Any passing idiot would have noticed me."

"Did the boyfriend show?" Rich Delancy asked.

"No, goddamn it." Scowling, Charlie cradled his mug of hot coffee and dipped his face almost into it to savor the rising heat.

"I can cheer you up," Bran said.

He stopped. "How?"

Everyone looked up.

"Come and look."

Charlie circled his desk and looked at the photo on the monitor. His eyes narrowed. "That's not the guy your girlfriend described."

"No, but I'd put money that it's the partner." Ignoring the eavesdroppers, he told Charlie about how Lina's memory had been triggered and then everything he'd done since.

"Jesus," Charlie murmured. "You have names. Have you called Novinski yet?"

"No." He rolled his tight shoulders. A thought popped into his head. "What do you want to bet I'll find a domestic violence call to that address?"

"The one Karl Ingebretsen told us about?"

"Yep." His fingers flew. "And there it is. Derrick and Melissa Cobb."

"Don't suppose there's any chance she's gotten tired of being smacked around."

"And left him?" A not-so-nice smile tugged at his mouth. "Now, there's a thought."

"I'm not coming up with anything current on him *or* her," Charlie said a minute later, from behind his own computer.

"Or on Tag or Taggart Jones." Bran stared at his monitor. "And—shit!—the social belongs to a Jones, all right, but not the right one." He kept reading. "Edgar Jones is fifty-nine and lives in Miles City, Montana."

"The father?"

"Huh."

Edgar Jones didn't answer his phone. Impatient, Bran called the Miles City Police Department and was lucky to hook up with a sergeant who admitted the population of his town was around 8,500 citizens. He happened to know Edgar Jones, who worked for a local company that did well drilling, irrigation, underground construction and trenching for pipelines. Within moments, the sergeant came up with a work number for Edgar, who answered immediately, sounding impatient.

"I have two sons. My older boy has gone into ranching. Haven't heard from the younger in a good ten years. He was a worthless kid spoiled rotten by my ex-wife."

Aware that Charlie was listening in, Bran asked, "And your younger son's name?"

"John Taggart. Always went by Tag."

"Were you aware that Tag has been using your social security number?"

"What?"

"You might want to check with your local social security office and find out whether any action on your part is required. Mr. Jones, would your ex-wife have stayed in touch with Tag?"

"She's dead," he said brusquely. "Passed away eleven years ago. I did my best with him, but he didn't want to hear anything I had to say."

He asked what that worthless son of his had done, and was disgusted at the possibility he might have robbed banks. "I washed my hands of him a long time ago," he said. "Anything else you need to know?"

"I'd like your older son's phone number, in case he's heard from his brother."

"Can't imagine. They were never close." But he supplied the number.

Nobody answered at that number, but Bran reached the voice mail for B & J Ranch. After leaving a message, he rubbed his face. His eyes were burning.

He'd always been a patient man, but he couldn't seem to deal with the brick wall he'd slammed into. He knew he was being unreasonable. The breakthrough was real: thanks to a brave and observant woman, they had the names of both men who'd pulled off at least five bank robberies before becoming killers, too. But he'd have sworn he *had* the scum-sucking son of a bitch. Instead, the unrelenting stress would continue to chew like acid at his stomach, steal sleep, break down barriers that held back unwanted feelings.

He swore. "Guess there's nothing to do but call Novinski."

"They do have resources we don't."

"Yeah. Shit."

The way this day was going, he wasn't surprised when she didn't answer her phone and he had to leave another message. Time to pick up Lina, and give her the good news: sorry, babe, your best friend's killer is still out there, still stalking you, and *I can't find him.*

BRAN FLATTENED BOTH hands on the scarred countertop that separated the public from the inner workings of the Clear Creek Police Department and leaned toward the fat ass on the other side of it. He must look as pissed as he felt, given how Detective Scott Wiegand shrank back.

Bran had figured Zach deserved to be here, too. They'd both gotten the run-around often enough from the CCPD, who had investigated— if you could call their bumbling around that— Sheila's murder. After talking to Zach, he had decided this should come ahead of confronting Rob Greaver again.

The empty waiting room was Wiegand's only lucky break so far. The only audience was the desk sergeant.

"Here's how it goes," Bran said, voice low but projecting all the menace he could summon. "Either you cooperate now, or we take one of two other options. Number one, we get a court order. Two, we go to the press. Either way, your whole department will look bad. You have my personal guarantee."

Scott Wiegand had put on some serious weight in the twenty-five years since he was primary investigator in the murder of Sheila Murphy. Sweat dripped down his face and darkened the underarms of the white shirt that stretched across a substantial belly.

"Threats won't get you anywhere," he blustered. "You don't have any jurisdiction here. Why don't I just pick up the phone and call your boss."

"Feel free. But, you know, since we're here as private citizens, I don't see how Sheriff Brown can help you."

"We ran an honest investigation. It's too damn bad we couldn't make an arrest, but you know why that was."

"Yep." Bran straightened. "You decided right out of the gate that my father was your man, and you never looked very hard at anyone else."

"You can't prove that." The detective's voice didn't come out as strong as he'd probably been hoping.

Hearing his cue, Zach slapped down a familiar manila envelope on the counter. The meager contents were the sum total of what the detectives had accomplished back then—or what they were willing to admit to having done. And he'd acquired even that limited info through a back door. "You're the one who has to do the proving," Zach said. "What's in this file is laughable. But we're willing to go easy on you about that. You and Nolte were young. This is a small police department. It could be you didn't get the training you should have had." His voice hardened. "But this is an open case. If you can't produce all evidence collected from the murder scene, I'd call that actionable." He shrugged. "Or if we go the route of getting in touch with KOMO or KING 5 news, I'm going to guess some heads will roll here. You might want to start thinking about early retirement, Scott."

"It's not going to look real good if you have a lead you're not sharing," he shot back.

The man actually had a point there, Bran reflected, but he and Zach had given Wiegand plenty of opportunities to join them in reopening the investigation.

"Oh, we have leads." Zach was on a roll now. "But see, *we* developed them. In the absence of cooperation from the Clear Creek Police Department, which is apparently afraid the original investigation might look inept if it were to see the light of day."

Wiegand snarled an obscenity and launched himself at the swinging half door that separated him from getting his ass kicked. A scuffle wasn't what Bran had had in mind, but burying his fist in that tub of lard might release some of the tension wound so tight he was ready to snap.

A man appeared from the short hall behind the desk sergeant's domain. Detective Doug Easley moved fast, clamping his hand down on Wiegand's shoulder.

Wiegand whirled on him, a fist lifted.

"Whoa." Stocky and half a head shorter than his fellow detective, Easley took a prudent step back. "It's just me."

"This is none of your goddamn business!"

Easley stayed rock steady. "Sure it is. I have a stake in this department. Now, don't make me call the chief down here."

"Butt out!" Wiegand snapped.

"Let's have a quiet word." He looked at Bran and Zach. "If you gentlemen will excuse us."

"We'll be waiting," Bran promised. Battle-ready, he didn't like standing down, but this behavior wasn't like him. And, damn it, Bran had had dealings with Detective Doug Easley before, and found him to be competent.

Turning his back on the desk sergeant, Bran

kept his voice low. "You knew Easley. Did you ever ask *him* to check what's been saved?"

His brother shot him an impatient look. "Of course I did. He said Wiegand is the detective on record, and I needed to deal with him. And we know how that went."

Zach, constitutionally unable to hold still, took to pacing. Better able to hide his own tension, Bran leaned against the counter and watched the wall clock. Waiting for the minute hand to inch forward was agonizing. He wondered if he was getting an ulcer.

Easley reappeared and pushed through the swinging door. "Let me walk you out."

Zach stiffened, but Bran laid a hand on his shoulder.

His first breath of the cold air burned his lungs. Dusk had fallen, he realized, and the temperature with it. Where was their usual Northwest winter weather? It should be rainy and forty degrees, not clear and arctic.

Easley waited until the door closed behind them to say, "Detective Wiegand has agreed to make me his liaison to you." He cleared his throat. "I wasn't around when your sister was killed, but I've seen Scott work. You may not want to believe it, but he's thorough."

Sure. Bran's frustration rose again. "There's a manila envelope on the counter in there that says otherwise. We were told it was everything on Sheila's murder. Take a look, Easley, and see how *thorough* you find it."

"The record-keeping here hasn't always been the best." Easley jerked his head toward the granite block building behind him. "The place hasn't been remodeled since I came to work here. The town grows, money goes to adding patrol officers, not a more efficient evidence room or a new records clerk. You should understand that."

"I understand," Bran said grudgingly. Zach grimaced his agreement.

"Here's the deal. I'll dig in Evidence and find whatever we kept. Scott says your sister's nightgown is there. He's…felt threatened for no good reason, or he would have told you that much. I'll let you know what I find. I won't hesitate to send the nightgown off to the state lab for DNA testing." His voice hardened. "In return, once you have a viable suspect, you need to share whatever you know with us. The arrest will be ours, not yours."

Bran exchanged a glance with Zach, who nodded slightly.

"We always wanted to work with your department. We're well aware neither of us has jurisdiction to make the arrest. We have a couple of strong possibilities right now." He hesitated. "One of them is dead, but his wife is still in the same house, and I doubt if she got rid of everything of her husband's." Which meant, with a warrant they could probably come up with DNA to check for a match.

The detective sighed. "What's your next step?"

"A second interview with the son," Zach said.

"Any chance you want to include me or Detective Wiegand in that?"

Bran shook his head. "I knew him when we were kids. He's torn right now, but this is an old secret he needs to unload. He understands why this matters to us. With one of you there, it becomes a police interrogation."

Easley grunted unhappily, but said, "Okay. I can buy that." He looked the two of them over. "I'll hold you to your word."

Unmoving, Zach stood with his arms crossed. "And we'll be waiting to hear what you find."

The standoff ended with nods all around.

# CHAPTER FIFTEEN

WHEN BRAN CALLED to say tersely that he'd be home in a minute, Lina was caught off guard. "You decided not to go to Seattle?"

After a moment of silence, he said, "We put it off."

Seconds later, the key turned in the lock. He walked in the door with a stony expression that failed to hide his weariness. The lines on his face aged him.

Her heart stilled. "Is something wrong?"

He looked at her as if she were a stranger, said, "No," and walked right past her into the bedroom.

She gaped after him, dismissed. She felt unimportant, small.

Between classes today, when the students were writing, even when someone was talking and she should have been listening, Lina hadn't been able to stop herself from reliving too many terrifying moments. The moment when she'd seen Maya murdered. The car accident, in color and detail sharpened by the morning's near miss. The boy on the bicycle looking over his shoulder when he heard the clashing metal, nothing in his expression suggesting he knew how close he'd come to getting hit.

And then, fresh again, the man in the autobody shop looking at her, assessing her with what she suspected now was sexual intent. It was her discomfort that had embedded that otherwise meaningless moment in her memory.

After Bran told her what he'd learned that day while he drove her home, it got worse. She'd been alone in the silent apartment now for over two hours, waiting for him to come home.

She knew he was already dealing with the pressure of keeping her safe and investigating one of the worst crimes ever to happen in this county. This had to be the worst timing for him to confront a man who might possibly have raped and strangled his little sister, but she understood why he couldn't hold off. The crime had haunted him since he was a boy, and now answers were tantalizingly close.

What scared her was imagining the impact on him, no matter what he learned. What would it do to him if he struck out and eventually had to give up? But if he was able to arrest this Rob Greaver for a murder he committed as a boy not much older than Bran had been then, would the resolution change anything meaningful for Bran and Zach? They'd lost so much besides their sister. She ached with the fear that they both hoped for too much.

But...they hadn't gone to Seattle after all? Then what had he been doing for the last two hours, to make him lock down like that?

Staring at the empty hall, unable to hear a sound from the bedroom, Lina tried to draw her knees up to hug them. With the baby in the way, she had to give up. Her knees weren't getting anywhere *near* her chest.

As she put her feet back on the floor, her rare temper flared. Was that all the answer she deserved?

Her jaw set. He had damn well better be in there pulling himself together, calming himself so he could talk to her.

The baby cartwheeled in excitement. Guiltily, she wondered if adrenaline made it through the umbilical cord.

Now it felt more as if she was jumping up and down on a trampoline that happened to be her mommy's bladder. Lina really had to pee, but no way was she going to be in the bathroom when Bran emerged from seclusion.

And there he was, having shed his jacket and the shoulder holster. She doubted he'd locked up his handgun, however; increasingly, he seemed to keep it within reach. And, yes, as he walked past her as if she was invisible, she saw a lump in the waffle knit of his henley shirt at the small of his back.

He went around the wall into the kitchen, where he opened and closed the refrigerator. "Have you eaten?" he called.

"No."

Silence. "I can order a pizza."

"Do whatever you want. I'll make myself a salad."

"Fine." A moment later, he was talking to someone, presumably putting in his order. Then he reappeared, a beer in his hand, his blue eyes trained on her. "You feeling okay?"

She rubbed her belly in a futile effort to soothe her energetic baby. "Peachy. Until you walked in the door with a dark cloud hanging over you."

He looked at her as if she was crazy. "What are you talking about?"

"You might as well have come from your brother's deathbed. But is anything wrong?" She imitated his flinty delivery. "'No.'"

His eyes narrowed. "Nothing's wrong. I have things to think about, that's all."

"Think away," she snapped, unable to decide if the burning in her chest was emotional or pregnancy-related heartburn. After struggling up from the couch, which seemed way more dif-ficult than it had been only a few weeks ago, she went to the bathroom, taking pleasure in stabbing the stupid little button that locked him out.

She stayed long enough to pee, then had to pee again, before deciding she needed to be grown-up enough to try to talk to him.

He had his feet up in his recliner and seemed absorbed in what some talking heads had to say about the upcoming Super Bowl, which if she wasn't mistaken was still weeks away. And since the Seahawks hadn't made it through the play-offs, she doubted he cared that much about the preparations for the game anyway.

Lina stopped in the middle of the living room. "I take it you'd rather be alone."

He turned that maddeningly unemotional gaze on her. "Did I say that? But is a play-by-play going to be a requirement when I walk in the door every day?"

This was what it felt like to have her hopes crushed. Now her sinuses were on fire along with her heart or her esophagus or whatever it was.

"I'd call it sharing," she said, proud of how cool she sounded. "But if I have to demand anything from you, it's not worth having."

Determined not to let him see how hurt she was, she marched past him to the kitchen and pulled all the vegetables she could find out of the refrigerator. She had no appetite whatsoever, but putting a salad together gave her something to do.

She could poke at it for a few minutes, then dump it in the garbage. He'd never notice.

The cucumber looked suspect, but maybe—

Bran mumbled something that was probably obscene. Lina started peeling, watching curls of cucumber skin drop to the cutting board.

He stalked around the corner. "If that's how you feel about it, maybe you should have tried waiting instead of jumping right in with a demand."

The nasty edge to his voice stiffened her back. "Asking if something had upset you seemed innocent enough to me."

"Things are getting to me, okay? Is that what you want to know?"

Her back to him, Lina closed her eyes. "I don't expect anything of you, Bran. I never did. That's why—"

"You had no intention of telling me you were pregnant?"

"You really want to fight, don't you?" And she knew suddenly that she couldn't stand it. Did he care about her a little too much? Was that what precipitated this? Pushing her away was the only way he could prove to himself that she didn't mean anything to him? Amazing how well it worked.

"All I wanted was to come home to some peace and quiet," he said tightly.

"But here I am."

He swore again. "Lina, you're overreacting."

Her laugh sounded like shards of glass to her ears. "I'm overreacting." She shook her head, gathered herself and turned to face him. "Bran, your intentions were good. You've been as…kind as you know how. But you don't want to live with anyone else, unless she makes no demands on you whatsoever."

"No demands?" His blue eyes were thundercloud dark. "You've consumed my life since you barely missed taking a bullet! Or haven't you noticed?"

She could not let him see her tears. Sucking in a deep breath, she spun to face the salad-makings spread out on the counter. Her hands shook until she curled them into fists, her nails biting into her palms. She had to breathe. *In. Out. In. Out.*

"Damn it, Lina!" he said behind her, in a completely different voice.

She had to look at him to say this. His mouth was twisted with what might be regret, and he held out a hand to her. She ignored it.

"I need to finish out the week. But tomorrow I'm going to give my notice. The district can find a substitute now instead of in March. Going home is the right thing for me to do. It'll remove a distraction you don't need right now. I'll be safe there."

*You'll have your life back.*

"Later…" She faltered. "We can talk about what contact you want to have with your daughter."

Shock registered on his rough-hewn face and his hand dropped to his side. "You don't mean that."

"I do."

"Lina." He made an indescribable sound. "I was in a bad mood. That's all. And you're going to give up on me?"

She didn't know how it was she hadn't crumpled to a ball in the corner. How she held on to her dignity. "You are a really good man. I have no doubt about that. But all you ever share is what's on the surface. You don't trust me. Maybe you can't. I don't know. I've tried. I thought—" She swallowed. Oh, God, maybe she couldn't finish this. Her voice emerged as a whisper. "I thought—"

"You thought?" he repeated, with unmistakable urgency.

Lina found the strength to say what had to be said. "That someday you might love me. But that isn't going to happen, is it?"

Clearly thunderstruck, he backed up a step, seemingly unaware when he bumped the wall. "You know how hard that is for me."

"You mean, impossible," she said softly.

She should put away the vegetables, but she couldn't. She just couldn't. Instead, she pushed by him, not stopping until she was in the middle of the living room where she said, "I'm asking you to sleep on the couch." Then she rushed for the bedroom, closing the door and wishing it had a lock even if he wouldn't have any trouble picking it.

But it didn't matter. Because he wouldn't be opening that bedroom door.

BRAN HADN'T MOVED from where he'd stood, not quite in the kitchen. He wanted to slam his fist into the wall, but he knew what that felt like. After Mom and Zach left, after he'd watched their car disappear down the street, he'd gone up to the attic bedroom he'd shared with his brother and punched the wall, over and over and over, until he hit a stud and broke half the bones in his hand. Dad had had to take him to the ER. He'd worn a cast for almost six weeks.

The holes in the wall were there until he'd renovated to sell the house after Dad's death. Those holes had served as a reminder. Symbolic of losing everything, and how poorly he'd handled the loss.

This time, he had a hole in his chest. The pain was excruciating, the hollow sensation almost worse.

What had he done?

He'd asked for it, that was what, and he had no idea why. It was as if he'd wanted Lina mad at him. So he didn't have to talk to her, tell her how complicated everything had become, how confused he was, how tangled in the past.

*Well, good going, dude; you got what you wanted.*

Except he hadn't wanted anything like this. He'd wanted...space.

Easily achieved. He could have gone over to Zach's instead of coming home. Lina hadn't even been expecting him yet. Tess was good about giving him and Zach time alone when they needed to talk.

*Except you didn't want to talk, right?*

His muscles ached, forcing him to realize he was as tense as if he was gearing up to confront a violent offender. He groaned and stumbled a couple of steps, flattening his hands against the wall beside the door, leaning his forehead on it.

She was crying in his bedroom. He knew she was, even though he couldn't hear a thing. He could go after her right now. Except...she couldn't have been any clearer. And...he didn't know if he could make anything better, not when he didn't know what to say.

*I'm sorry?*

That wasn't even close to good enough.

The pressure had been building inside him for

days. Weeks. He'd called it fear for her, but was driven now to admit it had always been more than that.

He remembered that strange moment after she'd been shot, when she was sitting on the bumper of the ambulance, hands wrapped, shivering because they'd taken away her coat. Wearing the gold pendant he'd given her, after being distraught when she thought she'd lost it. He'd known the medics would take good care of her, that she had to get checked out at the hospital. But for that moment, he hadn't been able to tear his eyes from hers.

In a way, it was as if she'd stripped bare for him. The unsettling part was that he'd felt as naked.

That was when it started, he thought, a deep down terror he had refused to acknowledge because it took him back to a time he hated to remember.

It was as if he was a little boy again, instead of the nearly thirteen years old he'd actually been. *Mommy, don't go! Zach!*

To this day, he could close his eyes and see Zach's face pressed to the car window, the shock and grief as he looked back as great as Bran's own. Did either parent have a clue what they'd done to their two boys?

Of course not. Even Dad, for all his regrets, for

the hurt that never left him, didn't seem to notice what happened to the son who stayed with him. They just…didn't talk about any of it. Dad held up his head and pretended he didn't notice what people were saying. Bran came home from school with raw knuckles and black eyes, and Dad never asked what the fights had been about.

Even later, when Bran became a detective and told his father he was thinking of reopening the investigation, all his father would say was, "No." The second time Bran raised the subject, Dad looked him in the eye and said, "I'm asking you. Your sister is gone. Let it lie."

*So easily*, Bran thought, *I learned to keep it all inside.*

A knock on the door made him lurch back from the wall and reach for his weapon until he remembered the damn pizza. He scraped a hand over his face and composed himself enough to face the delivery kid. Fortunately, he had enough bucks in his wallet. He put the pizza straight in the refrigerator. Eating had become a foreign concept.

Eventually, he used the bathroom, brushed his teeth and turned out the lights. He grabbed the pillow and blankets he'd stowed in the linen closet and sprawled on the sofa, one knee bent, one foot on the floor. And then he stared at the dark ceiling, waiting for the tiny sounds Lina would make as she sneaked out to the bathroom, hoping he wouldn't notice.

Inside his gut, it all kept churning. And all he could think was, *I'm not the man I thought I was.*

BRAN LOOKED WORSE than she felt, which was really something. Lina had winced at the sight of herself in the mirror before she got in the shower. Her eyes were red and puffy, but otherwise she was colorless. It was as if some of her life force had leached out of her during the sleepless night.

She did the best she could with the hair dryer and makeup, but the result wasn't good.

It ceased to matter when she saw the misery and exhaustion on Bran's face. His hair stuck up every which way, and he looked gaunt, as if he'd dropped twenty pounds overnight.

He sat on the sofa, wearing only knit boxer shorts and a T-shirt, his elbows braced on his knees and his shoulders slumped. He looked up when she came out of the bathroom. "Lina."

"Good morning." Her voice didn't sound quite right, but neither did his.

"Can we talk?"

Oh, God. She knew they had to. She even knew she owed him an apology. He'd been right—she had overreacted. All her fears had suddenly coalesced. It was as if she'd been waiting for him to give her an excuse to run. But she also knew staying was perilous, and not because Maya's killer was still out there.

"I'm sorry," she said hurriedly. "You were right. I was pushy because—"

His bloodshot eyes stayed on her face. "Because?"

"The day sucked, okay? Thinking about the accident and then remembering where I'd seen *him* freaked me out, and I kept seeing Maya and—" She stopped. "I wanted you to come home, and then when you did—"

"I was an asshole." His voice sounded as raw as she felt.

Lina didn't say anything.

"Too much is happening. I don't know how to feel about any of it. I just…wasn't ready to talk, and I didn't know how to say that nicely."

She shook her head. That was the part that still hurt. "It was more than that. You were angry that I was here. That you had to interact with me."

"No. I was angry because—" He didn't finish.

"Because?"

His turn to shake his head.

"I'll do my best to stay out of your hair the rest of the week. Unless you have an idea where I could go."

He closed his eyes and pinched the bridge of his nose hard enough to make his knuckles show white before looking at her again. "Don't go, Lina. Don't give your notice." There was a noticeable pause before he could squeeze out the last word. "Please. Please don't leave."

God help her, she didn't want to go anywhere. "What good will staying do?"

"Give me a chance." The plea in his eyes might be more powerful because of how terrible he looked.

She remembered thinking that Bran Murphy would never beg for anything, but that was what he was doing. She hated that she was responsible for making him do it.

She had some doubts about her own part in last night's debacle. David had damaged her ability to trust more than she'd understood. Taking that out on Bran was unfair. He might not love her, but he *was* trustworthy. She was staking her life and her baby's on him. She couldn't believe he'd ever break a vow the way David had.

So she bit her lip and nodded. "I won't make any decisions yet. Last night was my fault as much as yours. I…usually know when to back off."

"And I believe you would have told me about the baby. I'm ashamed of myself, but I was lashing out."

If any more regret carved his face she wouldn't be able to stand it. "People squabble. That's what we did." She raised her eyebrows. "You know, if you plan to go into work, you could really use a shower and shave."

He grimaced and rubbed the dark stubble on his jaw. "Yeah. Okay."

"I think we have time for pancakes, if you want some."

"Yeah," he said hoarsely. "That would be really nice."

Lina went into the kitchen, hoping by the time she saw him again he would have smoothed out some of the cavernous lines in his face carved by regret.

ZACH BACKED HIS pickup into the parking space so he and Bran could see the trucking company headquarters without getting out. Today was a little warmer than the last few had been, but not by much. The slight warming and the milky color of the sky presaged snow. He hadn't looked at the newspaper this morning or turned on his radio to find out what was predicted, but he'd bet his next paycheck the first flakes would appear tonight.

Clearly preoccupied, Bran had been quiet during the hour drive from Clear Creek. He had said that even the two FBI agents were coming up empty-handed when they tried to figure out where Tag Jones and the Cobbs were hiding out. Zach knew Bran would have liked to believe they'd hightailed it out of Clear Creek, but they both figured that wasn't the case.

Lina represented the death penalty to Jones. She hadn't just seen him holding a gun on her friend, she'd seen him pull the trigger. The drawing was great, but this was a case where a picture was *not* worth a thousand words. If Lina was gone and the investigators couldn't come up with any physical evidence, he could shrug and say, "We all have look-alikes out there. All I can tell you is, that's not me."

Getting rid of Lina had to be his number one priority. Which made it surprising Bran had agreed to leave her long enough to follow up with Rob Greaver.

"Shit day?" Zach asked eventually, after turning off the engine.

Bran bumped his head a couple of times on the headrest. "Shit night."

Zach frowned.

"Lina and I went at it. I was a jerk, she told me she was giving the school district only the rest of the week for notice, then flying home."

"That…might be the safest thing for her to do," Zach said, thinking it through.

"Or incredibly dangerous."

"Yeah. That's possible, too," he had to concede. "But how can you stop her?"

"She's already said she'll put off deciding what to do. We agreed it was a stupid argument, we both overreacted."

"Uh-huh." Zach wasn't buying it.

"I don't know if I can be what she needs," Bran said abruptly.

Zach shifted behind the wheel to stare at his brother. "You shouldn't have to transform yourself for anyone."

"You didn't make any adjustments for Tess?" his brother scoffed.

"I had to quit running from what I felt, that's all. You know what happened when I got scared. She almost died because I wasn't there for her." The single worst moment of his life—and that was saying something—was when he'd seen the flicker of orange flames from outside her house, when he'd known she might already be dead because he wasn't in there to protect her the way he should have been. "I learned my lesson."

"There he is."

Looking toward the building, Zach saw Rob Greaver. Just like the last time, he carried an insulated lunch container. This time, he wasn't alone. Another guy wearing the same uniform was with him. The way they were laughing as they crossed the parking lot, they had to be friends.

Bran jumped out and Zach joined him. The sound of their doors slamming made Rob turn his head. Angry color suffused his face, but he didn't stop until he was a couple feet from them,

Zach blocking his way to the driver's-side door of Rob's truck.

His friend stuck with him. "Hey, what's this about?"

Rob ignored him. "Shit, you just won't give up, will you?"

The epitome of relaxation, Bran lounged against the tailgate of Rob's pickup, arms crossed. "Nope. Mom and Dad gave us both the same middle name."

Zach grinned despite the tension. Bran was on to something there. "Stubborn," he said helpfully.

Greaver rolled his eyes. "You're comics."

"You need a hand here?" the friend asked. He was shorter and leaner than the Murphy boys, but Zach had to give him credit for being gutsy enough to stand up with his buddy.

Rob finally spared him a glance. "Thanks, Chad, but I've got this. Unfortunately, I know these two."

Chad appeared doubtful, but finally nodded. "Okay. I'm off then. I'll probably see you tomorrow."

Nobody spoke until he got into his own car and the lights came on.

"I talked to your sister the other day." That seemed as good an opening as any to Zach.

Rob barked a laugh. "Bet Mary didn't have anything good to say about me."

"Nothing that bad. We got reminiscing. You know how it is. The two of us talked about how it feels to hear someone sneaking out of your house during the night, and to have to spend all the years that follow wondering."

A nerve jumped in Rob's cheek. "That's a lie. She never said anything like that."

Actually, she hadn't, but Zach had learned to read what wasn't said as well as what was.

"Then she mentioned you and your dad fighting the next day. She said things got rough between the two of you."

His shoulders jerked. "I was a teenager. My father wanted me to toe the line."

Hard to miss the way he said *father*. As if it fouled his mouth. Had he even mentioned his father the last time they talked? Zach couldn't remember.

"And you did everything you could to enrage him," Bran contributed.

"Yeah, so? Half the kids in any high school are at war with their parents."

Which was also true enough, but Zach thought Rob's rebellion had a different cause.

"Your mom has always had her doubts about you, hasn't she?" Bran mused. "Lot of tension there."

"She took his side no matter what." His mouth

clamped shut as if he realized he had skated the line there.

"You know I found Sheila, right?" He had to make this guy understand who counted here, and Zach didn't know how else. "I can still see her. They always say this, but she did look like a doll. Broken. Naked."

Rob swallowed. "Don't tell me. It's got nothing to do—"

Zach rolled his shoulders and took a step forward. "Was it you, Rob? Did you rape my sister and then wrap your hands around her neck and squeeze until you knew she was dead? *Was it you?*"

"No!" The color had risen to his cheeks again. "God, *no*," he said more quietly, even as his free hand balled into a fist, loosened, fisted again.

Good. He was feeling the pressure.

"Or did you hear your father go out that night? Did you confront him the next day?" Zach asked, voice almost silky, until he snarled, "What did he say, Rob? Did he tell you what he'd done?"

"Jesus." Face convulsing, Rob fell back a step, swung away from them. "Jesus."

With startling speed, Bran launched himself from the truck and grabbed the man's shoulder, yanking him around to face them. Showing his teeth, Bran leaned in. "What did he tell you?"

Expression tortured, he looked from one to the

other of them, as if searching for an out. Any out. He started shaking his head. "I can't—I can't tell you!"

Still with his hand on Rob's shoulder, Bran said in an astonishingly gentle voice, "There are some things that shouldn't be kept quiet, Rob. You have to know that by this time. Never being able to get something like that out will eat you alive sooner or later."

Rob Greaver groaned in anguish. His eyes were wet as he looked at Bran. "How could I tell anyone? He was my dad. How could I?" And then he broke down completely.

# *CHAPTER SIXTEEN*

As FAR AS Lina was concerned, this day had so far been no improvement on the previous one.

Bran took her to school and then picked her up after the last bell and drove her home. As usual, there wasn't a lot of conversation, but he looked tired rather than grim, which was something.

Once inside, he asked politely about her day and volunteered the information that Agent Novinski thought she might have a lead on the Cobbs. He seemed pleased to have made an arrest on another case he'd briefly told her about. After checking the lock on the sliding door in the bedroom and wiggling the bar that made a backup lock, he asked if she was sure she'd be okay while he and Zach went to talk to Rob Greaver.

"I probably won't be back for close to three hours," he warned.

But she'd always been self-reliant, and this was no time to become dependent on someone else's company.

"You told me that this morning," she said. "I'll be fine."

"You won't open the door to anyone."

"I promise I won't."

So he'd left. The minute the door closed and she heard it lock, Lina let her smile drop away. Oh, boy—three hours of stewing.

She was instantly mad at herself. Having time to herself meant being able to read, or watch a TV show Bran would hate, or paint her toenails, or… There had to be a million things she could do to entertain herself.

She was in the middle of an old Tony Hillerman mystery she'd taken from Bran's shelf. Ten minutes after settling on the couch with it, she realized how many times she'd had to go back to reread paragraphs and knew it wasn't the author's fault. Unfortunately, this book finally, a few pages later, did grab her attention in a big way when Sergeant Chee found a gunshot victim. She didn't need Hillerman's description to see the scene in hideous detail.

Lina closed the book. For once in her life, she regretted not having a pile of tests to grade.

She really ought to do some yoga, or at least a few exercises. But she couldn't seem to make herself get up off the sofa.

Finally, she gave in to the inevitable, closed the blinds in the bedroom to dim the daylight and snuggled into Bran's bed for a nap.

She woke suddenly in a panic. It had to be a

noise… The key turning in the lock. Bran must be home. Despite the burst of adrenaline, she felt fuzzy. It was weird waking in the dark, and yet having her clothes on.

Out of curiosity, she went to the slider first, turning on the balcony light and pulling up the blinds to see whether it had started to snow yet.

It not only had, the sight of all that white also momentarily dazzled her eyes. Wow. The weatherman on the morning news had mentioned the possibility of three or four inches, but this was looking more serious than that. And she'd only been asleep—she checked the clock—two hours.

"Lina?" Bran called, an urgency in his voice making her suspect it wasn't the first time.

"I'm here." Not bothering with shoes, she went out in the hall. "Give me a minute."

Two hours was about the outer limit for her bladder these days.

When she went to the living room, she found Bran sitting on his recliner staring into space. Her chest contracted at the sight of his face. She hadn't thought he could look worse than this morning.

"Bran?" she whispered.

He turned dazed blue eyes on her. "It was Rob Greaver's father. He killed Sheila."

"Oh, my God." She stood where she was. "How— He *told* you?"

"Yeah," he said roughly. "We applied a little pressure, but I think he needed to get it out. He's spent a lot of years trying to bury what he knew."

"Mr. Greaver is dead, isn't he?"

He nodded. "I don't think Rob would have said anything otherwise, no matter how we leaned on him."

"So…" She tried to interpret his expression. "There's nobody to arrest."

"No."

"Do you want…um…would you rather not talk about it?"

"What I'd like is for you to come here." His voice was ragged. He rocked forward to put his feet on the floor and held out an arm.

Lina threw herself onto his lap, secure in his arms closing around her. She pressed her cheek to his, feeling moisture, and thought, *Oh, no! I'm crying.* Only then, she knew it wasn't her. "Oh, Bran," she murmured. "I'm so sorry. So sorry."

Shocked that he would let himself cry, she rubbed the back of his neck, smoothed his hair, held him tight.

"At least you know. You and Zach. After all this time, you know."

"Yeah." He took a deep breath and let it filter out. "We know."

Taking a chance, Lina straightened enough to see his face. "You're sure?"

He pulled an arm from around her to wipe his face on his shirtsleeve. "Damn. I can't believe—"

"Everyone cries. Or they should anyway."

He gave a short laugh. "This is a first for me. At least since I was a boy."

"You didn't cry when your dad died?"

Bran shook his head. "It…didn't occur to me."

"Oh, Bran." Now *she* was going to cry. She pressed her lips against the corner of his, then her cheek to his again.

They sat like that for several minutes. Eventually, she realized he'd set the recliner to rocking. It felt so good, being cradled like this, holding him in turn.

A man who hated being emotionally vulnerable, he had let her see him cry.

Lina was willing to bet that neither he nor his brother had displayed a whole lot of emotion during their drive back to Clear Creek. Would Zach cry in Tess's arms?

Finally, Bran started to talk. "I didn't tell you that yesterday Zach and I went into the Clear Creek police station and got tough. A detective named Easley who Zach knows promised to find any evidence still stored from when Sheila died. He called this morning to tell me they had her nightgown. He says there's a stain that could be semen."

His hand moved over her back in soothing circles.

"I'm going to pay to have it tested. Because the suspect is dead and there won't be any trial, the state lab is unlikely to be willing to do anything, or at least it'll be at the bottom of their list of priorities."

She understood that, too, even if she didn't like it.

"It's worth a little money to be absolutely sure."

"How will you get Mr. Greaver's DNA for comparison?"

"Easley said he'd get a warrant based on Rob's testimony. Chances are good Mrs. Greaver hasn't cleaned out all her husband's stuff. All we need is a hairbrush or a comb or, hell, something he spit on."

"How did Rob know?" she asked. "Did he hear his father sneaking out, or what?"

"More than that. Greaver had a telescope. Rob saw him stop Sheila the day before when she was riding her bike. He thought it was strange, so he sneaked up on them and heard him telling Sheila he'd let her look through his telescope some night so she could see all the stars. Greaver was kind of a grump, not that friendly to neighborhood kids." Bran was speaking in a near monotone.

"Then that night, Rob heard the front door open and close, and he looked out to see his father carrying the telescope across the street. He says he thought maybe our dad had given permission for us all to get up and look through it."

Bran had to stop to collect himself.

"The next day, Rob heard. He got his father alone and said, 'I know you were there. Did you talk her into coming out alone to meet you?'"

Fingers pressed to her mouth, Lina listened in horror. She could see it so easily—a little girl who didn't know bad things could happen, tempted into an adventure that was supposed to be a secret. Seeing the stars up close would have sounded exciting. She could keep herself awake until after everyone else was asleep, then tiptoe to the back door and let herself out to meet the nice neighbor who had brought his telescope. It was awfully dark out there, but he'd said not to turn on a light, and there he was, just as he'd promised. The telescope was set up on a tripod, pointing at the clear night sky...

And, oh, Lina wished she *couldn't* picture it so clearly.

"He told Rob he just wanted to make her feel good," Bran said dully. "She was such a pretty girl."

Lina shuddered.

"Only she fought and she said she'd tell her

daddy, and things got out of hand. He didn't mean to hurt her, he claimed."

"How could Rob stay silent?"

"His father said his mother wouldn't be able to get by without him. Think about what would happen to their family. Rob might end up in foster care. Greaver said Sheila was already dead. Telling wouldn't make anything better. He promised never to put himself in a position for anything like that to happen again. He said, 'I love you, son.'"

Bran's chest heaved with something close to a sob.

"Rob was fourteen. Scared. He says he told his mother anyway and she slapped him. He was making up stories. How could he do that to his own father?"

Lina shook her head. She remembered when it came out that a girl she'd taught had been molested by her father for years, and the mother had refused to believe her. Instead of standing for her daughter, she'd chosen her husband. And Rob... he'd been a boy, faced with a terrible dilemma.

In that horribly expressionless voice, Bran said, "Rob thinks his father molested his sister, too, although Mary would never admit to it. Odds are, there've been other girls."

"But he didn't kill them."

He rubbed his cheek against her head. "No," he said tiredly. "Maybe Sheila was his first after his daughter and he hadn't yet figured out how to ease her into believing what he was doing was normal. It takes practice to terrorize a kid into silence, I suppose. Maybe if Sheila had kept her mouth shut, he'd have let her live. I don't know."

A lump in her throat, she nuzzled his neck. "Your parents would have believed her, wouldn't they?"

"Damn straight."

"You're sure this Rob wasn't lying?"

"If he was, he should move to Hollywood. He'd win an Academy Award with his first movie." Bran was silent for a moment. "He knows we have the nightgown. I didn't tell him there's any doubt about whether that stain is semen or not. If his dad's doesn't match up, Rob has to know we'll be back to ask him for his."

"I'm so sorry," she said again. "I wish it had never happened. I wish—"

"Thank you for the thought."

"I mean it," she said passionately, starting to push away from him again.

The smile he gave her was crooked but real. "I know. But maybe things are meant to happen the way they happen. At least Zach and I found each other again." He paused and searched her face. "I found you."

Lina felt an odd unfurling of warmth inside her. She'd been an idiot. Bran might never be able to tell her he loved her. He probably didn't *know* what he felt. But tonight, he had demonstrated that he could change. In his anguish and confusion, he'd come to *her*. He had opened himself to her in a way she couldn't imagine he'd ever done before, for anyone. He'd wanted her arms around him, her comfort, her understanding.

Yes, there would be times he'd hurt and exasperate her when he closed himself off. But, in so many ways, he had proved that he put her first in his life. What more could a woman ask from a man?

It came to her that the lesson she should have taken from her ex-husband was that words alone meant nothing, however passionate or romantic they were. Promises could be empty, but actions weren't. And from the minute Bran crouched beside her in the manager's office at Walgreens, he'd showed her she could depend on him.

"You did find me," she told him, her own voice shaking.

He went still. "Lina?"

She took a deep breath for courage. "If you're sure it's what you want, I'll marry you."

*"God."* He snatched her even closer and his mouth found hers. His stubble scratched her, their teeth bumped, she thought *he* was shaking, but none of it mattered. Eager, frantic, clumsy, he gave her everything she needed.

Despite her ungainly body, she scrambled to straddle him, using her hands and lips and tongue to give him everything *he* needed.

He had to lift her off him to work her pants down her legs, but didn't bother with her shirt or socks. Her eager hands dealt with the fly of his jeans. Their joining felt so unbelievably good, they both went still for a minute, only looking deep into each other's eyes. And then her inner muscles tightened and he gripped her hips, lifting her, pulling her down hard, setting a rhythm that had her whimpering and him groaning. They exploded together.

Lina melted against him, feeling boneless. She might never move again. Bran's heart hammered against her breast. He buried his face in her hair.

And then her stomach lurched.

He jolted. "God, I hope she doesn't know what we were doing," he said, clearly horrified.

Rubbing a hand gently over her stomach, Lina giggled. "I think she's complaining because we quit doing it. She likes to rock."

"*I* like to rock," he murmured, voice husky, sexy.

Of all times, now she had tears in her eyes when she smiled at him. "Me, too."

BRAN WOKE BEFORE his alarm in the morning. After he and Lina had dinner, they'd gone to bed to make love again. However ridiculously early the hour, he'd fallen asleep fast and hard. Since his body was still spooned around hers, he wasn't sure he had moved all night long. The nightmares he'd anticipated hadn't materialized.

Lying still for a minute, he wrapped his mind around everything Rob had told them. Bran had wanted to be enraged, to punish Rob for the damage his silence had done all of them, but had only felt pity. Rob, too, had been living a nightmare. In every meaningful way, he'd lost his parents that day. Yeah, if he'd had the guts to speak up, Bran's life would have been different. How different, he wasn't sure. It was Mom's sexual promiscuity more than Sheila's murder that had doomed his parents' marriage. Maybe the outcome wouldn't have changed, him believing in Dad, Zach in their mother. And…Bran and Zach both had reason to understand why a teenage boy would have felt he'd be betraying his father to tell what he knew.

Trying not to wake Lina, Bran reached over her to silence the alarm, then eased out of bed. He'd hardly slept the previous night, and he doubted she had, either. The nap she'd taken hadn't made up the deficit. He wished he didn't have to wake her up.

Struck suddenly by how quiet it was, Bran went to the sliding door and parted the blinds to see out. He laughed quietly. He'd turn on the radio for confirmation, but felt sure school had been canceled. The snow had to be a foot deep, and it was still coming down. Lina would be able to stay, cozy, in bed.

Unfortunately, he didn't have the same luxury. Cops didn't get snow days. He was only glad he wasn't still on patrol. This would be a bitch of a day out there on the roads.

In the kitchen, he turned on the radio at low volume while he poured himself a bowl of cereal. Fortunately, Clear Creek wasn't too far down the alphabetical list of school districts in the Puget Sound region that were closing today. After turning the radio off, Bran ate his cereal where he was, leaning against the cabinet. The coffee still wasn't quite ready, so he picked up his phone while he waited.

"Charlie? Any chance you could give me a lift today?"

His fellow detective said with good humor, "Don't trust your fancy little car out in the snow?"

"I think it would be headlamps deep today," Bran admitted, not minding his friend giving him a hard time.

"Yeah, I'll be there in fifteen," he said, and was gone.

Bran poured his coffee, then went down the hall. As much as he'd like to kiss Lina goodbye, it would be kinder just to leave her a note.

But when he reached the bedroom, she rolled over and said sleepily, "Bran?"

"Hey." He sat on the edge of the bed and smoothed her hair back from her face. He loved the high arch of her forehead. This was what he'd really wanted—just to touch her. Kiss her before he left. Have her drowsy smile to picture all day.

She said she'd marry him. His relief felt bottomless. To go from the devastation of the night before to her surrendering completely was still almost more than he could let himself believe. It made him a little nervous that he wasn't 100 percent sure what he'd said or done that had led to her capitulation, but rumor had it men never entirely understood the women in their lives.

Her lips curved now. "Time to get up?"

"Nope." He leaned over and kissed her gently, lingering for a moment. "Snow day."

"Really?"

He laughed. "There has to be a foot or more out there. Go back to sleep, sweetheart. Think of me struggling through the drifts."

"Oh, no! I'll bet your Camaro doesn't handle very well in snow, does it?"

"I'm afraid not. Charlie Warring is picking me up. He has four-wheel drive."

"Oh, good." She sighed. "Sad to say, I have

to go to the bathroom, but then I think I will go back to sleep."

"Damn, I wish I could get back in bed with you."

She disentangled one arm from the covers and slid her hand over his thigh to the ridge beneath his zipper. "Mmm. Because you're so sleepy."

Bran laughed ruefully. "No. But, unfortunately, I have to go. Charlie will be here any minute. You take care. I'll call later."

He kissed her again. Their lips clung long enough to raise his temperature, but he finally tore himself away.

The snowfall had slowed, flakes drifting down to land softly on the white blanket on the ground. Given the covered parking, he was able to get in Charlie's Subaru without wading through a foot of the stuff, but the drive was slow going. He saw signs that the snowplows had been out working all night, but what they'd cleared had begun to fill in again. Side streets remained pristine except for a few tracks where hardy folks had managed to drive out. The snowplows might reach them by late afternoon—if the residents were lucky.

"Hell," he said, "maybe we should have both worked from home today."

"I thought about it," Charlie admitted. Then he grinned. "I could have worked from a ski hill, too. This may not be powder snow, but it's lighter than we usually get around here."

"I've never skied or snowboarded."

"Seriously?"

"Nope. My father didn't make that kind of money."

Charlie grunted. "Who does? Do you know what ticket prices are these days? Almost seventy bucks for a weekend day at both Stevens Pass and Crystal Mountain. Then there's the gas to get there and the equipment." He shook his head.

"Not that much worse than an evening out in Seattle," Bran observed. "Although if you get hooked and want to go every weekend…"

He was cheered to see that the parking lot outside the sheriff's department and courthouse had been plowed, and not that long ago. The current shift of deputies on patrol had already gone out, Zach presumably included. He knew from experience that they'd spend the day untangling fender-benders, calling for tow trucks to pull vehicles out of ditches and rescuing stranded motorists who invariably hadn't dressed warmly enough for the day.

His phone rang even before he'd sat down behind his desk. Novinski.

"Count your blessings," she grumbled. "Most of your county is flat. Downtown Seattle might as well be a demolition derby this morning. A metro bus skidded down a hill and took out half a dozen parked cars. Why won't people stay home?" she asked plaintively.

"Because they're in essential jobs. Because their bosses expect them to show up." He grinned. "Because they're convinced they're so important, the city will slow to a stop without them."

"It's because of them this city *has* slowed to a stop." She huffed out a breath. "My lead on the Cobbs took me nowhere. They're either using a false identity or are just staying off the radar."

"My bet is that they're staying off the radar," he said slowly. "They're not sophisticated people. Chances are good they wouldn't know where to go to buy forged identity papers. They could have friends they're staying with, who maybe are even letting them borrow driver's licenses in case they get pulled over."

She didn't argue. "You know they're narrowing down their choice of the next bank to hit by now."

"Cobb may be."

"Because he's the decision maker."

"And because Jones is otherwise occupied."

"You really think he knows where you're keeping Lina and is watching." Damned if she didn't still sound doubtful. She still thought he was shying at shadows.

And...nothing had happened, so maybe she was right.

Yeah, but if she was wrong and he eased up?

If Lina died? A hole opened in his gut. Nope, he wasn't backing down.

"Unless he's stupider than I think he is, yeah. We might have had a chance if she hadn't insisted on going back to work, but I can't blame her."

"It has dragged on."

"Four weeks yesterday."

"I'll keep on it," she said. "I assume you'll do the same."

"Oh, yeah." He ended the call wondering if she had guessed the baby that Lina carried was his.

That got him to thinking about whether Lina would like to be surprised with an engagement ring, or pick out her own.

Charlie and he had been the first two arrivals among detectives, but the lieutenant had appeared while Bran was on the phone, and now Delancy and Sperling walked in, both looking as if they'd traipsed from the North Pole.

"It's coming down harder again," Sperling said, unnecessarily since his head and shoulders were dusted. He pulled off a fleece scarf and shook snow off before hanging it on the rack by the door. It was a surprise he hadn't found an excuse not to come in. Talking about taking his retirement, Sperling didn't do much but go through the motions. Bran suspected he wasn't the only one to hope he'd just do it. A unit as small as theirs didn't need dead wood.

Delancy had unzipped his parka when his phone rang. "Shit," he mumbled before he answered.

Engaged in a computer search, Bran quit paying attention until he saw Delancy zipping up again. He had been next up in the roster, Bran remembered.

Typical of the jackass, he was complaining loudly. "Who'd go out and kill someone in this weather? Why freeze your ass off and risk ending up stuck in a drift with the cops surrounding you?"

For once, he'd asked an intelligent question. Crime did usually nose-dive during blizzards. Hand still on the computer mouse, Bran looked up. "Not a domestic?"

"Doesn't sound like it." He looked around. "Sperling, you want to come with me?"

Lieutenant Arnold stepped out of his office. "You're still here?"

"We're going." Delancy pulled on gloves as an unhappy Sperling reached for his scarf.

Warring had swiveled in his chair, too. "Who's dead?"

"Woman named Andrea Young."

Bran expelled what air he'd had in his lungs as if he'd been slammed by a 2x4. Warring turned to look at him.

Delancy opened the door.

"Wait." Bran pushed himself to his feet. His

heart had taken up an irregular rhythm. "I know her. Who's the responding officer? What did he say?"

Everyone had turned to stare.

"Josh Orr. Dispatch says this Andrea cleans houses. A customer called her this morning to find out if she was coming. In the middle of their conversation, she heard the housecleaner say something like, 'Who are you? How'd you get in?' And then she heard a gunshot. After that, nothing. She hung up and called 911."

"Jesus." Bran ran for the door. At the last second, Delancy stepped aside to let him by.

"Murphy!" his lieutenant snapped. "What are you thinking?"

He turned, wild with fear. "She cleans my place. She has a key to my apartment. She...labels them." He swallowed. "Lina's home because of the snow." Sleeping in. God. She wouldn't even hear that bastard coming.

Compassion transforming his homely face, Lt. Arnold said sharply, "Put on a vest. Take someone with you. I'll call the CCPD and have them send the nearest patrol unit."

Charlie had already grabbed his coat. "I'm driving."

God. He'd forgotten he hadn't driven today. Terror swelled in him as they took the time to pick up department-issued Kevlar vests and ran out to Charlie's SUV and jumped in. Charlie put it in Reverse and backed out fast enough to send them into a skid, then accelerated. They rocketed forward.

Bran called Lina's number. Had she brought her phone into the bedroom last night? If it was still buried in her purse... The call went straight to voice mail. He cursed.

"Her phone is off. It's probably charging."

"You don't have a landline?"

"No."

"We'll be there in about two minutes."

"We don't know how long it took the first responder to get there. If he had to break in or get a neighbor to let him in—" His right foot was drilling a hole in the floorboard, even though Charlie was already driving faster than was safe. "He's had time." Too much.

*I'm too late.*

No, he couldn't think that way.

They fishtailed around a corner.

## CHAPTER SEVENTEEN

TOWEL WRAPPED AROUND her head, Lina sat on the edge of the bed and pulled on her socks. To stay warm, she'd have to dry her hair next, but she took a moment to savor how fabulous she felt. Amazing sex and all the sleep her body could want combined to fizz like champagne in her veins.

Now if only Bran had been snowbound with her. Think what a lovely day they could have had, making love and talking.

She wrinkled her nose. Okay, maybe not talking.

She fully expected Bran to retreat from last night's high emotion. He probably thought everything that needed to be said had been. Certainly about his sister's murder, and likely about his and Lina's relationship, too. After all, she'd agreed to marry him. His plan was back on track.

And…to be honest, maybe there *wasn't* anything else to say, beyond practicalities like setting a date and deciding if they were going to have a church wedding or civil service. Of course she'd have to call her parents. They'd want to be there, no matter how simple the ceremony she and Bran chose to have. They'd *especially* want to come check out the man she was marrying.

Lina had pulled off the towel and was shaking out her hair when she heard the familiar scrape of a key in the lock. Happiness warmed her from the inside out. Bran must have convinced his lieutenant that he could work from home today.

She jumped to her feet and hurried for the bedroom door to meet him, but then came to a sudden stop. He always called to warn her when his arrival was unexpected.

Which he'd probably tried to do. She'd turned off her phone last night when she plugged it in to charge. Bran *couldn't* call. And who else would have a key?

From the hall she saw the apartment door swing open. That hint of nerves made her hesitate still, hovering where she was. With the only windows in the two bedrooms, it was mostly dark in the living area since she hadn't turned lights on yet. But the man who stepped in was briefly illuminated by the hall light behind him. It gleamed off his bald head, which turned as his gaze swept from the kitchen toward the living room.

Stifling a cry, Lina leaped back into the bedroom. Terror balled in her chest. *Not him. Oh, God, not him.*

As silently as possible, she closed the bedroom door. Her teeth chattered as she looked frantically around. With her phone in the kitchen, she had no way of calling for help.

The bedroom light must show beneath the door, letting him know where she was. No—she'd left the bathroom light on, too. He might look in there first.

Whimpering, she hurried to the far side of the bed and shoved the mattress forward until it tipped almost off the springs, then raced around and wedged herself behind it, pushing again until, with a thump, it fell against the wall, covering the door.

The handle rattled, and the door pressed against the mattress.

Desperate, using strength she hadn't known she had, she tipped the whole bed over until it lay against the mattress.

There was a funny *pop, pop*, and the mirror above the dresser behind her shattered. Lina screamed.

Bullets had passed right through the mattress and springs. And he must be using a silencer, like he had at the high school. If neighbors were home, they wouldn't hear a thing.

Her screams. They might hear those.

But then she saw what had lain on the carpeted floor beneath the bed.

IN THE CONFINED space of the passenger seat, Bran wrestled on the vest, then kept trying to call, in case she picked up her phone.

"Damn it, Lina, *answer*! Wake up!" Don't be dead already.

Charlie remained silent, driving as fast as he dared in risky conditions.

Needing to do something, Bran called information for the complex manager's office.

Voice mail.

He swore, a low, hoarse litany of fear.

He heard a distant siren, but couldn't tell where it was coming from. God, let it be pulling up to his complex.

Ahead, a car slid through a stop sign and glided into the intersection directly in front of them. Now it was Charlie swearing as he skillfully braked and swerved. It took a minute to regain traction and accelerate.

A minute they couldn't afford. A minute that had Bran sweating.

LINA SHOVED THE bed back against the wall, trying to keep herself to the side, where bullets wouldn't penetrate. *Pop, pop.*

Abandoning the effort, praying the weight of a king-size mattress and springs would buy her just a minute or two, she snatched up the escape ladder from the floor and raced for the sliding door. She kicked away the bar and unlocked the door with a shaking hand. Impervious to the cold, wearing only socks on her feet, she stepped out in the snow, hung the hooks over the balcony rail, and let the rungs fall. *Clank, clank, clank.*

Oh, God. Just getting over the railing seemed impossible with her bulky body. *I'm sorry, baby. So sorry.*

Suddenly, she was weirdly calm. *Think of this as getting out of a swimming pool, easy as pie. Hands on the railing, push yourself up. Swing your leg over. That's it.*

For a second she straddled the railing, heart pounding, excrutiatingly aware of the four-story drop to a snow-covered concrete patio below. If she slipped and went over…

But then, out of the corner of her eye, she caught movement in the bedroom. Jerked out of her momentary panic, she emulated a gymnast on a balance beam, swinging herself around, and groped with both feet for a rung on the ladder.

There it was!

*Go! Go! Go!*

She scrambled down, her last sight through the railing of *him*, face contorted with fury as he scrambled over the bed he'd now toppled back into the room.

She reached the balcony below, but vertical

blinds were drawn, and she saw only darkness past them.

Sobbing for breath, she kept going.

"Jesus! That has to be her!" Charlie exclaimed.

They were a block away, approaching the backside of the block of apartments. Bran wouldn't have thought he could even pick out which window and balcony were his.

Except a woman hung suspended on…yeah… an escape ladder. The one he'd bought in an excess of paranoia because of Tess's close call. Above her, a man was stepping out onto the balcony. Even from this distance, Bran saw the gun in his hand.

Bran's Glock was already in his, but he was too far away.

*I'm going to see her shot. Fall to her death.* Not a praying man, he prayed now.

Charlie accelerated, sending them flying forward, skidding, weaving from side to side, but they'd be there in seconds. Only, the son of a bitch was already out on the balcony. In seconds, he'd be able to lean over and pump some bullets into the woman hanging below him.

Her stocking-clad feet kept slipping on the metal rungs, and Lina couldn't feel her hands anymore. With her pregnant belly sticking out, this was so hard. Her baby did somersaults, un-balancing her further. She didn't have the breath to scream, although some kind of sound squeaked out with every exhalation. Synthesized terror.

A car was coming fast. *Please let the driver see me. Please.*

Knowing she was completely exposed to the man above her, Lina did the only thing she could think of. She reached clumsily around the back of the ladder, held on as well as she could and wrapped her right leg around, too. The ladder swung wildly.

Lina risked looking up and, oh God, there he was, smiling down at her. So sure he had her.

She hadn't thought her pulse could race any faster, but it managed.

*Pop.* The bullet pinged off the metal railing just below her. But she'd done it! Somehow she'd maneuvered her body around the straps that sup-ported the rungs and now clung to the back of the ladder. The third floor balcony above her would block any easy shot. Only, suddenly, she was paralyzed. Done. Shaking, teeth chattering, she couldn't make herself move. She looked down at the balcony below her—and at another dark slid-ing door. No escape.

Then the ladder shook, and she knew he had started down after her.

THE INSTANT CHARLIE's Outback slithered to a stop, both men threw themselves out, Charlie scrambling for the back. Bran left his door open as a shield.

"Police!" he yelled. "Drop the gun!"

Tag Jones hooked his left arm over a rung, turned and fired his semi-automatic. Once, twice, three times.

Swearing viciously, Bran dropped behind the door. He heard glass crumbling, the distinctive sound of a bullet hitting metal.

"Charlie!" he yelled, knowing his partner hadn't had time to put on a vest.

"I'm okay!" Charlie yelled back.

Crouching, Bran stuck his head around the door. The window inches above him exploded. He took a breath, another…and pulled the trigger. He got off at least three shots within the space of a few heartbeats.

The gun dropped from John Taggart Jones's hand. Seemingly in slow motion, he toppled from the ladder and plummeted almost the full four stories, landing with a hard thud, facedown in the snow. His handgun had already settled a good ten feet from him, vanishing into the virgin snow.

He didn't move again.

Charlie ran for the body, Bran for where the ladder ended ten feet above the ground.

GUNFIRE. LINA HUGGED the ladder as it gave a great heave. Now she was sobbing but dry-eyed. A body flew past her, outstretched as if doing a swan dive. She saw blood, and a vacant expression.

And then she looked down, where two men ran forward. Bran came to a stop, directly below her. She had never, and prayed she would never again, see that expression on his face. It echoed all the terror she felt, and so much more.

"Lina." He didn't sound like himself. "Are you all right?"

Unable to form words, she tried to nod. All she could do was hold on tight, every muscle in her body rigid and shaking.

"Sweetheart." Somehow he'd steadied his voice. Deep and strong, it soaked into her. "Can you let yourself down just a few feet to the balcony?"

She shook her head hard, even as she knew she had to.

"We'll call the fire department. They can bring the ladder truck."

But, shaking or not, she made herself loosen her grip. She could do this. She could. She reached down with her right foot and finally found purchase. She thought. It was hard to tell, with her feet numb now, too. But it held her weight, so she dared to move the other foot, too. Then one hand, and the next.

He stood below her, anguish in his eyes.

"That's it, honey. Now another step. You're almost there."

She *was* there, except her foot had come down on the balcony railing because the ladder hung outside it. Lina closed her eyes and whispered, "We're alive, baby. We'll get out of this. We will."

Depending entirely on upper body strength, she lowered herself to a near-crouch, then twisted enough to set her butt down on the top of the railing. Still clinging to the ladder to slow her descent, she dropped to the floor of the balcony and teetered on legs that didn't want to hold her up. But she was able to look down and wave reassurance at Bran.

She spread both hands she couldn't feel on the swell of her pregnancy and rubbed. "We made it," she murmured. "We're safe and sound."

WHEN BRAN OPENED the sliding door an endless ten minutes later, Lina flew into his arms. And, God, she was cold. It was like hugging a snowwoman. Making a pained sound, he pulled her into the bedroom of the apartment two floors below his.

"You broke in," she mumbled against his chest.

He'd have laughed if he hadn't still been bone-deep, bowel-loosening scared. "Nope. The manager called the woman who lives here. Instead of us having to wait for her to rush home, turned out she had a friend in the complex who had a key."

Her teeth chattered and she shook.

"God, Lina." He knew he was holding her tighter than he should, but he couldn't help himself. He bent forward so his forehead touched hers, closed his eyes, and struggled for calm. Finally, he swung her off her feet and said, "Warm bath for you."

She didn't argue.

Bran insisted on carrying Lina through the stranger's apartment and past two gaping strangers. She tried thanking them, but he didn't slow his stride. Looking at her stocking feet covered with snow, he didn't set her down in the elevator, either. Moments later, he had her back in his apartment, where he carried her straight to the bathroom. He ran a warm bath for her, then gently peeled off her clothes and lifted her into the tub.

It just about killed him to watch as her hands and feet defrosted, but the pain passed quickly and she sighed her relief. She had been outside long enough for her wet hair to start to freeze. After asking for more hot water, Lina sank down to immerse her head, too.

Eventually, Bran helped her out of the tub and dried her carefully. He'd brought the warmest clothes he could find for her to put on, including a pair of fuzzy, school-bus yellow socks. She did most of the work, but let him kneel and put on her socks for her. Then she sat obediently on the closed toilet and let him dry her hair. Something he'd never done for a woman before, it occurred to him, but then Lina was introducing a lot of firsts into his life.

She glanced at the splintered bedroom door as she came out of the bathroom, and said indignantly, "He shot your mattress."

"I noticed."

Jones had shot at Lina. Bran couldn't imagine how she had escaped. Bought time for him to get to her. One bullet, and she could have been gone.

It took him a minute to pull himself together well enough to put the bed back together as a temporary measure. Even though the damage wasn't as noticeable on the mattress itself, he thought it would be worth the money to replace the damn bed.

That wasn't a memory he'd want hanging around.

He asked if she'd had breakfast. *Before the homicidal maniac broke into the apartment.* When she said no, he set about scrambling eggs and toasting bread for both of them. He poured her a hot cup of herbal tea and himself coffee.

Nothing like a meal to restore a sense of normalcy, right?

A couple of bites later, he pushed his plate away. "I can't eat."

"I'm...not sure I can, either." Lina's eyes had never looked bigger, more haunted. "I was so scared."

He was around the table, scooping her up, before he knew what he was doing. Then he sat in the recliner and just held her, curled on his lap.

"I've never been so scared in my freakin' life," he told her. "When I saw you dangling there—" His throat seized and he pressed a kiss to the top of her head.

She burrowed even closer and mumbled something.

Bran tipped his head. "What?"

"My hero."

"We almost didn't make it in time," he said roughly. "Another thirty seconds—" His throat seemed to spasm, choking off the unthinkable words: *you'd be dead.*

Not just her. The child they'd made together. The one he could feel moving where her belly rested against his.

And, yeah, he wanted this baby, their little girl, but it was Lina who'd shaken him to his core. There'd been an instant there, when he saw her hanging above a two-story drop-off, an armed man climbing down after her, when Bran would have sworn the world had stopped. He hadn't been able to breathe, suspected even his heart had quit beating. Dying must feel like that. The end.

Lina twisted suddenly to look at him. "How did you know I needed you?"

"Jones murdered my housekeeper for the key to our apartment. The detective it was assigned to mentioned her and I knew right away."

"Oh, no." Lina pinched her lips together, distress clouding her eyes. "She died because of me."

Bran shook his head. "She died because a man with no conscience wouldn't stop until he killed *you*. He'd have done anything to get to you, just like he was willing to do anything to walk away from that bank with the money." He saw that she was remembering again, thinking of her friend, and nodded. "He was a monster, Lina. *He* was the killer."

"I saw his face as he was falling."

Well, shit. That had come out of left field. He kissed her temple and waited.

"I think he was already dead. It was you who shot him, wasn't it?"

"Yeah." He cleared his throat. "Charlie got us there, but he hadn't had a chance to put on a vest. I was in a better position to put myself out there a little."

Her eyes told him she knew he'd have done exactly the same thing if he hadn't been wearing the vest. That she knew he'd have done anything at all, if he could save her.

Her forehead crinkled. "Shouldn't you be out there? Won't they need to interview you and… I don't know, whatever else happens after a shooting?"

"Yeah," he said again, still hoarsely. "They will. Lots of theys, because we're inside the Clear Creek city limits here, and the FBI will eventually show up, too, since he was one of their bank robbers. But they can all wait."

Lina sat up, fire lighting her eyes. "If any of them have the nerve to say you were wrong to shoot him, they'll hear from me!"

Both amused and completely turned on by her ferocity, Bran kneaded her nape. "No, I'm pretty sure no one will. Charlie was a witness, remember. Charlie's SUV is now pocked with bullet holes, which proves Jones was shooting at *us*. And this is the guy *you* saw shoot and kill Maya. It's just routine, Lina. I'll probably be on administrative leave for a few days."

"Oh." She relaxed again. "Okay. That will be nice. Having you home, I mean."

"Yeah, I think I need that, too," he admitted. "Considering you scared me spitless."

"What do you mean, *I* scared you?" she asked in mock indignation. "It wasn't my fault."

"No. It was mine." He couldn't believe he was going to do this. It was a hell of a lot riskier than sticking his head out where a gunman could blow it off. But the tightness deep in his chest wouldn't let him off the hook. He had to say this, and he had to see her face when he did, or he'd have to learn to live with this discomfort that verged on pain.

"Yours?" Lina planted a hand on his chest to once again sit up enough so she could see his face. "What are you talking about?"

"Not what happened. I don't mean that." He swallowed, feeling like his damn Adam's apple had swollen to twice its usual size. "I mean that I don't know how I'd have gone on without you." Admitting that much was bad enough. Getting the rest out...

Her eyes widened and he was sure she'd quit breathing.

"I've never loved a woman before. Except my mother, I guess."

"And she let you down," Lina said softly.

Trying really hard not to squirm, he moved his shoulders. "I thought she did." *Thought?* He shoved aside his surprise. He'd have to think about that later. "The thing is, I started to love you without knowing what was happening." Fast, before he could chicken out, he said, "I do love you. I'm not easy to live with. I know that. But...

I'll keep trying. And I swear I'll never let you down, not in any of the big ways."

Tears filled her gorgeous gray-green eyes. "I know you won't, Bran. I never doubted that. Not once." She laid her hand on his cheek and jaw, her skin so soft. She smiled tremulously. "And of course I love you. Surely you'd guessed."

"I...hoped." He turned his face to press a kiss into her palm. "Can we get married soon? Until we do, I think I'll keep—" Cutting himself off seemed smart. He didn't have to tell her he'd keep being scared until the deed was done. Scared he'd blow it. Scared she'd come to her senses. Scared her *I love you* was really gratitude.

Scared she'd cancel the wedding two days before it happened.

No, he hadn't loved Paige, but he hadn't needed one more person walking out on him.

"I won't, you know."

He blinked. "What?"

"Change my mind. That's what you were thinking, isn't it?"

God, she'd pulled his thoughts right out of his head. Which *should* scare him, but for some reason didn't. "Yeah," he admitted. "I told you the truth. I'm glad Paige was smart enough to realize something was missing. But even so..." He hesitated.

"If it happens to you once, you've got to wonder the next time," Lina concluded for him.

He grimaced. "Plus, it's you. I don't want to be without you, Lina. I want you to stay. Don't move back to your apartment."

"No, although…" She was the one to hesitate this time. But then she said in a rush, "Could we move to *my* apartment instead? At least for now? I don't ever want to go out on your balcony again, or even look out the sliding doors."

He shook his head. "See? I should have known you'd feel that way. Of course we can move to your place. We can grab enough stuff for tomorrow and go now. I'll come back for the rest later. I kind of thought we should buy a house before the baby comes anyway."

"I would love that," she said, her eyes shimmering. "And let's do go now. Because I'd really like it if you'd make love to me, and *not* on that bed."

He cupped one of her breasts and squeezed gently. "Seems to me this recliner worked just fine last night."

Lina arched her back to push her breast more firmly into his hand. "You're right. This recliner has no bad memories at all."

"Only good," he said huskily, starting to divest her of the clothes she'd put on only a few minutes ago. But, hey, he'd let her keep her socks.

Bran helped Lina up the front porch steps, then slid the key in the lock and ceremoniously opened the front door of the 1940s bungalow.

"Home, sweet home," she said with satisfaction.

"All ours," he agreed.

The house was only the third they had looked at. Lina had loved it at first sight. That it was less than three blocks from Zach's house was a bonus. After having him do an inspection, they had put earnest money down the same day they saw it. Because Bran had both the proceeds from his childhood home and substantial savings from his salary, he had been able to pay cash, allowing them to close on the house in only two weeks. Lina's more modest savings were slated to pay for some of the remodeling they intended to do.

Most of the work could wait, this house was dated but, unlike Zach's when he first bought it, livable. They had decided to go ahead and refinish the hardwood floors before move-in day. Lina just hoped to be in the house before the baby came.

And married.

She was still having nightmares, but at least no one was out to kill her anymore. After Bran shot Tag Jones, Clear Creek Police had located a car no one recognized in a visitor spot at the apartment complex. The key they found in his pocket fit. The registration that was in the glove compartment and the borrowed driver's license in his wallet led a combined county and FBI SWAT team to a house up a long, rutted dirt road in the northeast corner of the county, tucked in the Cascade foothills. There, they surprised the Cobbs, as well as the couple renting the house who were arrested for aiding and abetting.

Enough of the stolen money was recovered to make the banks happy.

Charged with a long list of crimes including first-degree murder, Derrick Cobb went to jail. Even though everyone concerned suspected Melissa Cobb qualified as a battered woman, she faced charges, too.

Detective Tom Sperling had announced his retirement. Zach was one of many to apply for the position that was opening, and already knew he'd been selected. He'd only been with the department a year, but the two years he'd worked Homicide for the Portland Police Bureau trumped anyone else's qualifications. Lina knew Tess was relieved, because in theory detectives were less likely to be killed on the job than patrol officers. In practice…well…the bullet that took out the window in Charlie Warring's Subaru had come very close to striking Bran in the head.

Lina, for one, was glad Bran worked for a rural county sheriff's department, and not in an urban area, where serious crimes were so much more common.

Today, they wandered through the house, Bran relaxed and indulgent. With it empty, their footsteps and voices echoed. Lina could hardly wait to start hunting for antiques to supplement the basic furniture they already owned. Fortunately, she'd have plenty of time once the baby had come.

Today she stopped in the middle of one of the smaller bedrooms, taking in the way the winter sun fell through the old-fashioned sash window, and said, "This one will be hers."

"Good choice," Bran said, then cocked his head. "Sounds like Zach and Tess are here."

Tess was the first to appear. Looking around, she said, "I love this place. You know Zach and I aren't ever going to be able to move, don't you? Not now that you'll be living so close."

Lina laughed. "Adding on a bedroom or two to your house would be a snap."

Framed by the doorway, Zach groaned. "Adding on? We're already trapped in the never-ending remodel."

"It's fun," Tess insisted.

She and Lina started talking wallpaper. Just a border in here, Lina decided. Bran was determined to have the basics done so they could move in before the baby came. Zach had volunteered to sand the floors, after which he'd help Bran stain and finish them. Lina didn't care if they got anything else done before they moved in, except for the baby's bedroom.

"Maybe I should paint before Zach starts on the floors—"

Bran had been talking to his brother, but he turned at that. "I'll be doing the painting in here. The fumes can't be good for a pregnant woman."

"But my doctor said—"

He crossed his arms and just looked at her. She quit wasting her breath.

"And no ladders for you," he added. "At least until after the baby comes."

Tess laughed at Bran. "Detective Domineering."

Without altering his stance, he stared his sister-in-law down. "Maybe. But she's not climbing up on a ladder anyway."

Lina got the giggles. She might have taught Bran Murphy to love, but there was only so much you could change a man.

And, truthfully, she wasn't all that enthusiastic about ladders of *any* height at the moment.

Their wedding was less than a week away. She suspected Bran was more nervous than he admitted about meeting her parents, who were flying in Thursday ahead of the Saturday ceremony. She, in turn, was a little nervous about meeting his mother, who would be staying with Zach and

Tess. Bran himself had called his mother to invite her. Even though he hadn't asked, Lina left him alone in the living room for that call. He'd talked to his mother for a long time, his voice quiet.

After, all he'd say was, "She was a lousy wife, but a good mother. I...lost something when I cut her off. As you and Zach both have pointed out, I have a chance for a do-over."

She had hugged him, something he so obviously needed from her, and often. "And Anna Grace Murphy will have two grandmothers."

Now, dreaming, she wandered over to peer out the window at their yard, thinking this spring she'd plant a rose beneath the window. Bran came up behind her, enclosing her securely in his arms.

Smiling, she turned her head to see that they were momentarily alone. "We've come so far," she murmured.

He nuzzled her neck, said, "Yeah," and looked at her with naked honesty. "You're the best thing that ever happened to me."

Blinking back tears, she whispered, "Ditto."

Even as he kissed her, he caressed her stomach with one big, warm hand, as if to be sure baby Anna knew she was part of everything good, too.

\* \* \* \* \*

# LARGER-PRINT BOOKS!

## GET 2 FREE
## LARGER-PRINT NOVELS
## PLUS 2 FREE
## MYSTERY GIFTS

*Love Inspired*®

### Larger-print novels are now available...

LILP15

# LARGER-PRINT BOOKS!

## GET 2 FREE
## LARGER-PRINT NOVELS
## PLUS 2 FREE
## MYSTERY GIFTS

*Love Inspired*®
## SUSPENSE
RIVETING INSPIRATIONAL ROMANCE

### Larger-print novels are now available...

# LARGER-PRINT BOOKS!
## GET 2 FREE LARGER-PRINT NOVELS PLUS
## 2 FREE GIFTS!

**⊕HARLEQUIN®**

*super romance®*

## More Story...More Romance

# READERSERVICE.COM

## Manage your account online!

- Review your order history
- Manage your payments
- Update your address

---

*We've designed the*
*Reader Service website*
*just for you.*

---

## Enjoy all the features!

- Discover new series available to you, and read excerpts from any series.
- Respond to mailings and special monthly offers.
- Connect with favorite authors at the blog.
- Browse the Bonus Bucks catalog and online-only exculsives.
- Share your feedback.

*Visit us at:*
## ReaderService.com